Third in the Paul

THE TWINS

OTHER BOOKS BY PHILIP TULLIS

NON-FICTION:

CHRISTIAN OR IN NAME ONLY?
GOT ATTITUDE? SO DO I!
THANK GOD FOR ATTITUDE (coming soon)

FICTION:

Under the Pen Name Bruce Blanton

CONFLICTED

The Paul Bannachek Series
PROGRAMMED
SHIFTED
THE TWINS

THE TWINS

BRUCE BLANTON

JENTUL Publishing, LLC
Helena, Montana

The Twins
Copyright © 2020 by Bruce Blanton, aka Philip W. Tullis

For more information write or call JENTUL Publishing. 8409 Hillview Drive | Helena, Montana 59602 | USA 1.406.458-8884 |

ISBN: 978-1-7357186-6-8

Library of Congress Control Number: 2021904242

Published by Jentul Publishing, LLC
Helena, MT 59602

First Printing March, 2021

Printed in the United States of America

DEDICATIONS

For Mr. John Wall.
Great Boss. Great Leader. Great Teacher.
We really made a good team.
Too bad the company made stupid decisions!

To Emma and Ellana, you are like the
granddaughters we never had.
Our love for you is without bounds.

CHAPTERS

Even a child is known by his doings, whether his work [be] pure, and whether [it be] right. ~ **Proverbs 20:11**

It were better for him that a millstone were hanged about his neck, and he cast into the sea, than that he should offend one of these little ones. ~ (**Jesus**)**Luke 17:2**

Be sober, be vigilant; because your adversary the devil, as a roaring lion, walketh about, seeking whom he may devour.
~ **1 Peter 5:8**

"If you had not committed great sins, God would not have sent a punishment like me upon you" ~ **Ghenghis Khan**

"If everybody is thinking alike, then somebody isn't thinking."
~ **General George S. Patton**

"Light thinks it travels faster than anything, but it is wrong. No matter how fast light travels, it finds the darkness has always got there first and is waiting for it." ~ **Terry Pratchett**

"You mess with a child you mess with me!"
~ **Paul Bannachek**

1

Pushing Restart

Riding first class on American Airlines was more of a necessity than comfort for Paul Bannachek. He would have preferred not to fly at all. It was not that he had a fear of flying, he simply did not like being in a long tube with two hundred other people breathing recycled air. The necessity came about because it was the only seat his friend Johnny Alston could arrange for him. Paul's short three day visit to Memphis was not a surprise for Johnny. He knew Paul was coming, but he did not have the normal two-week notice. Johnny only received a two-day notification. Still, Paul thought Johnny had worked as he had always done, performing at high capacity, arranging what needed to be arranged. He had Paul's new identification set up with a passport and bank account matching his new name. Paul thought using the name of Stanley Frazer was kind of sick but also funny. After all, who would use the name of the man who hunted him for so many years?

Still using the new name might throw off his pursuers. They would probably think Paul would never use a name of one of their own. While in Memphis, Paul had shared his experiences in Germany with his friend Johnny. He told Johnny everything that happened including his loss of Alisa, but also the gratitude he had for God to allow him to have some semblance of a normal life—even if it was for just over a year. Johnny had listened and digested all of the information giving comfort to his friend Paul. He then broke the news.

"Paul, it is becoming increasingly more difficult to get you new identities. With all of the safeguards the government has placed into action, I am finding it dangerous to create new personas for you."

"Johnny, what am I going to do? You know I need to constantly change my identifications, especially with everything I find myself involved in."

"The best idea I can come up with is to start creating Canadian identifications. However, I also think you should not just destroy the ID's you have used. Destroying them is not the same as putting them to rest for a period of time."

"Not sure what you mean, Johnny."

"Simply put my friend, you can use an ID for a while and then switch to another and then another and then go back to the first. You don't have to just destroy that persona. They never really existed anyway."

"Don't you think that is kinda risky?" Paul asked.

"Of course, it's risky. But, if you use the same identification for missions, it will allow you to use the others for travel giving you cover."

"Agreed. For now, I will use this new I.D. Stanley Frazer for travel."

Johnny had transferred Paul's accumulated wealth to five separate identifications so that Paul would now be able to start fresh. He had also purchased a ticket on American Airlines for Paul to travel to the Bahamas for a week's vacation. After everything Paul had experienced in Germany, he wanted to re-charge.

He needed to rest emotionally as well as mentally. Laying in the sun for a week and swimming in the ocean was just what Paul felt he needed. Maneuvering through Memphis International Airport was stressful because he needed to avoid all the cameras. And when checking in he had to use his telekinetic ability to block the digital camera from filming the passengers. Paul was well aware of the facial recognition software the government had and was using, though it told the people it was a technology under construction. Like most technology the government had and used, the American people knew nothing of it until it was twenty years out of date. Paul felt sorry for the people of the world. The people just did not know the real technological world their governments had built around them. They had no clue as to what was coming. But Paul knew and understood!

As the DC-9 began its decent towards the Nassau airport, Paul wondered why the Spirit was sending him here. He had pulled out his new map back at the Munford Hotel in Munford, Tennessee and flipped his dime as usual. Only this time the dime rolled off the map. After several tries Paul understood he was going to some place outside of the US. All he could do was wait. It only took a minute or two until he received the impression he was to go to the Bahamas. Once he knew his destination, he walked to the Munford Library and signed onto one of the community computers to find a hotel. Not knowing why, as he never really knew why, Paul chose the Breeze's Hotel and resort. It was right on the beach and was all inclusive. Having three restaurants meant he would not have to leave to find meals. All he would have to do was pay for his $400 a night room and everything else was included. Still, he was not sure why that particular hotel was where he was supposed to stay. But like everything else in his life for the past forty-one years, Paul simply followed his intuition or listened to the Spirit within him. Usually, they were one in the same.

Stepping off the plane in Nassau, Paul ensured to block the

camera's in the terminal while he hailed a taxi. It was a balmy eighty-four degrees at 1 pm in the afternoon. Being November, the temperature felt wonderful. As he waited in the taxi queue, Paul thought about Alisa. He knew she would have loved to have travelled here. She would have enjoyed the beach and relaxation. On the other hand, he also knew that she could never have adjusted to the world he lived in. When he had told her about it, she had said it terrified her. He found himself missing his wife terribly, so he decided not to let himself think about her. At least not for a while. For now, he needed to get to his hotel, check in, find his room and unpack his backpack. He would then have to iron his slacks and button-up shirts. His jeans and undergarments he would place on top of the hotel dresser. The idea of bed bugs getting into his clothing was something that appalled him. Bed bugs, "the nature of travel," he told himself.

The cab ride only took nine minutes. Paul checked into his room, unpacked, ironed his wrinkled clothes and then changed into a clean pair of jeans and a pullover short sleeved shirt. He then left the hotel and walked the four miles into town and wondered about checking out the sites. He gave off the appearance that he was like most everyone else, but in reality, he was doing what he always did in a new location—reconnaissance. Paul studied the layout of the town. He memorized every road and alley. He calculated time of travel based on the various speeds he could achieve, and he looked for any possible threat he could conceive. After several hours of exploring and mapping the surroundings, Paul was satisfied he could maintain an escape if it became necessary. The only problem he would have would be getting off the island. If something were to happen, he could not just get on a plane nor could he just get on a boat. He could run the circumference of the island in about 40 minutes as that is what he could usually cover eighty miles in. Again, for Paul the idea of being on an island, with no real means of escape, bothered him.

On the way back to the Breeze's Hotel, Paul stopped at a store and bought a small roll of duct tape and a small container of one gallon freezer bags. He also purchased a couple of shirts, two pairs of shorts, and a pair of swim trunks. Then he stopped at another store and picked up a small radio. A typical AM/FM radio is all he needed or wanted. They were good for local news and weather. He could also manipulate them to pick up police channels and other secure channels using his telekinetic abilities. Once he had his supplies in hand, Paul walked back to the hotel, went to his room and changed his shirt. He then unpacked his additional identification, passport with wallet, cash and credit cards. Placing the emergency I.D. into a one-gallon freezer bag, he rolled it and folded it tightly ensuring the air was out and then sealed the bag. He placed that into another one-gallon bag and duct taped it to the toilet back. Paul could now relax.

One last step was necessary before joining the other guests at the hotel; Paul had to figure out who he was going to be. He needed to create Stan Frazer. Like so many other times he had to create a persona that was interesting but also boring. He would have to *become* someone. He sat down on the hotel bed and looked across the suite into the mirror. He saw a sandy blonde, blue-eyed, 24-year-old man. He had learned how to hide his now 59 years of life experience so that he could fit in. A chemist. He would be a recently graduated chemist from the University of Illinois, who had just graduated with his master's degree in Chemical Engineering. He would have graduated in August and had travelled to Memphis to visit his grandparents because he was orphaned at the age of twelve. They had raised him. He would also tell people he accepted a position with Pre-Finish Metals, a company in Elk Grove, Illinois and that he would be moving into his apartment in Downers Grove, Illinois within two weeks.

With his story committed to memory, Paul stood up from the bed and left his room taking the stairs down to the main floor.

His first night's dinner would be at the Reggae Café. It was an outdoor restaurant which served burgers, fries and local treats. Being a casual, all you can eat restaurant was just what he wanted. Plus, when he was done, he could take a few steps and be on the beach where he could walk and enjoy the fresh sea air. Walking past the pool area Paul noticed most of the people were couples. There were some singles who Paul studied carefully as he meandered towards the café. The men ranged in ages of 20 to 50 and the women's ages were about 25 to 40. He immediately noted those who were on the prowl for a partner and those who were simply there to rest and relax. Paul would of course attempt to socialize with the married couples, as that was safest for him. Still, he would have to be careful. Married couples could be strange people. Most were simple folk enjoying the company of one another, but there were those who would try to set him up with a daughter or niece or a friends' kid. And then there were the sickos. Thankfully they were few. Unfortunately for Paul, he had been born and grown up to be a very handsome man. His six-foot two-inch, 220-pound frame made him appealing to women and unfortunately to those men who like men. He hoped he could avoid both types.

Demolishing his triple bacon cheeseburger and chili fries, Paul slurped down his Dr. Pepper and then headed for the beach. He decided he would walk north for a mile as the sun was setting. Checking his watch and noting the time was 7 pm, Paul walked for about ten minutes, then turned and headed south past the hotel for another ten minutes. It was now 7:20 pm, so he headed back to the hotel and found the hot tub. Seeing the hot tub was larger than most, he figured he could fit in with the five couples sitting and soaking. Paul stripped off his jeans and shirt, folded them neatly and placed them on a pool chair. He had his swim shorts on underneath which fit tightly but comfortably. Stepping into the hot tub, he said good evening to the couples soaking in the bubbling, hot water. The older couple, who were in their mid-forties, responded with, "Good evening," while the other younger couples ignored him. He could see they were not married, and the women were clearly checking out his physique. Ignoring the younger couples, he gave the body language of being open to conversing with the older couple. The man in his forties started the conversation.

"You just check in today?"

Paul replied, "Yes sir. Arrived here about one thirty. How did you know?"

"Your skin. You're still very white. My name is George Wilkerson, and this is my wife, Sue," the man said extending a hand in welcome.

Shaking the man's hand, Paul said, "Thank you. My name is Stan Frazer." He then shook Sue's hand and asked, "Where you folks from?"

"We're from Wichita!" Sue exclaimed. "How about you? Where are you from?"

Paul stuck to his fabricated story so well that no one would even consider he was lying. Then the invariable question came.

"So, what do you do Stan?" asked George.

Again, Paul stuck to his story about being a recently graduated Chemist.

"How about you, Sir, what do you do?" Paul asked.

The man seemed nervous when he said, "I am a Rabbi."

"Cool," replied Paul. "It must be difficult to get away. I mean with having to do three services a week and all."

"You know about our faith?" asked Sue.

Just as Paul responded, "Yes, I have known many Jews in my life…," one of the men from the four other couples said, "Geesh, Fucking Jews! Can't get away from them." The four couples all laughed. Paul saw and felt the hurt from the Wilkerson couple.

Immediately George said, "Come on sweetheart, we have to rise early tomorrow for our flight."

Paul said, "Sir, don't let these manure-mouthed, scumbag

losers drive you off. They're just wasted, walking human flesh."

Just as Sue started to speak one of the men spoke up saying, "Hey ass-wipe, what did you just say?"

"Oh, you know what I said. I said it loud enough for you to purposely hear," Paul responded.

George stood up and said, "Young man, there is no need for this. We are leaving."

Paul interjected, "That's just the point, Sir. You and your wife, Sue have no reason to leave. Just because these human trash cans cannot stop the garbage that pours from their turd-filled mouths does not mean you have to leave. Sit, please, enjoy the evening."

Sue said, "Thank you, young man, but we are *used* to this. We will leave." She stood up, taking her husband's hand and led him back to their hotel room. As they left, Paul felt their pain and their anguish which made him angry!

"Okay folks, I hope to see you again before you leave in the morning," Paul said to their departing backsides.

The small group to Paul's left laughed. One of them said, "Hey we can send you some swine blood if you like. We'll have room service deliver it." Paul had had enough! He did not care what people said about him, but to abuse that nice couple was something he would not tolerate.

"So low life, you get a kick out of bullying innocent people?" Paul asked the larger man who'd made the pig blood comment.

"You know, you're not too bright, are you?" the man in the center of the small gang asked.

"I am bright enough to know that you four are nothing but punks with big mouths. And I am bright enough to know that if you are foolish enough to follow me down to the beach 100 yards to the right, I will hurt you. And I am bright enough to know that three of you will not learn your lesson when I am done making you bleed and cry for mercy. But you, Steven, you will have learned your lesson." Paul stood up from the hot tub, slowly stepped out and moseyed over to the pool chair which held his dry jeans and shirt. "I'll be waiting for you scumbags. But don't make me wait too long!"

Leaving the hot tub area, he heard the four men talking. He had left them no choice but to follow him. They felt they could not look bad in front of the women. Paul had diminished their supposed manhood in front of their women. And their women wanted to see them hurt Paul. He knew he would not have long to wait. Unfortunately for the four men, Paul had been right. They attacked him just as he was out of sight of the hotel! Just as the first man threw his first and last punch at the back of Paul's head, Paul used his left foot kicking backwards into the man's left kneecap shattering it. As the man screamed and began to fall, Paul quickly turned, grabbed the man's hair and pulled his face down towards Paul's upcoming knee which smashed the man's nose and mouth. The force of the knee blow threw the man back six feet where he landed flat on his back, spitting blood and crying from the pain. Paul then blocked the on-coming punch from the man on his right, spinning and driving an open-handed blow into the man's center rib cage knocking the air out the man while breaking several of his ribs. He then used both hands to give the man a double blow to the temples knocking him unconscious instantly. Spinning quickly, Paul used his right foot to connect with the third man's jaw, knocking out several teeth and driving him back several feet. Paul then jumped and kicked the man in the chest, breaking five of the man's ribs, forcing the man to land on his back.

Standing there was the remaining man. He started walking backwards putting up his hands saying, "Please mister, I don't want any trouble! I have a wife at home, okay?"

"You have a wife at home and you're here with another woman?!" Paul asked angrily. The man had the look of shame on his face. Paul then said, "You deserve this more than them.

They are just racist, ignorant bullies, but you're also an adulterer!" Paul ran up to the man and punched him square in the nose and mouth. With blood gushing from his face, the man fell to his knees as the pain went to his brain from the powerful punch forcing him to tear up! Paul was going in for another blow when the Spirit within him told him to stop! The Spirit within Paul told Paul he was there to give the man the chance to choose. It told Paul he was there for *that* particular man! Paul immediately stopped his attack, looked down at the sobbing man and spit on the ground next to him. "You make me want to vomit, Mister!" Paul told the man. "You have a wife at home and you're here whoring around! You have no idea of the blessing you have." He then reached down and pulled the man up and then punched him in his ribs breaking several of them. Paul then walked back to his hotel room where he took a shower and waited to see if the police would be coming or not. They never came.

John Danick sat at his office at the CIA's Office of Scientific Intelligence, waiting for Marc Boyd, his senior analyst on the Bannachek file now code named "Hunter." It had been named "Programmed" but was changed due to security. Marc had sent John an instant message stating they believed they had found Bannachek again. As he waited, he wondered what he would do this time to try and capture their elusive prey. If they really found Paul Bannachek, depending on where the man was, Danick figured he would send two massive teams of thirty men each. He would give orders that only side arms with repressors be authorized. He would also send two sniper teams, each with their new Rifle Electromagnetic Pulse, or REMPs, weapons. They had a range of 200 yards and would shut down any energy, or in Bannacheks' case, his energy field. The problem was the weapons needed a two-minute re-charge period before being able to fire again. He looked up as Marc Boyd entered his office with a manila file marked "Top Secret Crypto."

"Boss, I think we have Bannachek," Boyd said as he handed the file over and across Danick's large desk.

"What do you mean you think? Have we found him or not?"

"Well sir, we believe he is in Nassau at a hotel named the Breeze's."

"Okay Marc, explain and please be concise."

"We do not know how Bannachek managed to avoid the cameras at the Memphis International Airport or the cameras at the Nassau Airport or even the hotel security cameras, but we are pretty sure he is at the hotel."

"I asked you to be concise, Marc. Tell me how you found him?"

"Sir, the facial recognition system recognized his picture from the DC-9 American Airline Flight from Memphis to Nassau. Once we had his picture and seat number we backtracked and found he did depart from Memphis under the name of Stanley Frazier."

"Frazier? You have got to be kidding! Is this guy taunting us or what?"

"I wouldn't know sir, but a man did check into the Breeze's hotel in Nassau under the name of Stan Frazier."

"Okay Marc, I want you to see if we have anyone down there working for the agency. If so, get him or her over to the hotel with Bannacheks' picture for a confirmation. Then..."

"Already done sir. The agency has an operative there who works as a tourist guide as their cover. I have taken the liberty to contact the woman and have sent her a picture of Bannachek. She has already responded that she has laid eyes upon him and the hotel."

"Marc, you did great. Who is this asset?"

"Her name is Karen Huruska. She is attached to the Foreign Intelligence Desk on Russia."

"Okay, I do not want you telling her anything about Bannachek. She is to observe his movements only. Then make contact with some of our teams. I want two thirty-man teams in the air by this evening, and make sure each team has a sniper and spotter. I want both those snipers armed with REMPs. Understood?"

"Understood Sir. How do you want the teams armed?"

Taking a moment before responding, Danick sighed and said, "No heavy armament. Side arms with repressors only. I do not want a blood bath down there. Besides, if we can hit Bannachek with the REMPs we may be able to weaken him enough for the teams to take him in hand-to-hand. If we are able to take him, have three medical personnel with each team. I want his blood drawn. As many vials as possible. Understood?"

"Yes sir. I will get right on it. I should be able to pull teams from Florida and Missouri, have them meet in Miami and have one of our charters take them in by the next afternoon."

"Hold up there, Marc. I want them flying in at night. We want as little attention as possible. Get them there late tomorrow evening, but not too late. If they arrive by 2200 hours they can set up and begin their operation by midnight. Since it is November there are less tourists, which means less late-night partiers."

"Got it, Sir. Less witnesses."

Sleeping until 0600 was unusual for Paul. He was normally up by 0430 every morning. The additional sleep felt good and yet it made him feel groggy. Looking at his watch, Paul figured he would be able to shower and get his breakfast by 0645. He laid there a moment thinking about the night before. The confrontation he had had bothered him. How was he supposed to help that man make a choice? He did not like the man at all. Then again, he did not like the gangbanger, Jerome Waller at first either and that kid made his choice—a wonderful choice. But the man last night was everything Paul detested. He was a racist and an adulterer. He was also a coward. Put the three together, as far as Paul was concerned, you had a waste of human flesh. But Paul also knew he was born to serve, protect, heal and provide the opportunity to choose. It was not his decision who he was to help. Still, it seemed he had helped a lot more of what he considered undesirables than that of plain decent people. He was starting to learn that God did not work in a way that man could understand. He worked in His way, with His plan. All Paul could do was obey and act.

After his ten-minute hot shower Paul stood in front of the mirror shaving. He thought about Alisa and how he had awakened the previous night several times as he had reached over for her in the bed. He missed his wife terribly. Paul knew he would never get over that loss. He knew he would always feel the emptiness of Alisa being gone. But he also felt his love for her and hers for him. Theirs was one of those rare, once in a lifetime, perfect loves that if one is blessed, gets to experience it. He knew she was his blessing and though he was angry at her loss, he was also grateful to God for the time he had with his beautiful Alisa. It seemed strange to Paul he felt the emptiness and at the same time the warmth and joy of her. He lied to himself thinking he wished he felt nothing. He knew he was feeling sorry for himself and yet it somehow helped him accept what God had commanded. For Paul, as difficult as it was on so many occasions, he always put God first; no matter how much it would hurt!

Meandering down to the pool area for breakfast Paul noticed the three men he had encountered the evening before. The women they had been with were not at their breakfast table. As Paul walked by the men, they looked at him with fear in their eyes. He walked over to the bar where breakfasts were being ordered and served. Paul ordered a five egg, cheese and mushroom omelet with four sausage links and a coffee. As he stood there waiting for his order, Paul looked around the breakfast area surveying the hotel guests. Clearly, from what he was able to pick up, the guests knew something had transpired the night before, but they did not know exactly what had occurred. After receiving his order, he walked over to the table with the three men and sat down.

"Good morning, gentlemen," Paul said as he addressed his quarry from the previous night.

The men did not say a word. They just looked at him briefly and then lowered their heads.

"I want you guys to know that as far as I am concerned, last night never happened. I am hoping all can be forgiven, but hopefully, *not* forgotten."

One man finally spoke saying, "Yeah we're sorry about last night too."

"Well," Paul said, "Why don't we all just go about our business and enjoy our vacations?"

"Sounds good," another man spoke up.

"By the way," Paul asked, "Where are your companions?"

The first man spoke saying, "Oh, they went back to their own hotel last night. Doubt we will see them again."

Paul asked, "So where is your friend?"

The second man said, "Steve went snorkeling about twenty minutes ago. Why?"

"I was hoping to speak with him today," was all Paul could say before he heard the scream!

"Shark!" a woman screamed out.

Looking over his left shoulder towards the beach, Paul could see the man from the previous night struggling as a large Caribbean Reef Shark attacked him! Paul was immediately on his feet running at his fastest speed towards the water. Within seconds, he covered the 600 yards, dove into the cold 60-degree water, swimming at his fastest pace to reach the man. He could not worry about witnesses! They had already seen his speed as he ran to the water so he could not worry about them seeing his speed *in* the water. He reached the shark's morning meal just before the 8-foot shark had been able to rip off the man's leg. Paul grabbed the shark's mouth ripping it open to free the leg and then split the shark in half. He threw the creature 500 yards out into the ocean before turning his attention to the smaller 6' sharks drawn in by the blood in the water. There were five circling in for the kill of the wounded snorkeler. Paul fired five explosive plasma energy shots obliterating each of the fish. Standing in the bloodied, red water Paul knew he had to act fast or the swimmer would surely die.

Pulling the man into his powerful arms, Paul swam and then ran as fast as he could to the shoreline. He looked into the dying man's face and saw he was the man from the previous night. Taking only a couple of seconds to cover the 600 yards to the shore, Paul laid the victim on his back and began healing the torn off leg. The man's right leg hung from his body by a small piece of skin tissue. The leg was crushed! The femoral artery was ripped open, gushing blood at tremendous rate. Laying his hands on the artery, Paul concentrated on repairing it, sealing the artery together to stop the loss of any more blood. He then concentrated on the bone. Slowly, he was able to repair the bone forcing energy from his own body into the shark's attempted meal. Paul then began healing the missing muscle, forcing new muscle to grow. Once the muscles were repaired, he began on the tissue, building new tissue. Paul had to stop when he realized there was now a crowd circled around him and the victim.

Looking around, he saw how people had vomited and some were in absolute awe seeing what he was doing for the victim and what he had done in the water. While he wanted to finish healing the man, Paul knew he had to make a quick exit. Laying his hands on the man's forehead he said, "You are healed in the name of Jesus, the only Son of God, my Lord and my Savior!" Paul then stood up, looked at the crowd around him and he took off at full pace! He knew the man would live. He heard the ambulance and police cars coming. The ambulance would take the man to the local hospital where they would finish stitching him up and place the man on fluids and a blood transfusion once his blood type was matched. What worried Paul were the witnesses.

They would all tell various stories of what they had seen which would be placed in police reports and then recorded in a computer. It would not take long for Langley to get the information which meant the CIA would know he was in Nassau and they would send a team.

Tearing up the beach, Paul used his telekinesis sending out electronic pulses to every camera and camera phone he had seen. People had been recording what he had done. The last thing Paul wanted was photographic evidence of him and what he could do. Besides, he figured the less people knew about him the safer they were. Like so many others over the years they could only tell stories but provide no evidence. Running at full pace now Paul headed south and then east into a private gated community. He continued east through the community across the main road into the wooded area. His best hope was to get deep within the foliage and keep himself hidden until that evening. Then he would sneak back to his hotel room, grab his belongings and try to stow away on one of the cruise ships docked in port. If he could not do that, he doubted he would be able to get off the island shy of stealing a private plane or boat.

Finding a hiding spot Paul sat down and began to relax, breathing in deeply and slowly. He felt he had used a good thirty percent of his energy. And while seventy percent energy level was sufficient, Paul wanted to get back to 100 percent. That meant rest and food. Since he had not been able to get more than a bite of his breakfast, Paul was hungry. Deciding to forgo the feeling of hunger he just sat and relaxed. Once it was dark, he would attempt to enter his hotel. But the Spirit within him told him otherwise. Paul was told he must make entry into the hospital to visit the man he had rescued. Paul must explain to the man he would have to make a choice. For some reason, which Paul did not know, the man was important. Of course, Paul never knew with the exception of Piotr, Alisa, Diane and Johnny. They were the only ones Paul ever knew the reason for being involved in their lives. All he could do then was eat fruit from the trees and rest to regain energy while waiting for nightfall.

The EADS CASA 295 plane landed at the back end of the Nassau airport. It had been given the country's highest clearance for landing. Airport personnel were instructed not to go near the plane and that the plane did not exist. It was 2210 hours as the two teams of thirty-three men off-loaded the plane and piled into the eight trucks on loan from the Bahamian Government. The team leader's comm device squawked in his ear as he stepped off the plane. It was a voice transmitting from Langley via satellite. The voice wanted to know the team's status. The team leader informed the voice he was dispersing his teams at the hotel and the wooded area near the hotel. "Negative," was the response he received. The leader was told to send one team to the hospital and establish a perimeter and to send a five-man team to Frazer's hotel room and wait. The remainder of the second team was to setup around the hotel as best they could. At no time was any member to use their side arms unless absolutely necessary. The snipers had been given permission to fire on sight. The team leader acknowledged his orders, though he clearly did not approve of them. For the leader, he and his men were trained to seek and destroy. Not being permitted to carry their full implement of weaponry was bad enough but having to wait for permission to use their side arms was ridiculous. He had been briefed on their target, at least somewhat, and he did not like endangering his men.

The CIA man, Marc Boyd was with them on the flight. He had given the team leader a psychological profile on Bannachek. He had told the leader that Bannachek would not resort to using violence unless he was cornered, and he would only kill if pushed to that level of danger. Since all of the team members were experts in hand-to-hand combat, they should be able to take Bannachek down without weapons. Boyd also told the teams that the snipers were authorized to fire upon sight and that the team members should take cover if the snipers fired. The snipers were ordered to request advice prior to taking any shots so the team members could disperse quickly. They needed to be about 200 yards from Bannachek if they fired at him. Boyd's comm device crackled in his ear.

"Yes, Sir," he said.

"We have a report that Bannachek saved a man on the beach from a shark attack. It is suspected that Bannachek will attempt to visit the man at the hospital. I have given the team leader instructions on how to deploy his men. You are to make entry with the five assigned team members into Bannachek's hotel. Wait for him there."

"Sir, what am I supposed to do if he shows up?"

"Stall Bannachek. Try and convince him to come in. Use as much time as you can get so the sniper can get set up. If we can get a few shots into Bannachek we might just be able to take him."

"And how am I supposed to stall him, if he shows up, Sir?"

"You have read his psych profile. You know he does not want to fight. See if you can get any information on him. See why he will not work with us. Anything will help Boyd!" Giving the affirmative to his orders Marc Boyd went off with the five assigned team members to Bannacheks' room. He hoped he could meet the infamous Paul Bannachek, but deep down he recognized the fear within himself. He really did not want to meet Bannachek at all. He would rather have Bannachek destroyed. A man like that roaming around, uncontrolled was simply too dangerous for anyone.

Checking his watch, Paul entered the Princess Margaret Hospital at 2210 hours. He checked in at the main desk and found the man who had been attacked by the shark was named Steve McCormick. He was on the second floor in room 212. Making his way up the stairs to the second floor, Paul stepped out of the stairwell scanning the hallway. It was relatively quiet in both directions. Seeing the room numbers posted on the wall he turned left and headed down the hallway, past the nurse's station to room 212. It was a four bedroom, but luckily for Paul there was only one patient. The patient was the man from the beach, Steve McCormick. Quietly, Paul stepped into the room and locked the door behind him. He walked over to the man's bed and gently nudged him until he opened his eyes. "You awake now, Steve?"

Focusing his eyes, Steve said, "It's you! You saved me. How will I ever be able to repay you?"

"You can't. Besides, I did *not* save you. I only rescued you! But you do need saving Steve."

"What do you mean?" the recuperating man asked.

Paul told him, "I want you to listen to these words. I want you think about them and then I will tell you what I mean. Understand?"

"Yes," the man responded fearfully.

"I have a message from God in my heart concerning the sinfulness of the wicked, there is no fear of God before their eyes. In their own eyes they flatter themselves too much to detect or hate their sin. The words of their mouths are wicked and deceitful; they fail to act wisely or do any good. Even on their beds they plot evil; they commit themselves to a sinful course and do not reject what is wrong." Then Paul asked, "What does that tell you Steve?"

"I am not sure. Are you some sort of Angel?"

"No, Steve. Believe me when I tell you, 'I am no Angel!' I am a man like you only I differ in two ways."

"How is that?" Steve asked.

"First and foremost, I serve God and his Son Jesus *my* Lord and Savior! Secondly, while I am a man like you, I am different because I can do things others cannot."

"So why did you save me, I mean rescue me, if you're telling me I am sort of an evil man?"

"It is not me telling you you're evil, Steve. What I just said came from the Bible. It comes from Psalms Chapter 36. I am only sharing with you what I am told to share with you. It is not for me to judge you. And you should be glad it is not up to me. If it was, I would not have rescued you!"

"Why? Aren't you judging me?"

"No, Steve. I made a judgement of your actions. You cheated on your wife! You verbally attacked that nice man and his wife simply because they are Jews. That, in my opinion, is evil! But hey, like I said, I am not your Judge. But if you search your heart, you know who your judge is."

Steve turned his head as he began to cry. He said, "Lord God, forgive me."

"Stop!" Paul exclaimed loudly. "If you are going to speak to God, I will help you to your knees and then leave the room. What you say to God in Heaven is between you and him. Not me. It is your relationship with God. Do you want help?"

"Yes, please," Steve said reaching out his hand. So, Paul helped him out of his hospital bed and then helped him lower himself to his knees. He then left the room and stood outside in the hallway as Steve McCormick pleaded to God for forgiveness and made his peace with the Lord. Paul looked in through the door's windowpane and then re-entered where he helped Steve back into his hospital bed.

"Why me?" Steve asked. "Why me?"

"I do not know," replied Paul. "But if I may make a suggestion."

"Yes, by all means. Tell me what you can."

Paul then said, "For some reason God has anointed or selected you Steve. There is a Bible in your bedside table. Start reading from Genesis 1 and do not stop until you read all 66 books. Go home and love your wife, live with honor and serve God and his Son Jesus. I promise you; it will not be easy! As you get closer to God, many things will be thrown at you by the adversary. When that happens, you will know that he is frightened you will never come back to his dark ways. Lead your wife and your unborn children to God. Rely on the Lord Jesus and he will help you. But you must trust. Do you understand?"

"I do. And I will. I promise you before God, I will."

"Again, do not promise me! I am simply a man. And if you make a promise to God, know that he will not take it lightly if you do not keep that promise."

"I understand. By the way, who are you?"

As Paul turned to leave the hospital room, he looked over his shoulder and said, "My name is Paul Bannachek." He then smiled at the man and left the room.

Checking his watch as he left the entrance of the hospital, Paul noted it was now 2310 hours. The parking lot was almost empty with only the late shift hospital staff vehicles parked in the small lot. He was almost at the end of the lot towards the wooded area when it hit him! He was not sure what it was, but his energy shield had engaged just before it hit him. The force knocked him back several feet and had lifted him off his feet. There had been no sound. Just an unbelievable force. As he lay there on the sand mixed parking lot, Paul felt dizzy. He could not think! Struggling to clear his mind, he saw the men rushing towards him. He thought he counted twelve men charging towards him. They were clearly professionals, as they were dressed in black uniforms. No insignias were visible. Paul managed to get to his feet just in time to defend himself.

Paul's energy was only at 90 percent when he was hit by whatever it was that hit him. He was concerned now because the weapon had reduced his energy to 75 percent. Still more than enough to defeat the onslaught of trained killers coming at him. He decided to use his full strength and speed to defeat his enemies as they attacked. While they were well trained, they were no match for his speed and strength. The training Mary had provided him years ago, in conjunction with his abilities, enabled Paul to wipe out the attack force in less than two minutes. Scanning the downed men, he saw that he had killed none. Many were unconscious in bloodied heaps and many were lying, moaning in pain, but he had killed none. About four minutes had passed from the time he had been hit with the strange weapon and the time it took to incapacitate the twelve men. Just as he turned for the woods he was hit again, knocking Paul six feet back and down to the ground.

Dizziness again surrounded Paul's brain. He fought hard to regain full control of his senses, this time taking only ten seconds. He felt his energy capacity was now down to 60 percent. Using his mind's eye, he searched and found the sniper and his spotter with their strange looking rifle. He fired a lethal plasma energy round at their nest destroying them and everything within 50 feet! At that moment Paul's started receiving small arms fire from every direction. He saw men coming out from every possible hiding place, firing repressed pistols, their bullets hitting his shield! He figured there must be eighteen of them. They fired their weapons until empty and would drop the weapons magazines and reload on the run still firing. Having enough and being weakened by the strange new weapon, Paul returned simple lethal plasma shots killing every man firing at him. Three men turned and ran for cover. He let them live. The rest, however, had forced his hand and gave their lives for nothing!

Charging through the woods, Paul was still woozy from the new weapons used on him. Concentrating, he forced himself to use energy on his mind's eye. There had been a total of 32 men who had attacked him. He killed 20 all total. The other 12 would be out for a couple of hours, but, he figured, there may be more lying-in wait for him. They may have another strange weapon they could use on him! He used his mind's eye to scan as far as he could as he ran through the woods. Thanks to the strange weapons used on him in Germany his mind was much more powerful. He could now see almost two miles in any direction vice his old half mile ability. There they were about a mile and a half out. They were waiting for him. Some with viewpoints of his hotel and some watching the woods. They had night vision glasses on. Paul decided he would not wait to be attacked again and yet he did not want to be forced to kill again.

Finding that there were twenty-four men in the woods Paul began concentrating on their locations. Once he was 200 yards out, he opened fire with twenty-four plasma stunning rounds in a rapid-fire movement. Each plasma round finding its target easily, stunning the man and placing him into an unconscious mode for several hours. Then he was hit again. Another pulse from the same sort of weapon. It could not be the same weapon since Paul had destroyed it with his blast of plasma and energy mix. He fired at the first sniper's nest. Laying on the ground in immense pain, Paul had to force himself to concentrate on where the shot came from. Fighting the groggy dizziness, he found the sniper's nest 150 yards to his south. They were in a tree. They had a perfect view of the hotel and the woods. Having enough of this, Paul fired another explosive plasma energy round at the tree exploding it and its inhabitants to nothing. He then lay there for another two minutes trying to maintain focus. Even with the small arms fire recharging him he was now down to 50 percent power. If they had another weapon like the new ones just used on him, he may not make it out! He had to get back to his room, get his ID taped in the toilet and get off the island. Somehow!

Still dizzy, Paul made it from the woods to the beach and then to the back of the Breeze's hotel. He decided to jump to the third floor where he was able to grab the ledge and pull himself up. He then slowly climbed to the sixth floor and over to his room's balcony. Once there he sensed there were people in his room. He waited. Using his mind's eye, he saw one was in the closet, one was in the bathroom and two were posted around the corner of the entrance way to his room. The other man was sitting on his couch working a small radio. Paul slid open the screen door and fired rapid fire stun plasma rounds hitting four of the five men. The fifth man on the couch jumped back from his position, instinctively grabbing for his pistol in the shoulder holster he carried.

"Don't!" Paul hissed at the intruder.

Looking around his room Paul walked up to the man on the couch. The man appeared to be about 30 years old. His radio was chirping from someone calling himself the team leader calling for help. Paul smiled at the man and said, "Just in case you don't know, my name is Paul Bannachek."

"I know who you are, Bannachek," the man said angrily. "You going to kill me like you did them?"

"Paul looked at the unconscious men and said, 'Oh, they are not dead. They are near comatose but not dead. Don't worry, they will be up and around in a few hours. That gives you and I some time to talk."

"I have nothing to say to you Bannachek. Only, you better get out because we have two more teams coming as I speak," Marc Boyd said lying.

"Oh, I don't think so Mister," replied Paul. "I think you and whoever is on the other end of that radio is just about all there is. So here is how it is going to go. I am going to ask you questions and you are going to answer those questions. Every time you refuse, or you lie, and believe me, I will know when you're lying, and I will hurt you. How does that sound?"

"Bannachek, I know about how you make people talk. Do whatever you feel you need to do; I do not care how much you hurt me because I know in the end you will heal me! So, go ahead, do your best or rather your worst. You cannot help who you are and that is your weakness."

"What do you mean I cannot help who I am?"

"I have read all the reports on you Bannachek. I know a great deal about what you have been doing and all the people you have helped. You are pathetically weak in your need to help others and that will be your downfall. With all of your abilities and all of your knowledge, you could have anything you wanted, but instead you go around creating dissent even among Christians who you seem to believe are special."

"Mister, you have no real idea of what I do. But it is nice to know you and those reports are full of disinformation. If you really knew who I am you would either want to help me or destroy me. Instead, you and those in your agency try to capture me. I will never allow that to happen. Ever!"

"How long do you think you can keep this up Bannachek? 30 to 40 years ago you had the advantage. But now with all the technology we have at our fingertips, there is nowhere you can go where we cannot find you. We found you here, didn't we?"

"Yes, you did. Now how about telling me how you got here so quickly. You had two teams here in less than twelve hours. You could not have gotten the news of the shark attack for a couple hours after it happened. I know a little about how you people operate too you know. So how did you find me so quickly?"

"Like I said Bannachek, I'm not telling you anything. Go ahead, hurt me! Then you can heal me."

"Huh," is all Paul said before firing a stun plasma round into Boyd. He then walked over to the man and placed his hands on Boyd's unconscious head. Using his telepathic skills Paul began searching Boyd's mind. He learned everything about the man in a matter of a minute. Paul then decided to punish Boyd. He began wiping Boyd's memory of everything for the past thirteen years. When the man regained consciousness, he would think he was twenty-one and just out of college. He would never regain his memories and the agency would not be able to help him retrieve those memories. Marc Boyd would have to restart his life.

Upon gaining the information he needed, Paul found his other identification taped in the toilet in his hotel bathroom. It had been unmolested. He raised his shirt and taped the documents and money to his flat belly using the duct tape. Paul then quickly grabbed his clothing and stuffed them into his backpack, placed it on his back and jumped from the sixth-floor balcony to the beach. He figured the only way off the island now was by boat. Paul began running north on the beach towards the marina he had seen on his reconnoiter the day before. He hoped he could find a fast boat that had enough capacity to cover the 185 miles to Miami. A larger boat could make it easily, but they did not have the speed he would need. Paul needed to find a fast, small boat. As he ran towards the marina Paul destroyed his current identification. Knowing that the passports and driver's license had RFID technology he now knew he could be tracked by satellite. Once they were destroyed by the fire from a plasma blast Paul, activated his shield. No satellite could track him now.

The marina was quiet at 0345 hours. Paul took his time as he crept around searching for the perfect boat. It did not take him long to spot two Mercedes-Benz AMG Cigarette racing boats. The boats were refueling and both boats had four men on and around them. Paul figured they were drug smugglers refueling for their next run. One boat would be perfect, but to get around the heavily armed men would mean he would have to use his telepathy. Surveying the men's minds, he knew the larger black boat had the cash from the US and the blue boat was for security. As quickly as he could Paul made it to the refueling boats and fired non-lethal stun plasma rounds into the eight men. He pulled the men off the boats and then wiped their memories. Leaving the security boat undamaged, Paul untied the mooring line of the black Mercedes boat and slowly headed out to sea. Once he was at sea, Paul opened up the throttle traveling at 130 mph. He would make Miami by 0530. Once he was a mile offshore, he would destroy the boat and swim inland. He hoped he did not run into the coast guard. If he did, he would have to use more of his energy to escape them. Since he was now down to thirty five percent Paul knew he could not afford to use more. He needed to eat and sleep so he could re-charge.

2

Finding Alisa

Exploding the Mercedes-Benz AMG Cigarette racing boat had
provided Paul a much-needed charge. He had been at below 30
percent energy when the kinetic energy from explosion the boat
provided Paul a 20 percent boost. His energy shield absorbed the
blast allowing Paul to expend enough energy to swim the mile
to shore without draining himself too much. He made it to the
shoreline at 0550 hours. It was still dark, and the tide was high.
Avoiding the fisherman, Paul swam north by northwest coming
ashore in the town of Miami Gardens. He walked up the beach
about a mile and then headed west into town. He spotted a
Denny's Restaurant where he sat and ordered his normal steak
and eggs with coffee and milk. It felt good to eat since he had
not had anything since his one bite of breakfast at the Breeze's
hotel and the scrounged fresh fruit from the trees where he had
hidden himself. After his breakfast, Paul hailed a taxi and asked
to be taken to the nearest Motel 6 which was in central Miami.
Paul did not want to be centrally located but he understood that
a Motel 6 would not have as many cameras. He knew he would

not attract as much attention arriving with only a backpack too.

The cab ride took a quick 15 minutes since it was only 0630. Paul checked into his room where he could get some sleep. He had not slept for almost 28 hours. His head hurt and while the meal had re-charged his energy, he needed rest. Paul set his alarm for 1500 and passed out. When the alarm woke him, he took a shower and ordered a pizza from the nearest Domino's pizza. He ordered an extra-large deluxe pizza with a chef salad. Sitting in his room waiting for his food delivery, Paul thought about the last couple of days. He thought about what he had learned from Marc Boyd. Searching into the man's mind had taught him a great deal. He now knew that trains and most planes had hidden cameras on board which recorded travelers. Those faces were constantly fed via satellite to massive computers programmed with facial recognition systems that constantly searched for various possible threats. Once a face was selected, it was immediately sent to Langley or to other agencies depending on who was doing the search. Paul now understood that if he was to fly, he would have to mentally disable cameras on board the airplane to hide his presence. Even buses were becoming too dangerous for Paul. His best mode of travel would be cars and freight trains.

Eating his fresh, hot pizza Paul thought about the other information he had learned from Boyd. He now knew that the new man in charge of the Office of Scientific Intelligence was named John Danick. For some reason Boyd did not like Danick. He suspected that Danick was a Christian but hiding his beliefs. Boyd also suspected that Danick did not believe they should be hunting Paul but did so as those were his orders. Wondering if that was true, Paul thought he may actually have an ally within the government that has been hunting him for over 40 years. What Paul found most interesting was the agency had never bothered to search for "Paul Bannachek." Maybe it was because he had never used his name since Mary had taken him as a young teenager, or maybe it was because the agency figured he had killed off his own identity. It was useful to know he could use his own name, if for anything, for travel. The new weapon they possessed bothered Paul. He had no defense against it. His only advantage was after the weapon was fired at him; it took several minutes to re-charge. And it only had a range of 200 yards at the maximum. But it was new, and they could improve it!

Falling asleep Paul thought about Alisa. He ached for her! He missed the little things of their marriage like always holding hands. He missed her sense of humor. He missed her scent. Most of all he missed her faith. She had this uncanny devotion for being new to the faith. It almost seemed to Paul as if she was created to have the faith she had. He missed her strength and her fortitude. He missed making love to his wife. Paul knew she had been his blessing and his onetime gift. There would not ever be another woman in Paul's life, he was sure of that. He felt grateful to God for allowing his marriage. But he also somewhat resented that he had lost Alisa because of what he was created to do. He would never, nor could he ever resent God or his Son Jesus. That old feeling of emptiness over Alisa's loss contrasted the warmth that filled his chest for his love of God as he passed out.

A presence in his room awoke Paul from a deep sleep. He felt there was someone there as he jumped out of his hotel bed in the dark room. Strangely his shield had not activated. As he focused his eyes, he saw her. There standing across the room was Alisa! He told himself it could not be her. It had to be a dream. Yes, he had to still be dreaming! Or was she an aberration of some sort? No, he had to be dreaming! Then she spoke.

"Paul, my darling husband, I have missed you for so long. And now I have been given the opportunity to see you!"

As Paul tried to reach out to his wife she said, "No Paul. You cannot touch me. I am here to tell you that you must come find me. Come find me Paul!"

"Baby-Girl! Where are you?"

"Kaliningrad, Paul. I am at Kaliningrad. Come find me, Paul. Please hurry. You must come find me!" Alisa then disappeared as if she had never been in the hotel room.

Sitting back down on the bed, Paul was in shock. Had he dreamed what he had just seen? Or had Alisa somehow been permitted to show herself to him? He knew she had died or rather had been killed in 1962 by the old KGB. How could she just appear now? Why had she been allowed to appear to him? Paul had no real understanding of Heaven though he did know that Angels could travel through what he called portals. But Alisa was not an Angel. All Paul could do was take it on faith that he was supposed to go to Kaliningrad. But why hadn't Michael shown himself. Then Paul remembered that Michael would only come when the Lord sent him. Paul was to listen to the Spirit within him most of the time. He was to depend on his faith when he was being led where God wanted him to go. For Paul, that was, at times, so very hard to do. He had seen so much in the past 40 years and he had been tested so many times. What was worse was the dark forces that tried to mislead him in ways he sometimes did not understand. But since Alisa showed herself, he would go to Kaliningrad. He would search for her. He felt the Spirit within him jump with joy, so he believed he was making the right decision. He would go to Kaliningrad and find his wife.

Paul decided he needed to find a travel agent. They were almost non-existent anymore in the age of computers. Paul hailed a taxi one block from the Motel 6 and requested the driver to take him to a travel agent. The driver told him the only agent he knew of was a 20-minute ride away. Paul handed the driver two $50 dollar bills and said, "Fine. Take me there." The driver drove Paul to a small mini-mall and dropped him outside a place called Finol Ever after Travel. It was 0930. The agency was just opening so Paul opted to walk over to the coffee shop two doors down and ordered a large coffee with cream and sugar and a pastry. He ate his pastry and walked back to the travel agency with his large half-drunk coffee. As he entered, he noticed two young women at their desks. Both of them seemed to be attracted to Paul as he entered. Not caring which agent he dealt with, Paul asked if either of the women could help him. The brunette spoke first so he walked over and asked if he could sit down.

After about ten minutes of small talk Paul produced his passport with the name of Troy Tomlin and one of his two credit cards. The round-trip airfare would cost him $2700.47 US currency on Polish airlines LOT. Normally the cost was about $1750 US, but Paul was leaving in just three days and he had been able to get the last business class ticket available. The flight would depart on Saturday the 28th and return on the 18th of December. He was sure he would be flagged by Homeland Security because of the timing of his purchase and his departure. Paul told the travel agent he was visiting a sick friend who may not survive the illness. That information was typed into the computer as well. Paul was told to pick up his tickets at the airport on the morning of his flight. All he had to do was sit in his hotel room for three days and stay out of trouble. He hoped that was possible during his taxi ride back to his motel room. For some reason trouble always found Paul. It was his nature.

The travel agent had booked Paul a room at the Hotel Kaiserhof, which was rated as superb. The cost was only $83.00 per night. Clearly a good price but then that was US currency. The flight would be nineteen hours at a good price and the room was more than fairly priced Paul thought. It did not really matter to him though. Each of his credit cards had a $50,000 dollar limit and he had access to just under $90,000 dollars under his Troy Tomlin identification. He had $8,000 cash on him, but he would need to get to a local Miami bank the next day to pull another $5,000 using his debt card. There would be a charge of course but not more than three percent. He did believe he needed to purchase luggage and some additional clothing. Russians were security cautious and naturally inquisitive. Paul had to appear as an American tourist visiting for vacation. The Americans would think he was visiting a sick friend and the Russians would think he was a tourist. If the two government's security agencies communicated Paul would deal with that problem if and when it arose. For now, he needed to do what he hated - shop.

After completing the dreaded task of shopping for clothes, Paul went back to his motel room and washed everything after removing all the RFID chips. After drying and ironing his clothes, he went to work on his new Kenetrek boots. Removing the soles of the shoes first and setting them aside Paul went to work on carving the hard rubber pieces he had purchased at a small hardware store. He made sure they were an exact fit for his new boots. He then painted each side with red lead paint he had picked up at a nearby marina. Paul created a small heat bloom to dry the rubber and then wrapped them in plastic which he subsequently melted and shaped using his mind. Once the inserts were dry, he placed the five gold coins he had purchased at a rare coin shop into the rubber inserts and then wrapped them in plastic again. His final phase was to put another coat of red lead paint onto the rubber and dry them. He placed them into his new boots and resealed the soles to the bottom of the boots. Now he was sure the airport detectors would not pick up the coins. No matter what happened he had his $10,000 dollar emergency fund on him just in case he lost his wallet, or worse. All he had to do now was eat and sleep to ensure he was at full capacity for his flight on Saturday.

The flight to Kaliningrad was perfectly timed at nineteen hours and six minutes. Paul had taken no chances at either airport. He engaged his shield to its lowest level thereby blocking the cameras from being able to see him, but also being invisible to the naked eye. He had used his telekinetic ability to disable the hidden cameras on the plane as well. The cameras would simply appear as though they malfunctioned. Clearing customs in Russia was more difficult than in the US. Paul had to use his telepathy on the Russian security personnel so that their screens appeared to indicate that he was a tourist vice the actual information he had provided in the States—that he was visiting a sick relative. He also had to place thoughts in the Russian's minds that he was not worth investigating. Once outside the airport, Paul hailed a taxi and enjoyed his scenic route to the hotel Kaiserhof. Paul knew the cabbie was literally taking him for a ride, but he did not mind. He used the rip-off ride to study and memorize every street, alleyway and building. It struck him strange how much Kaliningrad had changed in 80 years! Though in actuality, it had only been a year since he had last been there. He still could not get use to the time travel experience he had had. Once at the hotel, Paul tipped the driver an above average amount and thanked the man in Russian saying, "Thanks for the *ride*," he said in a sarcastic tone that let the driver know that Paul knew they had taken an excessively long route to the hotel.

Entering the Hotel Kaiserhof, Paul dismantled all of the hotel cameras using his telekinesis. He basically made every camera inoperable as well as the system they were connected to. Hotel security would have to replace the entire system, but first they would have to investigate how the problem occurred. Paul figured he would have at least three days before the cameras were replaced and operable again so he could relax or a bit. He checked into his room, leaving his passport at the front desk as required by law, and took the elevator to the top floor. Finding his room, Paul entered, quickly unpacked, and changed his clothes. He put on the new Aviator leather jacket he had purchased at a military surplus store. It was almost an exact match to the one he lost in Italy when the HERO was sunk by the German U-boat. Unsure of where he was going, Paul secured his passport from the front desk and headed out into the city. He figured he would let the Spirit within him lead him wherever he was going.

Having walked almost the entire city, Paul ended up at the

Church of St. Andrew the Apostle. Once there, he was led inside by the Spirit within himself. The church was old and had many religious statues and memorabilia. Remembering that St. Andrew was the brother of Simon Peter and a disciple of Christ Jesus who had recognized Jesus as soon as he saw him, Paul wondered if the church had some sort of special meaning for him. Why was he led there? What purpose could the old church have in finding Alisa? As he pondered these thoughts, Paul walked into the Sanctuary, chose a pew in the middle of the holy room, and sat down. He looked up at the Altar. There was a large, beautiful cross with a replica of Jesus nailed to it, hanging there with His blood flowing from the wounds inflicted by the Romans. To Paul it was such a sad yet beautiful representation of how our Lord sacrificed himself for mankind. He had never seen anything quite like it in any of the churches he had ever visited.

Sensing someone was watching him, Paul dropped to his knees and began to pray. His prayer lasted only three minutes before feeling a hand touch his left shoulder. He was surprised he had not sensed anyone come near him! Paul looked over his shoulder to see a man of about 80 years old standing next to him propped up with a wooden cane. "Hello Paul," the man said gently.

Shocked and dismayed, Paul literally jumped to his feet saying, "How do you know me, Mister?"

Smiling, the man said, "Paul I have been waiting 58 years for you to come here."

"What? What are you saying, Mister?"

"Please Paul, come with me to my office. I have something I have been holding for you. Something you may find has great value."

Paul felt the Spirit within him jump with joy as he followed the old man to the back office of the old church. Once in the office the old man closed and locked the door, and slowly walked over to his large wooden desk. Once seated, the man offered Paul a glass of wine, which Paul gladly welcomed.

"Sir, would you mind explaining yourself please?" Paul asked.

"Of course, Paul. My name is Metropolitan Alexander Bromhofsky. I have been the head of this church for almost 40 years now. I have been waiting for you, hoping you would show so that I may retire."

"Waiting for me?" Paul asked.

"Would you care for that glass of wine now, Paul?"

"Yes Sir. I think I need one."

"Fine. Would you mind going over to the large cabinet over there and getting the large crystal wine decanter and two crystal glasses please," the Metropolitan said pointing." Paul stood up from his large cushioned wooden chair and did as he was instructed. He came back to the desk and poured a glass for each of them.

"Now, if you do not mind, I will start from the beginning, the old man said in a wise, yet peaceful tone.

"Please do."

"I met Alisa in 1958. In those days I was a young, and as you Americans would call, a snot-nosed priest. I worked as a cobbler by day to support myself, and I preached into the late evenings secretly."

"In secret?" Paul asked.

"Yes, Paul, in secret. In those days the KGB arrested and even murdered many of us who were not sanctioned by the state. Only those approved by the government were allowed to preach and even they were watched closely to ensure the government's teaching was the only word preached. Of course, those of us who truly loved God and his Son Jesus would never go along with that. I met Alisa one day when she came into my shop. I recognized her immediately as Alisa Bannachek, one of the most wanted criminals in Russia."

"Criminal? My Alisa could never be a criminal! And what do you mean you recognized her?"

"Paul, Alisa was *deemed* a criminal by the state because of what she was doing."

"Well, what was she doing?" Paul nervously asked.

"She was doing God's work, Paul. Alisa was helping Jews escape to Israel. And she was hiding Christians and protecting them from the KGB."

"I knew she had a mission, but I was not exactly sure what she was going to be doing," Paul said.

"She was truly wonderful and giving Paul. Alisa had rescued over one thousand Jews and funded their way out of Russia. She utilized what she called the Russian "Underground Railroad." She said you had taught her about America's own Underground-Railroad for the slaves from your early and middle 19th century."

Chuckling, Paul said, "Sounds like my Alisa."

"Yes. She was an amazing woman. She was an amazing fighter too. Alisa had risked her life hundreds of times fighting soldiers and KGB Officers. Unfortunately, she also had been forced to kill on numerous occasions. And I want you to know Paul, while many men tried, not one was able to win her affections. She was devoted to God, his Son Jesus, and you every day until the KGB killed her."

Feeling his emotions welling up to the forefront, Paul took a large gulp of wine and asked, "How did she die?"

"Paul, I am sorry to say she died sacrificing herself for me, my beautiful pregnant wife Rominiska, our one-year-old son, and the twelve Christians I was giving communion too. The twelve and I were able to escape but regretfully, my wife, our unborn child and our son died with Alisa."

Tears filling his eyes, Paul asked, "How?"

"We were at one of many of Alisa's safe houses here in town. She had many throughout Russia. We were there, as I have said, so I could give communion. Someone informed on us. The KGB arrived just as I was giving the blood of our Lord Jesus. The KGB broke down the back door, entering with drawn weapons. Alisa immediately drew her pistol and began firing. She killed three while the fourth one escaped. Alisa directed us to the escape tunnel in the kitchen while returning fire with the many KGB and soldiers outside at the front of the house. We were able to get the twelve out before it happened."

"*What* happened?" Paul asked.

"The KGB launched a grenade through the front window. Alisa dived on top of it just before it exploded. We were saved, but she was blown apart, Paul. I snuck out from the tunnel and pulled her torso out of the raging fire and into the tunnel."

"Why. Why would you not let her be cremated?" Paul asked.

"Because Paul. I had promised her just a few weeks before that night, if anything ever happened to her, I would bury her body in secret."

"In secret? Why was that necessary?" Paul asked.

"Paul, Alisa had told me that when she died, she wanted to be buried in secret so her grave would not be defiled. She told me that one day you would come for her and she wanted you to take her home to America to be buried with your family. She also gave me two envelopes that I was never too open. She told me that when you came, and she said you *would* come, I was to give them to you."

At that moment, the Metropolitan turned white and crossed himself as he peered past Paul's shoulder. Paul turned to see Michael standing there. "Greeting's from those who are proud of you Paul," Michael said. "I have come with instructions for you."

Paul sat there and thought a moment before he asked in a sarcastic manner, "And what exactly are those instructions?"

"I have been sent to tell you that you must leave this place and go to St. Petersburg. They are attempting to create *the* formula and you must go there and destroy the place."

"You are not Michael!"

"You dare to question me and my authority!"

Paul replied, "I never question Michael. But you are not he! I command you in the name of God's Son Jesus to show your true self! Now!" The entity twisted and contorted as it changed forms into another being while screaming, "Do not use that name before me!"

Paul then said, "I command you in the name of God's Son Jesus to go back to where you came!" The entity then disappeared into an opening in the room's atmosphere.

The Metropolitan sat there looking as white as a sheet. He began choking and breathing. Paul ran over to his side of the desk and placed his hands on him to say, "You are healed in the name of Jesus, the Son of God, my Lord and Savior." Using his energy, he concentrated on the Metropolitan's heart, slowing it to a normal pace and easing the blood flow. The Metropolitan began to ease his breathing as his color returned to normal. After several minutes, he was finally able to speak again.

"Paul, what was that?"

In a gentle voice Paul said, "That was one of the many fallen. It was trying to trick me."

"But how did you know?" asked the Metropolitan.

"I have been blessed to have visits from God's Angel, Michael. He comes to me from time to time to warn and to instruct me."

"But how did you know it was not him? Didn't he look like Michael?"

"Yes, he appeared to look as Michael does, but he did not speak as the Angel always speaks."

The Metropolitan asked, "How does he speak to you?"

"Michael is an Angel of God. Every time he comes to me, he always greets me with "Greetings from God, Praise His Glorious Name, and from the Lord Jesus whom you serve." That was how I knew it was not Michael." Paul went further to explain that

Michael, along with the Holy Spirit within him, guided him. He told the Metropolitan that Michael was always gentle with him even if he questioned the Angel. What he had to figure out is why the dark fallen angel tried to convince him to go to St. Petersburg. He then asked the Metropolitan, "Do you not know scripture?"

"What do you mean, Paul? Of course, I know scripture!"

"Well then, I ask you to think of Ephesians 6:12 where it is written, 'For our struggle is not against flesh and blood, but against the rulers, against the authorities, against the powers of this dark world and against the spiritual forces of evil in the heavenly realms. And I ask you to think of Romans 8:37-39 wherein it says, 'No, in all these things we are more than conquerors through him who loved us. For I am convinced that neither death nor life, neither angels nor demons, neither the present nor the future, nor any powers, neither height nor depth, nor anything else in all creation, will be able to separate us from the love of God that is in Christ Jesus our LORD.' And did not Jesus himself say in John 14:30 'I will not speak much more with you, for the ruler of the world is coming, and he has nothing in me.' Does this not warn you about the fallen and the dark forces released against all mankind?"

"I know those verses and more Paul. It's just that I have never seen anything like what I just witnessed!"

"Sir, if you truly trust in the word then you should not be surprised when you do see things like what you just witnessed. The Nicene Creed is quoted many times in churches. Are you saying you do not believe what you say in the Sanctuary?"

Feeling perplexed and guilty, the old man became quiet. Paul felt compassion for the old man and told him he should not fret. "Many believers do not truly believe in the realms around us. They do not understand because they were not meant to understand. You have been blessed to witness this. Now, may I see the envelopes?"

The Metropolitan placed the two envelopes before Paul and sat back in his chair still bewildered at what he had witnessed. Paul reached over and picked up the envelopes feeling one was light and the other was heavy and bulky. He decided to open the heavy envelope first. Gently tearing it open from its side, Paul let the contents fall out into his hand. There in his hand sat a gold-roped chain with a 3 inch by 4-inch crucifix attached to it. On the front of the crucifix was a replica of Jesus, with a thorn crown and red blood coming from his small hands, feet and side. Affixed on the back, was a ring. The ring contained a small engraving on it which said, "Paul and Alisa Bannachek blessed marriage by God and His Son Jesus." Shaking the envelope again, three small pieces of paper fell out. Paul read the first small note.

"My darling and loving husband Paul. I had this made for you after the war ended. I have kept it knowing that someday you would retrieve it. I love you! ~Alisa." Paul's eyes welled up with tears as he held the heavy present in his hand. He opened his shirt and placed the chain and crucifix around his neck and then buttoned it back up. Regaining control of his emotions, Paul opened the second envelope and read the one-page letter.

"Paul, my love, if you are reading this then you have come for me. I am so grateful that I have always known you would come for me. Because I know, and have always known, that you love me for me and not for my appearance. I could never ask for a better husband Paul, and I am truly sorry for the way I left you. I had to leave because I knew you would never leave my side. You can never place anyone before God, Paul. Ever! And though I understand how hard your life has been and will continue to be, I want you to know that I believe you have been blessed by being who you are. Just as I was blessed to be your wife and to have my mission in serving God and his Son Jesus our Lord and Savior! Be strong and courageous and keep your hope in the Lord. One day we will be together again. I love you my darling and I always will love you! Your adoring and faithful wife, ~Alisa." Folding the letter, Paul could no longer contain his emotions. He began to weep!

The Metropolitan struggled to get up from his desk, and walking over to Paul, placed his arm around Paul's shoulder. He tried to comfort Paul while he wept but Paul was inconsolable. The old man told Paul he was truly sorry for Paul's loss and knew that Alisa was watching them at that very moment. "Alisa would want you to be strong, my son. She would want you to carry on. Remember your faith Paul! Remember why you are here and what you were created to do!"

Paul's weeping slowed and finally stopped. Angrily he said, "What do you know of me, Metropolitan? What do you know about me or what I have lost or how I am forced to live?"

"Paul, Alisa told me *all* about you. She told me about your life, your parents, and how you are hunted in our time. I would never want your life Paul, but I, at least, recognize you are blessed."

"Yeah, some blessing! I feel as though I am cursed. Why is that Metropolitan? Why?"

"Because you are a man. Because while you have been given great wisdom and powers or abilities, you are still just a man. But you were created for the purpose of defending and fighting for those who deserve the opportunity to choose, Paul. You know that. I believe one day, when you finally get to Heaven you will see just how much good you have done."

Paul remained silent. His anger quickly subsided, and he immediately felt guilty for his outburst and harsh words. He asked to be taken to Alisa's grave. The old man explained that Alisa no longer had a grave. He and his son had unburied her back in 1996 and had her remains cremated. He walked back to his desk and pulled out a small, beautiful oak box and handed it to Paul.

"These are Alisa's ashes Paul. And in the box is the wedding band you made for her in the woods." Nervously Paul accepted the box. He opened it to see the white dust-like material and the wedding band he had placed on Alisa's finger almost eighty years ago. Although for Paul, it was just over a year.

He then picked up the third piece of paper and read it. It was dated March 31, 1957. "Paul, Michael instructed me to open an account for you with $500,000 francs. He said you would have need of this in your time. I have therefore done as I was instructed. The Bank is the same one we deposited the gold in. The account is numbered which I know you will understand. Your loving wife Alisa." The number read 03-22-20/20-31:10-31/07-22-60. Paul immediately understood the code. It was Alisa's birthday followed by the twentieth book in the Bible, which is Proverbs, the thirty-first chapter, verses 10 thru 31, followed by Paul's birthday. The Bible verse was that which he quoted to her on the train from New York to Cincinnati, Ohio back in 1941. It was the Proverb of a good wife. Sitting there for a few minutes, Paul slowly digested the letters and the gift before him. He decided he would take Alisa's remains and bury them with his parents at the Homewood, Illinois cemetery. But first he would have to get to the UBS bank in Switzerland! He would have to transfer the funds to the account which Johnny would direct him to. He quickly ran the numbers in his head realizing that the $500,000 francs in 1957 would be worth over $4.5 million dollars now. He really did not need the money, but Alisa specified that Michael had instructed her to do it. So maybe he would need the cash

Looking up at the Metropolitan, Paul felt an overwhelming sense of gratitude flow over himself. The old man had kept his word to Alisa. He had taken many risks in his life for God and for the Lord Jesus. Paul thanked the old Metropolitan and told him he needed to leave immediately and get to Switzerland. He asked where the nearest train station was. The old Metropolitan asked why Paul didn't fly. After explaining his difficulties in flying and staying hidden, the Metropolitan understood. He gave Paul directions to the train station and then asked, "Will I ever see you again, Paul?" Paul said he might stop by on the way back but that depended on a lot of variables. He then stood up and shook the old preacher's hand, thanking him for his friendship towards Alisa.

Walking out of the old church, Paul began to wonder how the dark forces had known where he was. He wondered if those forces always knew his whereabouts. He thought, "Why didn't Michael show up? Had Michael abandoned him? Was God no longer going to help him? Had he angered God because of his constant complaining?"

Arriving at the Kaliningrad train station Paul followed his normal routine of engaging his shield to its minimum strength in order to block all cameras from seeing him. He then purchased a round trip ticket to Geneva, Switzerland on the Polregio train line. The round trip only cost him $820.00 US currency. The trip would only take 22 hours. It was plenty of time to eat and sleep and plan his visit to and escape from the UBS bank in Geneva. He knew they would have an excessive number of cameras and figured if he disabled them all, the bank may shut down. His only hope was to engage his shield before departing the train and keeping it engaged for the entire time he was in Geneva. If a street camera or ATM or business camera located him, it would only be a matter of hours before the CIA had a team or two on the ground hunting for him yet again. And he knew, with their new REMP weapon, his risk of being captured increased. He could not allow that, ever!

Once Paul was on the train he began walking through every car, disabling the cameras. Once he was sure all surveillance was disengaged, he turned off his shield. He could not risk bumping into another passenger and them to feel the small shock if he touched them. It would not harm them, but it could cause them to wonder about him. He located his seat in coach class, sat down and began to think. Paul understood that this trip, in the eyes of many, would seem like an unnecessary risk; but for him, it was about keeping his promise to Alisa. It was about ensuring she was buried with his family. It was about the love and honor he had for his wife, whether she be alive or in Heaven. Besides, he told himself, he now knew that not only was the CIA and every other intelligence agency in the world was tracking him, but also the dark forces. That meant he really had no safe place to hide. All he could do was run and try to avoid them all. Since that was not possible, Paul accepted that with the newer and improved technology readily at the fingertips of Government's fingertips, he would have to fight a great deal more than he had. He felt so tired from all the fighting! All he wanted to do was be left alone and to help those he was meant to help. Paul still had not grasped the battle he was in the middle of.

Sleeping for six hours, Paul awoke refreshed but also felt famished. He decided to walk toward the restaurant car to get some much-needed nourishment. Finding an open seat at a table, Paul ordered two chef's salads with extra egg, a large baked potato with extra sour cream, bacon bits and chives along with two bottles of water, non-gas. Paul could not stand carbonated water and could not understand why Europeans enjoyed it so much. As he waited on his meal, he listened to the various conversations going on around him. People spoke Russian, Polish, French German and one American couple spoke in English. It always baffled Paul how people were so ignorant of the world in which they lived. None of them seemed to understand that it was all just temporary, at least temporary in God's time. Thousands of years had gone by since Adam and Eve had been kicked out of Eden and yet that time was but a moment to God, His Son Jesus and all those in Heaven. People were so egocentric that they just did not seem to understand the truer meaning of life and what kind of gift life actually was. Instead, people seemed so self-absorbed. They only cared about what they wanted, and more often than not, did not really care about their fellow man. They cared about money, sex, power and possessions. He mused to himself the old saying, "You can't take it with you" wondering who came up with that expression. *Whoever it was*, he told himself, *they were very wise*.

Feeling completely nourished and totally recharged after his meal, Paul walked towards his car and decided to head towards the rear of the train to get some crisp, late November air. Stopping by his care, he grabbed his backpack and headed back. Upon reaching the frigid air outside, Paul began thinking of Alisa and their short but wonderful history. As angry as he was about losing her, he was grateful to God for the time they had together. Still, for Paul, the anger was ever present. He understood he had been given the choice long ago to forgo who he was and to give up his abilities or what some called powers. And he knew he had made the choice to continue on. He had to accept the responsibility of his decision. He also knew if he had chosen to give up who he was created to be, he never would have met Alisa nor would he have ever known what it was like to truly love a woman. At that moment Michael appeared.

"Greetings from God, **Praise His Glorious Name**," the Angel said.

"Michael! I am so glad to see you. Where have you been?"

"I have been doing battle for God, **Praise His Glorious Name**. Where else would I be?"

"Well, you could have been back at the church with the Metropolitan and me, that's where! Do you know that a dark one showed up claiming to be you?"

"Yes, Paul, I do know. And you handled yourself admirably. God, **Praise His Glorious Name**, is so proud of you. You did not let yourself be fooled."

"Yeah, well I may not have been fooled but I was scared! Why didn't you come?"

"Paul, God, **Praise His Glorious Name**, knew you would be

fine. You cannot become dependent upon me, Paul! You must trust the Spirit within you."

"Yeah, but..."

"No buts, Paul. I am your guide and that is all I am instructed to do. You have great abilities and powers, so you must learn to use them all. Learn to use them for the purpose you were created for."

Angrily, Paul said, "Fine! So why are you here this time, Michael?

"You should not be angry, Paul. Know that you are blessed."

"Blessed! Why do I feel as though I am cursed then?"

"Paul, you are human, and I must say you are acting like a child. You know you made your decision, and you know you were given the opportunity to have a normal life."

"Yeah, right. A normal life? You mean being hunted? That is not normal, Michael!"

Sighing, Michael said, "You impart so much wisdom from God, **Praise His Glorious Name**, to so many humans and yet you do not listen to your own words, Paul."

"Maybe that is because I do not get to see if those people listen to those words and make the choice. Has God ever considered that?"

"Paul, God, **Praise His Glorious Name**, knows all things and all thoughts and all actions. He knows your mind. I can tell you that *many* have chosen to go to His Son, Jesus the Christ the Savior. Now I do not have much time, Paul, so I want you to listen very carefully. After you finish your business at your destination, you must get back to your room and then back to your native land, America. You must find your brother Brian because you will need his help."

"Brian? Michael, my brother does not even know I am alive. He is a Navy SEAL serving his country. Why must I make contact with him?"

"Because Paul, Brian has been wounded badly. He will be put

out of the American military very soon. You will need to convince him to help you."

"Help me do what, Michael? What am I supposed to do now?"

"That I cannot tell you, as I do not yet know. All I know is God, **Praise His Glorious Name**, says you must find Brian, heal him and convince him to help you."

"Fine. I will get my sister Rachel to assist me. As soon as I have transferred the money from Geneva, I will fly back to the States from there."

"Unfortunately, Paul, you must go back to Kaliningrad first."

"Why?"

"Because you did not sanitize your room Paul. You simply left the Metropolitan and took this train. You know you must always sanitize your room so no evidence may be found of you. I can tell you now that the FSB of the people you call the Russians, are already planning on securing your quarters. They are hoping to find your DNA. They, like other Governments are still trying to create the serum, Paul."

"Okay, Michel. I will go back and sanitize the hotel room and then fly back to America to find Brian."

"It will not be that simple, Paul. When you arrive back there, you will be met by five entities. They are powerful, and they will try to destroy you!"

Paul asked what kind of entities Michael was talking about. Were they of the dark forces? Michael explained that the entities were man's creation. They are machines of great strength controlled by man. They have strength and weapons and were made of steel. They have an artificial intelligence. The FSB does not know that they learn at such a complex speed and will quickly lose control of their creations. Paul was instructed to destroy these creations and ensure they are totally obliterated. He also must make sure his room is sanitized. If any DNA is discovered, he would find himself back there in a year having to destroy another lab. Paul then asked, "Why had the dark forces tried to trick him into thinking one of them was really Michael?"

"Paul, they had laid a trap for you. If you would have gone to St. Petersburg, they may have been able to capture you."

"Who, the dark forces?" Paul asked.

"Yes and no, Paul. The forces of evil are working with certain factions of many powerful nations. They pass on forbidden knowledge to these Governments, and in return, the peoples of those governments give the fallen certain things believing the dark forces are beings from another world."

"There is no life from other worlds, Michael. I know at least that much."

"You are correct, Paul. But mankind chooses to believe there is life from other worlds, so man does not have to think about or acknowledge God, **Praise His Glorious Name**. They, therefore, work with the fallen, not knowing who they are really working with, and in reality, for. Now listen carefully, Paul. These man-made entities are very strong. They have weapons and a manner of thinking man calls Artificial Intelligence or AI. These entities will not distinguish between you and other men. Once they are released, they will destroy *every* living being they encounter. These entities' controllers will be unable to control them."

"So, I have to destroy these things?"

"Yes Paul. But their creators will believe they can alter the entities thinking patterns. Those men will fail. The newer entities will become even more intense."

"So, what do I do about them? Find where they are making them and destroy the place?"

"No Paul. Mankind is set on self-destruction and the dark forces are more than happy to help man achieve that goal. Destroy the five entities and get back to your native land and find Brian." Michael disappeared in his normal fashion through a hole in the atmosphere.

Paul did not like what he had heard! He knew that his time

was the end times for mankind, but he thought it would happen some other way. He had always figured before Jesus returned, that man would create pandemics and wars along with other natural disasters, but he did not think the dark forces would be involved. Maybe that is what the Bible meant by the angels "unleashing." The dark forces would entice man as they always have, and man would destroy himself with the help of the dark forces. The dark forces had already infected the world and God would not let it go on much longer. Paul wished every man and woman would turn to God, but he knew it would never happen. He knew from the prophesies that the majority would perish and spend eternity in hell. Only the few, maybe a billion he hoped, would be saved for the new heaven and new earth. For now, Paul had to get to Switzerland and then back to Kaliningrad, destroy the entities and then get home. He wondered how Brian would react when the two brothers met. The last time he met with his sister Rachel, she had told him that Brian was not a believer. That could complicate things. Realizing all he could do was rely on his faith, Paul decided to get home as fast as he could.

The trip back from Geneva only took a couple of hours since Paul decided to risk flying. Transferring the money from the UBS bank was easier than Paul had thought. He blocked the cameras as he had planned and transferred the entire sum of $4.5 million to Johnny Alston's escrow account. Paul then sent a text from his international burner phone to Johnny with a code. The code read t=4.5 0 distro P. He waited for a text back with a check mark as an acknowledgment. Paul then removed the sim card and destroyed the phone and the card separately. He figured his friend would keep his ten percent and hold the funds until Paul gave further instructions. In the meantime, Paul had to get back to the hotel and sanitize the room hoping he could avoid the confrontation Michael said would happen. Unfortunately, Paul had never been able to cheat his fate. What he found waiting for him was something he never could have imagined!

3

A New Form of Evil

Arriving at the Kaliningrad airport at 1545 hours Paul decided it would be safer to ride the bus back to his hotel. He believed he would have a better opportunity to reconnoiter the area without drawing any suspicion toward himself. He departed the bus three blocks from the Hotel Kaiserhof taking an easy stroll, as if he were a tourist. Ensuring to keep his energy shield on at the lowest intensity gave him a degree of comfort because he knew no camera would be able to detect him. The problem was ensuring he did not bump into anyone. The shock they would feel would be minimal, but it would attract attention to him which is something he needed to avoid at all times. Heading east along Oktyabrskaya Street, Paul noted that several Army trucks were parked on Generala Pavlova Ulitsa. With them were several large vans of which one had a dish on top of it. He figured the trucks each had the capacity of twenty men and the vans, which were probably communication and command centers, held about six men. All total there would be about 75 men waiting for him, if in fact they were there for Paul Bannachek.

Not wanting to take any unnecessary risks, Paul stepped into the Sharlotta Café, ensuring to turn off his energy field after checking for cameras. He took a seat at a table next to the window while he waited for a server to come take his order. As he waited, he watched and studied the area. From his view point he could see the hotel entrance but nothing else around the hotel. A young woman of about twenty came to his table and asked for his order. Paul asked what was *good*. The young woman told him they were known for their cheesecake. He ordered a slice with coffee as he continued to watch. While he waited, he began using his mind's eye, allowing him to see in detail the entire area. There were already men stationed at the back of his hotel and FSB agents in the lobby and restaurant of the hotel. He let his eye track all the way to his room. There he saw them. The AI beings along with two agents of the FSB. They were going through every inch of his room with black light scanners and some sort of other device. It appeared they were going over every inch. One of the AI beings had a clear plastic bag which seemed empty but when he concentrated his eye more intensely Paul saw they had one of his hairs.

How could they have one of my hairs? he thought. *I was not in the room long!* Cursing at himself for not sanitizing before departing the room, Paul told himself he had no choice but to get back what they *never* should have found. The server brought the cheesecake and coffee asking if there would be anything else, to which Paul replied, "No thank you. Just the bill please." The woman gave him the bill for ₽12 rubles or about 16 cents US. Paul paid with a US $10 bill saying, "Keep the change Miss." The young woman was ecstatic over the more than generous tip! The tip was more money than she made in a week. She thanked Paul repeatedly and told him to come back again, with a warm genuine smile. He smiled back saying, "Wish I could Ma'am, but I am leaving tonight." She walked away with a depressed kind of frown on her face while Paul devoured his cheesecake and quickly downed his strong coffee. Deciding he needed to continue scanning the area before confronting the AI beings, he saw that one of the vans had Metropolitan Bromhofsky sitting in shackles. His eye was blackened, and he had blood coming from his nose and his mouth. Clearly, the old man had been beaten. Paul felt his rage erupting! The Russians had violated one of his many rules. Never hit or abuse in any way a senior citizen, especially a man of the clergy! He told himself he would set the Metropolitan free after his confrontation. To ensure the Russians could not escape with Alisa's old friend, he disabled the Van's engine using his telekinetic abilities. For now, they were stuck and not going anywhere, which gave Paul peace of mind for his attack.

Departing the bakery/café Paul reengaged his energy shield and continued his walk east, concentrating with his mind's eye. He surveyed the entire area for escape routes and all potential threats. He then concentrated on the AI beings. There were five of them. Two were outside and three on the inside of his room. They *looked* human, or rather humanoid, but they had no discerning characteristics in their appearance. They each stood at about six feet five inches. They had hair and black, lifeless eyes. Their skin was solid white; whiter than an albino's would be. It almost had the look of plastic, though Paul suspected it was silicone. As he walked, he studied them, noting that they had quick movements which were fluid and precise. Paul had incorrectly assumed the AI's would be clumsy and slow since they were relatively new to the world. But he reminded himself just how advanced some governments had become. He knew that most people were completely unaware of the technological advancements their countries had made. As in America, the citizens were 20 years behind what was actually in existence. Paul also understood why this was. Very soon, the world would change, almost overnight. It would truly become an Orwellian nightmare and the people would either jump on board or be hunted down and enslaved or killed. First, however, the world was being gas lit via the latest pandemic.

Picking up his pace, Paul entered the hotel lobby with his shield engaged at minimal force so the cameras could not detect him. The FSB briefly men took note but did not appear to recognize him. As he made his way to the elevator, Paul scanned several of the FSB agent's minds. He learned that they were to take him alive and the orders were coming from the communications van. He also learned the AI entities were responsible for his capture—the agents were there for back up. Paul entered the elevator and rode it to his floor. He could see with his mind's eye that the entire floor was empty apart from the five AI's and the FSB men in his room and at his doorway. Wondering if the FSB had cleared the floor, Paul decided that he was going to step off the elevator with his energy shield in full mode. He felt the fear creep up his spine as well as in his mind. Then he remembered a verse he often times forgot. "Though an army encamp against me, my heart shall not fear" (Psalm 27:3). He also remembered, "Behold, God is my salvation, I will trust and not be afraid; For the Lord God is my strength and song, And He has become my salvation" (Isaiah 12:2). Still though, those verse's applied to men, didn't they? Paul told himself he had to put away his fear and be strong. His DNA could NEVER be taken, and he had to rescue the Metropolitan.

Upon stepping off the elevator, Paul's intent was to charge the two AI's standing guard at his doorway. Unfortunately, they had already moved towards him. Their speed was almost equal to his! They covered the 200 feet in less than five seconds. They were on him with a speed and strength the likes he had never felt. Their strength and agility were equally as quick as well. His shield knocked them back only two feet, unlike a human who would die if he or she had touched him at his full power. One of the AI's reached for his weapon then stopped. Paul could sense their thoughts, though they were not like human thoughts, with brain waves. These thoughts were electronic and seemed to travel between one another using something like Wi-Fi. He perceived their thoughts to say, "No, we must capture this human." Paul did not wait for their next action. He did a quick jump kick with all his strength, hitting the AI being on his right, smack in the middle of his humanoid face. The force of the impact was strong enough to crush the AI's face plate and knock its head off! Exposed were some sort of metal alloy with wires and an oozing fluid that was like hydraulic fluid. Paul did not wait to examine the wounded AI! He ran at full speed to his room, taking only a second or two to reach the entryway, only to be met by the three waiting AI. Paul sensed the AI's orders had changed. He saw the thought patterns were to kill him, just as the first AI pulled his weapon. The weapon appeared to be a smaller version of the REMP weapons the CIA had used against him in the Bahamas, though smaller. The AI fired a round hitting Paul squarely in the chest.

Landing on his back, Paul felt the immediate loss of energy. It was not as acute as when he was hit by the CIA snipers, but he still lost about five percent energy upon being hit. This weapon did not make him groggy at all. He was able to keep his thought process as he jumped back up only to be hit four more times by the weapon. Now he was groggy! His head throbbed as he fought to regain his cognitive abilities! Paul felt the large energy loss by the multiple shots. They equaled that of one of the rifle REMP shots. As he struggled to stand up, he saw the AI release some sort of magazine or package from the weapon, reach for another to reload and fired. This time Paul was fast enough to return fire with a lethal plasma round which should have melted and destroyed the AI! Instead, it simply blew the AI apart into multiple pieces. The shot did destroy the bag with his DNA evidence which gave Paul some comfort. He now had to get out of the hotel so that he was not captured or killed, and he still needed to rescue the Metropolitan! Then he remembered what Michael had told him - he had to destroy all of the AI's.

Charging into the room, he received multiple gunshots from the FSB men to which he responded with lethal force plasma rounds. The kinetic energy from their bullets hitting his shield only charged him five percent thereby re-energizing him to 80 percent.

As the three AI's reached for their weapons, Paul charged all three of them with his full force and strength driving the four of them out the hotel window. He kicked himself away from the two AI's which had grabbed hold of him and used an energy beam to slow his fall. They were on the ground before him. The Russian soldiers on the ground opened fire upon him, unloading several hundred rounds into his shield as he landed. The energy recharged him to 100 percent plus, enabling him to destroy another AI as he ran towards the front of the hotel with the other two entities chasing him. Their speed was close to his which amazed Paul! The remaining AI from the Hotel floor was already out-front waiting for him along with all the FSB men from the lobby and restaurant! The AI waiting for him fired multiple pulse rounds into Paul, weakening him and knocking him to the ground yet again. Simultaneously, the FSB men were firing at him, re-charging him. Recognizing the greater threat Paul fired at the AI destroying it as it had turned to fire upon the FSB men. The REMP destroyed humans as if they were spontaneously combusting. While they did not know it, those FSB agents gave their lives for Paul! Getting to his feet, Paul heard the screams of the people on the street. The remaining AI's had opened fire upon every human they saw. Paul sensed their communication among themselves saying kill all the humans. This communication was different. It did not come from the communication van. It came from themselves! They had become self-conscious. They killed the remaining Russian troops charging at Paul along with every human within sight. It was a blood bath that Paul had to stop!

Though he wanted to know more about these AI's and their capabilities, Paul could not let more innocent humans to be killed. He opened fire on the remaining two AI's, destroying them both. Unfortunately, he had not been quick enough to stop the carnage that killed over 300 innocent civilians. The idea that these AI's could turn on their creators and simply annihilate human beings was terrifying to Paul. He had to block the emotions he felt and get to the Metropolitan before the remaining Russian FSB were able to run off with the old man on foot. Charging the large van, Paul faced waves of Russian Soldiers exiting the trucks he had noted earlier. Firing their weapons as they rushed towards him, the soldiers quickly recharged Paul. He returned fire with lethal plasma rounds killing all 60 soldiers. He made it to the van in mere seconds, where he ripped the Van's sliding door off only to receive multiple rounds to the face from the FSB agents within it. His energy shield simply consumed the energy from the rounds, strengthening him even more as he fired multiple plasma rounds into the agents! Gently he helped the Metropolitan out of the van, took hold of the old man's wrist shackles and melted them off the Metropolitan. He then did the same for the ankle shackles. Paul picked up the frail old clergyman into his arms and ran at full speed until he was well away from the carnage and destruction.

Stopping at the Youzhny Rest Park, Paul set the Metropolitan down as gently as he could.

"Are you okay Metropolitan?" he asked the old man.

"I am fine, Paul. I have to tell you, the stories Alisa had told me about you, really didn't seem believable until I saw it with my own eyes!"

"Metropolitan, I wish you had not seen any of that. What I am is *not* something I like people to see."

"Why would you say that Paul? You are an instrument or rather a warrior for God our Father and his Son our Lord Jesus!"

"Not sure if I am a warrior, but I have accepted that I am a servant."

"Paul, I have to tell you that for me, you have been a blessing."

"A blessing? Metropolitan, if I had not shown up, none of this would have happened. It is because of me you were abused, and those innocent civilians died! How is that a blessing?"

"Young man, most of my life I have been preaching the word of God and the Gospel of his Son Jesus Christ, but until you showed up, I have realized I did not *really* believe!"

"How can you say that Metropolitan?"

"Remember the verse "For we wrestle not against flesh and blood, but against principalities, against powers, against the rulers of the darkness of this world, against spiritual wickedness in high places?"

"Yes. That comes from Ephesians Chapter six. Why?"

"Because Paul, until you came into my life, I did not believe in that. Therefore, my faith was weak!"

"Metropolitan, you need not worry about believing. Believing and knowing are two very different manners of thought. Now that you have seen what is almost always unseen, you now know. Because you now know you can have true faith!"

"Paul, I fear so many who follow my vocation do not believe. They preach, but do not believe. Therefore the people have been kept in the dark for so very long whichis why they do not believe today."

"You know Metropolitan, since my experience going back in time to Germany, I have come up with a hypothesis that those who are schizophrenic and others who say they see demons and Angels are not really crazy. I believe their brains are wired differently so they see what we cannot see. The rest of the world locks those people away in asylums saying they are mentally ill, so they do not have to think about it. I believe mankind does not want to know about the unseen. Man, simply wants to unbelieve!"

"It is our fault Paul. The fault of the Church. We have not taught the flock the truth. We have not done so because we want to stay in power, or we just want to keep the people in the pews. Either way my son, we have done great ill toward our brethren."

"No Metropolitan, it is not your fault. As Jude wrote in his small book, 'Evil has crept in through the side door.' But remember this old man, God allows those to see who he wants to see."

"I thank you Paul! I thank God and his Son Jesus for letting me see! Now you must go Paul. You must take Alisa back to America with you and place her with your relatives."

"What will you do Metropolitan? You cannot go back to the church or they will find you and imprison you."

"I still have a few friends from the old days who can help me Paul. I will hide until the Lord takes me home. But you Paul, you must leave me now! You must get back to America and fulfill your obligation to God! But before you go, I must share something else with you."

"What's that Metropolitan?"

"When Alisa told me about you, I only half believed her."

"You told me that already Metropolitan."

"Yes. But what I did not tell you is I use to fantasize about being you or like you with all your powers and abilities."

"What, and now you don't?"

"Paul, while I am in awe of what you do and have done. I can honestly tell you that I would not want to be like you. To be so alone and always on the run. To be always fighting for others. And yet I want you to know that I also believe God has a great place for you in Heaven, whenever you get there. I also want you to know that I will be there with Alisa and my wife and friends and children waiting for you."

"Well Metropolitan, let us hope that you don't go home too soon. You may still have work to do here…, Metropolitan?" Paul called out as the old cleric slumped over. Reaching out,

Paul discovered that the old preacher had died.

Cradling the old man into his arms, Paul carried the former preacher to a trail where he found a bend. Gently he laid the old man down, propping him up against a tree and then gently kissed his forehead. "You're lucky Metropolitan. You are finally home now." Paul stood up and walked down the trail thinking about all that had transpired. He wished Alisa was there. She had the innate ability to help him understand things. He wondered if she was watching him. He hoped she was proud of him just as he hoped he did not let down the Lord. Paul then wondered about the AI entities. He sensed something about them. It was the same feeling he had when the fallen had attacked him back at the cemetery before being sent into the darkness. That feeling of *bone chilling* cold. The feeling of death and evil. Darkness! Did the Fallen use the Russians like they had the Germans? Were they using the Americans or *all* the leaders of the world? Were the AI's going to be a part of the new world order before the return of Jesus? How could man fight them? He had a difficult time fighting the entities and he had the strength of 10 weightlifters and the speed of 20 sprinters combined. So how would an everyday human being fight these entities? Or would people even bother to fight? Would mankind ever recognize what was really going on in the world around them?

How could mankind not notice or recognize what was happening in the world around them? Paul wondered if only Christians could see, but then told himself even they wore blinders. So many of the Christians simply told themselves that the world was the way it was because God allowed it to be that way. As the world changed more and more towards darkness, Christians either left the church or simply withdrew even more. They did not seem to recognize or understand that they had a duty to stand up and fight as much as possible. This latest tactic by the evil one, the Pandemic, was being used to shut the churches, allow rioters to attack Christians and have governmental powers deny equal rights for Christians. Of course, Paul understood that everything happening was told to Christians by Jesus through his Gospels. The problem was many Christians did not read their Bibles and most of the churches did not teach about this upcoming event or even how the world was becoming increasingly darker as it waited for the return of Christ Jesus. The great falling way was now occurring.

Suddenly Paul felt the Spirit within him speak to him. The Spirit told him that his thoughts were correct to a point. Paul needed to understand that so many who call themselves Christian would simply walk away from the church because of what was happening and about to happen. Others would become even more faithful to the Lord, but many would be arrested, imprisoned and subjected to behavior modification. Many would succumb to this while the others would be killed. Still, others would run and hide forming small groups which would depend upon one another for survival in hopes of living until the Lord Jesus returned. Others, a minority of Christians worldwide, would fight back. In his native land of America, a civil war would start soon. Once that happened, America would fall allowing the forces of darkness to have world domination. The war would not last long as the military, for its own survival, would join forces with the new world government's military and it would stop the civil war in America. Only the Christians who fought and hid would hold out. Most of them would be killed, receiving their reward in Heaven though. Paul, was not to intervene except to help those who had not made a choice, be able to make their choice. For now, Paul was to get back to America as quickly as possible! He had to connect with his brother Brian, who was not a Christian, and get him to help Paul in what would be Paul's most dangerous mission.

"Brian?" Paul thought to himself. He never met his younger brother. How could he convince Brian to help him? What was this mission? And since Paul was serving God the Father and his Son Jesus, Paul's Lord and Savior, how could he get Brian to help him, especially if the mission is dangerous. All his missions were dangerous! He did not want to involve his sister Rachel, but he realized he may need her to get to Brian. Paul also wondered *why* Brian. He was a Navy SEAL. A decorated combat veteran or at least that is what Rachel had told him. She had also told Paul that Brian was a career man. So, if he was a lifer, as Paul heard veterans call career men, and he was not a follower of Christ Jesus, how could Paul convince his younger brother to leave the Navy to help? He needed to know what his mission was before he could contemplate anything. He needed Michael guidance, but as usual Michael was not around to answer his questions when he needed him to be. Paul felt guilty for thinking that way. He still had a difficult time accepting *everything* happens in God's timeframe, not his! Michael would show up when the time was right. Paul just had to accept that and remember that like all humans, he needed to depend on his faith in Christ Jesus to get him through the times of uncertainty, apprehension and fear.

Returning to his senses, he heard multiple sirens and helicopters coming his way, Paul decided to run. He needed as much distance from the small war zone as he could possibly get. The last thing he wanted or needed was an unnecessary confrontation with the Russian police or more soldiers. He suspected that a message had been sent to the leadership of Russian military and their intelligence agencies. They would do everything possible to capture or kill him, just like the CIA and so many other intelligence agencies and wealthy individuals throughout the world. While his power was at 80 percent, Paul knew he could run for at least 30 miles before becoming dangerously low on energy. Increasing his speed through the woods, Paul concentrated on his memorized maps. His best manner of escape was to jump a freight train heading west. Once he was out of Russia, he could figure a way out of Europe. He also thought about the civilians remaining back in Kaliningrad. Rather, he thought about the civilians remaining in the general area of his hotel. The Russian government would have to *cleanse* the area, so no information ever leaked out.

It took about eighteen minutes for Paul to reach the 204-freight line southeast of Kaliningrad. Thirty miles in that amount of time was not his fastest speed but it sufficed, considering he needed to conserve his energy. He knew from his memory of maps and timetables; he could reach Bismarck in North East Germany in two days. From there he would attempt to get a flight to London or maybe even Shannon, Ireland. If it was possible, he would then get a flight to Chicago so he could place Alisa with his parents. Shannon would be his ideal choice as there were many direct flights from there and it was not as security conscious as Heathrow Airport. For Paul, the fewer cameras, the lesser the possibility of confrontation was always best. He figured Johnny would be expecting him to call or arrive sometime soon and he did not want his friend to worry. Paul waited for several hours before the long 300-car train, carrying Russia's prized iron ore, passed by him at a steady speed of fifteen miles per hour. He jumped a car that was enclosed which had steel beams loaded within it. Steel being one of Russia's main exports, Paul had hoped the train was carrying some. He did not want to spend two days riding a coal car in the open environment. At least with the steel, he was in a somewhat clean, enclosed car providing him protection from the environment and any type of satellite surveillance systems.

Having a power level of 60 percent, Paul decided he should sleep. He was hungry, but not famished, and he understood from the years of experience that sleep would at least recharge him 15 percent. He would need food soon but jumping off the train for something to eat could delay him by several days. That was time he could not afford right now. He told himself it would be a fast, which he was long overdue on. Setting his backpack down for a pillow, he laid down on it to rest. As he was falling asleep, his thoughts drifted to Alisa. He craved her so badly! All he wanted was to hold her and to hear her voice. He wanted her to make him laugh like she always did! He wanted to smell her hair and fall asleep with her head resting on his chest so he could play with her hair. That was their thing. He loved running his fingers through her hair and then waking up to see her hair stand on end. She was so cute in the morning. As his breathing slowed, his eyes became heavy, Paul realized he would never forget Alisa and he would always miss her. He would always be married to *her* and he would always feel the emptiness of being without her. He began to wonder what his life would have been like if he had never been injected as an infant. Would he have lived like everyone else? Would he have grown up normally, gone to college, married, had children and now be retired?

Falling asleep he realized it was folly to think or wonder of such things. His life, like everyone else's life was his. It had purpose, like every other human being on the planet. If he had been able to change it, he knew he would not. If he had he never would have met Alisa. He never would have been able to be-friend Johnny Alston or help the hundreds he had helped. People like Diane. If he changed anything then Alisa would never have done the wonderful things she had done. And maybe the Metro-politan would not done what he had done. Or the thousands of Jews Alisa had rescued and smuggled to Israel would never have made it there. Or all the Christians she hid would never have been hid and therefore lost their lives or their faith. Paul was realizing that live was most assuredly like skipping a pebble in a pond. Every man woman and child's actions caused a ripple effect on the world. Bad and evil actions caused worse and evil actions whereas good God serving actions caused more such acts.

4

Finding Brian

The presence awakened Paul quickly. His subconscious mind had recognized Michaels' presence waking him, because his mind recognized Michael, his shield did not activate. Groggily, Paul opened his eyes. He was mentally spent from the past week of actions even though his power level was back to 65 percent. His nostrils filled with the aroma of cooked meat. Looking over at Michael he saw his guide squatting over a small fire in the corner of the train car opposite of Paul. Michael looked over at him saying, "Greetings from God the Father and Creator of all things, **Praise His Glorious Name**! Good morning my young friend. How are you this fine new day?"

Becoming more alert but emotionally spent Paul replied, "I am tired Michael. And, if I may say I am kind of ticked off."

"Why is that my young friend?"

Grumpily Paul replied, "First, why do you call me your *young* friend? I am almost 60 years old now!

"Paul, in the matter of time you are but an infant. Currently in your life, you have no understanding of time and reality. So, let me just say that those who are saved will live for eternity, then how young is 60 years old?"

Feeling foolish, Paul replied, "I guess I seem childish at times, don't I?"

"Not to worry my young friend. I understand or at least I try to understand. Remember I come in human form, but I am not human. That gift was given to all of you on Earth."

"I remember Michael. So why are you here this time? And before you answer that would you mind telling me why the Holy Spirt tells me things and you then you tell me other things?"

"Paul, after all this time have you not figured that out yet? I am surprised at you. Alas, I will explain it to you! I come with directions from God, **Praise His Glorious Name**, so you know what you are supposed to do and accomplish. The Holy Spirt is within you and he gives you information from the SON, The Lord Jesus. The SON wants you to be armed with certain knowledge and He wants to direct and protect you so you may serve His Father God, **Praise His Glorious Name**, successfully. The Lord Jesus is, after all, your biggest advocate!"

"So, tell me Michael, why does not my Lord Jesus just come and tell me Himself?"

"Paul! You know the answer to that! Jesus will not return until He is told by God, **Praise His Glorious Name**, and that will only happen at the appointed time. Come, eat this fine quail I have prepared for you. I know you are hungry and low on energy. Come, please sit with me. Eat!

Standing up, Paul walked the 12 feet over to where Michael was squatting and sat down beside him. He asked, "Are you going to eat too, Michael?"

"Thank you, Paul! Yes, I will join you. It has been over a millennia in your time since I actually ate food."

"You mean you do not eat in Heaven?" Paul asked.

"No Paul, we have no need for food in Heaven. We are sustained by God, **Praise His Glorious Name,** in all things. We can eat but have no need. I must admit though, it is nice to share food every now and then. Now please eat."

Looking at the five quail Michael had prepared, Paul peeled off some of the meat and ate. He marveled at how good it tasted, especially since he saw no salt or even pepper - the bird tasted wonderful. He watched as Michael eat his food finding himself surprised the Angel could savor it so much.

Paul wondered if he should ask about what the Holy Spirit within him had told him about what was coming. "What could it hurt?" he told himself.

"Michael, do you know what the Holy Spirit told me?"

"I do."

"May I ask you some questions about what I was told?"

"God, **Praise His Glorious Name,** knew you would be asking and has allowed me to share *some* knowledge with you. So, ask what you will, and I will answer what I may."

"Okay," Paul said. "I understood most of what the Spirit told me, but I am wondering just how bad it will become. Could you tell me more?"

"Paul, you know the current pandemic that is happening around the earth?"

"Yes."

"It is manmade. It has been unleashed so that man will relinquish his natural right of freedom. Man will lose all freedoms very soon. There will be a large war and your native land will change forever. Once that war is over, your native land will cease to exist, rather it will become part of one major land or government. Peace will come after that, though many will die, but that peace will be a false peace. Once that war is completed the world governments will elect one leader. That leader will establish many rules and laws which were foretold within the scriptures. You know these things Paul. So, for three and a half years there will be a perceived peace and then it will all change. Every man, woman and child will be slaves to their own desires and to that leader. Only the saved will not be slaves, but they will be hunted, jailed, and killed. Some will hide and fight in order to share the final chance at salvation for the heathen. Many of those who belong to the SON's Church will commit apostasy, which is the great falling away spoken of in scripture. Those that do commit apostasy will hate those of you who stay pure to your faith, even more so than the non-believers ever could! They will hunt your brothers and sisters and murder them even in their sleep. And they will be cheered on by the others. So many will become part of the beast through their bodies being taken by the many demons of the enemy."

"Wait a minute, Michael. Just how many demons are there? Not more than the ten thousand legions, right? And by ten thousand legions, that means a 100 million, right?"

"Oh, there are so many more! You see Paul, when those who are unsaved die and go to hell, their souls are destroyed, but some only partly. Those become demons. That means as of now there are well over a billion demons on earth."

"But Michael, there only about seven billion people on earth. How can one billion takeover seven billion?"

"Did I say they would?" You are using man's thought process again. Remember what Peter wrote in his second letter. Many were created to be destroyed. These are the ones who the enemy has no need to take over. They are the ones who are lovers of evil. Demon's take over those who could be saved. Some can still be saved if God, **Praise His Glorious Name,** decides to call or anoint them. Many have already been called throughout time and have been saved. That is why those who love and follow the SON evangelize too so many. Of course, many of those who evangelize should not as they are some of the hucksters which cause much apostasy."

"Michael, will I be used to evangelize?"

"Paul, your soul was created to protect, heal and provide the opportunity to choose. Hence your birth and all you have done.

Now I can say no more about this. Finish your meal so I can explain what you must do. Too much time has already elapsed."

Finishing his meal, Paul licked his fingers clean from the delectable meal Michael had made. He then wiped his hands on the plastic covering on the Russian steel, wondering what his full assignment was. He only knew he needed to do something extremely important. Paul believed that his coming for Alisa was a gift allowed by God. Instead of wondering any longer he simply asked, "Michael, what am I supposed to do and why do you say, 'too much time has passed'?"

Michael then said, "Paul you must return to your native land immediately. You must find your brother Brian since he will assist you in this truly important task from God, **Praise His Glorious Name.**"

"My brother? Michael, Brian has no knowledge of me. And from what my sister Rachel has told me, he is not saved and is not a believer. He is a combat veteran in the Navy SEALS."

"You will need Rachel's help in meeting Brian. He is in the hospital at the Navy base in Jacksonville, Florida. You will also need the help of your friend Johnny Alston and from the man you helped in the Bahamas. His heart is true, and he has become fully devoted to the SON."

"Why all this help Michael? I have never needed help before."

"Oh, Paul! With all God, **Praise His Glorious Name,** has given you; you believe you have not needed help? What about all Johnny Alston has done for you? What about Alisa and all she did for you? What about Diane who has helped you with so many children? I sometimes wonder about you Paul."

Feeling ashamed Paul meekly asked, "What are they going to help me with?"

"Paul, you must save and rescue two girls who are fraternal, ten-year-old twins. They are so important to what is about to transpire."

"Twins? Why are they so important?"

"Paul, these two children have special gifts given to them by God, **Praise His Glorious Name!**"

"What kind of gifts? Are they like me?"

"No Paul, your gifts were corrupt and manmade which God, **Praise His Glorious Name,** ensured *you* received. No, these girls have the gift of healing. On their own or separately they can heal various diseases and ailments. But together, when they hold one another's hand, they can heal anything and everything. They can also form an impenetrable shield that no manmade weapon or even that of the enemy can penetrate. They can extend this shield and they can enhance **you** Paul!"

"Me?"

"Yes Paul. They can recharge you. They have been taken just yesterday by your Government's people who serve the enemy. They, of course, think they are serving alien beings and being provided technology in payment. You must find and rescue the twins! God, **Praise His Glorious Name,** has great plans for these children. But first you must rescue their grandparents and move them to the place you call Montana. You must give them new lives so that they can protect the twins and hide them in plain sight."

"How can they do that if the enemy knows of these children?" Paul asked.

"Paul, the enemy does not know of them yet. They were taken as part of the experiments the evil one's of your Government are conducting at the behest of those who they think are their friends from alien worlds. That is why you will need your brother Brian. You will have to fight like you have never fought before. Without his help, you will not succeed, and the twins will be taken and tortured. Their abilities will be discovered, and they will be forced to use their abilities for evil."

"Okay. I understand. I must get back to America as fast as possible."

"Yes Paul, which is why I want you to place your hand on my shoulder."

"Why Michel? Why must I place my hand on your shoulder?"

"Just do it Paul. We have no more time!"

Paul did as he was instructed and placed his hand on Michael's shoulder. Immediately he found himself in a tunnel of light. It was so bright; he had to close his eyes and keep them closed. The tunnel was not like that which the fallen had sent him into, though he felt an energy around him that charged him to full capacity. The tunnel felt good! It felt of beauty and pure love. Unfortunately, the experience lasted only a few seconds as he found himself standing in a large, wooded area next to Michael. He looked east and clearly saw New York City! He was amazed at the speed they must have travelled in just a few seconds. Wondering how they had travelled almost ten thousand miles in just seconds, Paul asked Michael, "What was that!?"

"You have truly been blessed Paul. God, **Praise His Glorious Name**, has allowed you to see how we Angels travel amongst you humans upon his earth."

"But Michael, this was not like the tunnel I went through before. What is the difference? Are there more than these two tunnels?"

"There are two other forms however I am not permitted to speak of them."

"I do not understand any of this Michael. Just thinking about it gives me a headache!"

"Listen carefully to what I am going to tell you Paul. Do not share this knowledge with anyone except those the Spirit within you permits. What you call tunnels are part of creation. The tunnel the evil one's sent you into is that of time and space. All are forbidden to use that tunnel because the earth is part of that. God, **Praise His Glorious Name,** has forbidden access to that. The dark ones sent you into it thinking you would either die or spend eternity there. God, **Praise His Glorious Name,** released you back in Germany to correct what was supposed to be."

"What was supposed to be? What do you mean Michael?"

"Paul the dark forces had changed history. Your parents had been sent to the death camps for experiments, which is why your mother was terrified of doctors and hospitals. And, after you were taken by Mary, your parents had no other children. You changed history back to how it was meant to unfold. You rescued your parents thereby preventing them from the horrors of the camps. And because of what you did, your parents had Rachel and Brian after Mary took you. And because you did rescue your parents, Piotr was saved, and he became a leader of the newly formed Jews for Christ. Plus, because you rescued Alisa, she became a follower of the SON and helped saved thousands of people."

"But Michael, growing up, my parents only spoke of the camps twice to me. So how is it that I remember that, if they never succumbed to those experiences?"

"Listen Paul, you will never understand how time works. But there are alternate timelines. They are dangerous because they can change the outcome of human history, which is why God, **Praise His Glorious Name,** forbade them."

"If that is so, how is it that you showed up in Germany?"

"Because God, **Praise His Glorious Name,** sent me to guide you. No angel, whether of light or darkness can survive *that* tunnel. It is, as I told you, a foundation of God's, **Praise His Glorious Name,** Earth. The dark forces developed technology to traverse time. That technology was what you experienced in Germany."

"Have they travelled back in time to make changes before?"

"Yes Paul. Are you familiar with the Annunciation with Saint Emidius painted in 1486? That painting shows the fallen had been there and man had seen them. My brother Gabriel was sent to fight and drive them away."

"Michael, the tunnel we just went through, what was that?"

"That tunnel is how we Angels travel on earth. It has been closed to the fallen which is why they use their technology to travel at almost the same speeds and sometimes even faster. Now, I have explained enough! You must get on with your mission. The Holy Spirit within you will direct you on what to do next."

As Michael disappeared, Paul stood there nearly dumbfounded. He slowly began to understand just how wrong mankind was in its beliefs and scientific studies. There was so much truth to know and he wanted to know it. Paul understood he was only given bits and pieces of information, which was much more than most of mankind would ever know, at least until they got to Heaven—if they made it to Heaven. For now, he told himself, he had to get on with his mission. The simple fact that two children were in such danger angered him! He had to get moving. Those in the Government were going to learn that if you mess with children, Paul Bannachek would make you wish you had never been born! He needed to get ahold of his sister Rachel so she could make the arrangements for him to meet Brian. But he also had to transfer the money from Switzerland to the US. That meant he needed to find Steve McCormick, the man he helped make the all-important decision in the Bahamas. Steve could help him transfer the funds and then Johnny could do his thing with the money.

Heeding what the Spirit within him directed, Paul headed east out of the large park he recognized as Central Park. It was still dark out. He looked at his watch noticing it had stopped. He looked at the sky and the moon, estimating it was about 11 pm. Immediately his shield activated as he saw the two police officers approaching him. Paul figured the park was closed due to the hour and the curfew set due to the virus outbreak. He had great respect for the police but had no time to banter with them and over their trained suspicions. Paul fired two non-lethal stun plasma rounds into each officer causing them to collapse. He then walked up to them and wiped their minds of ever seeing him and then continued to the park's entrance. Recognizing Manhattan, Paul realized he was at 62nd Street. The Spirit led him to 175 East 62nd Street to a condominium building. His thoughts told him to make entry to the second floor where he would find Steve McCormick's flat.

With his energy shield still engaged at its lowest power level, Paul did not have to worry about the thousands of cameras along his journey nor did he worry about the building's security. He simply used his telekinesis to open the front entrance door, fired a non-lethal plasma rounds into the front doorman and the posted security officer before riding the elevator to the second floor. There were three condos on the floor. Paul, directed by the Spirit within him, turned left and walked the 70 feet to the front door of Steve McCormick's condo. Again, using his telekinesis, Paul unlocked the door, stepped inside and disengaged the alarm. Letting his eyes adjust to the darkness took but a few moments. He walked through the living room to the hallway leading to the first bedroom. It was small. Peeking inside, he saw a crib with a baby sound asleep within it. The baby seemed to be just a week old. Clearly from the decor and the sleeper the baby wore, it was a little girl. Smiling to himself at her fragile beauty, Paul made a mental note he must be very quiet as he continued to the next bedroom. It was made into a home office. As he continued, he passed the bathroom to the final room, the master suite. Peeking past the half open door he saw Steve and his wife sleeping.

Stepping into the large bedroom, Paul sensed a darkness. Immediately he scanned the entire room with his mind's eye. Seeing no threat Paul focused on the couple. Clearly the darkness was coming from the wife. While Steve had truly come to the faith and his mind and heart (soul) were now clean and devoted to the Lord Jesus, his wife was not! Paul had to be careful searching her mind as always, but when one was sleeping, he had to take extra precaution. Dreams could be very dangerous as he could be sucked into the dream and then have to fight his way out. Fortunately, his wife was not in REM stage. Paul was able to learn much from her in the matter of a minute. Her name was Maureen. She did not marry Steve out of love, rather, she married him due to his wealth and his up-and-coming career. She was also not pleased with his conversion to Christianity. She was angry because he had changed from his selfish ways. Maureen wanted her old husband back. She did not care if he cheated because she cheated on him. And she did not like that he was reading his bible every night nor did she like him telling her he was going to find them a church to attend. More disturbingly, she did not like the fact that he had given his three weeks' notice last week to his prestigious trading firm. She was very upset by his plans move their family to Willard, Missouri. He planned on buying a small farm! She was planning to divorce Steve and take everything they had, including their daughter!

Withdrawing himself from her mind, Paul fired a non-lethal plasma round into her ensuring she would not awaken until morning. He then quietly walked over to Steve and gently shook the man awake. Startled, Steve awoke quickly as he sat up. "Easy Steve, it is only me, Paul Bannachek."

"Mr. Bannachek, what, what are you doing here. In my bedroom?!"

"Steve, I came to ask for your help. And please call me Paul, okay?"

"What can I help you with Paul," Steve asked as he wiped the sleep from his eyes?

"Do you have access to your work computer from here, Steve?"

"Of course, since this virus thing I have been working from home. Why?"

Hesitating a moment Paul said, "I really need you to transfer some funds for me, but I need you to do it as stealthily as possible. Can you do that? More importantly will you do that?"

"Paul, I can do it, but I would like to know why, that is if you will tell me?"

"All I can tell you is that the lives of two little girls and their family depend on you helping me!"

"Do you mind if I get up and put on my robe? We can talk in my office."

"Sure thing, Steve. I would prefer that."

Looking at Maureen, Steve said, "I cannot believe she is still asleep. Usually, the smallest noise awakens her."

"Your wife will sleep until morning Steve. I have made sure of that."

"How? What did you do to her," Steve asked in a small, frightened voice?

"Using the same principle I used on you, when the Lord healed you from the shark attack, I made sure she will sleep soundly until morning."

"Oh, Okay. Would you like some coffee Paul? It will only take a few minutes to brew and it will take me that long to log into my work computer."

"That would be really nice. Two sugars and a cream please."

Donning his bathrobe, Steve said, "Sure thing. Funny, I take mine the same way. Can you tell me more about these children?" he asked as he led Paul back down the hall, checking on his newborn daughter before continuing towards the kitchen.

"Sorry Steve. The less you know the better off you will be."

"How's that?"

"Steve, you are new to the faith. Because of that you will be attacked, maybe from those closest to you. I cannot risk jeopardizing those children for anyone or anything."

"I understand or at least I think I do. Boy you're not kidding about being attacked! I think Maureen hates me for becoming a Christian! I mean she is really angry especially since I gave notice at my firm and told her we were moving to Missouri."

Wondering if he should tell Steve what he had learned, the

Spirit within him told Paul he must not. But Paul could give Steve precautionary advice. "You know Steve, when one becomes a Christian, many of those who were close to that person walk away thinking they are nuts or gone off the deep end. Some, however, stay close and thinking they will get you to change your mind. If I were you, I would take certain precautions."

"What kind of precautions Paul?"

"For one thing, I would make sure I had some money that was untouchable by anyone. I would also gain as much information on anyone who might try and take your daughter from you, just in case you need it."

"You're talking about Maureen, aren't you?"

"Steve, all I am saying is, you as a dad and as a man have a responsibility towards your family, especially your child. She must grow up with the knowledge of God and His SON Jesus so they can make a choice. That's all I am saying."

Giving Paul a strange look Steve said, "You know, I think I understand." Leading Paul to his office he sat down at his computer and logged on saying, "Where is the money coming from and where is it going?"

Giving Steve the information on the account in Switzerland and then the information to Johnny Alston's escrow account, Paul sat down and watched Steve work. First Steve transferred the funds to his firm where he bought four million in stocks. Then he placed an override on the account and immediately sold the stocks and sent the sale proceeds to an account he had created under a false name with a false social security number. He let the money sit there for ten minutes while he went back to the kitchen and made their coffee. Coming back to his home office, he handed Paul his coffee while he sat down with his own. He then completed the funds transfer to Johnny's escrow account. Steve told Paul that his firm would discover the transaction by 10 am in the morning, so he hoped Paul's friend Johnny would move the funds before then. If he didn't, the firm would probably cancel the last two transactions keeping the funds from Switzerland so it could sit on the funds awhile before investigating anything. Paul immediately asked Steve if he could borrow his cellular phone which Steve handed over to him from his desk. Paul sent an encoded text message to Johnny telling him to immediately transfer the funds to one of his accounts and that he would call the next day to confirm. He waited twenty minutes before he received a coded text saying it was done.

Finishing their coffee, Paul asked for the fastest way to Boston. Steve told Paul if he hurried, he could catch the 12:15 am and be in Boston by 4:30 am. Or he could take his time and catch the Amtrak at 2:40 am and be there by 8 o'clock. Wanting to save as much time as possible Paul asked for directions to the bus station. It was now 11:50 pm. Steve said he could make the flight if he called Paul a cab. But Paul politely declined and thanked Steve for all of his help and the directions. He wished Steve a wonderful journey on his Christian path before departing.

Paul ran the four miles with no problem. He made the Greyhound Station by 12:10 am. He purchased his ticket and boarded the bus, ensuring to avoid security and blocking the cameras. He had just enough time to purchase a burner cellular phone before stepping onto the bus and finding a seat. He took a seat in the very back on the nearly deserted bus.

After the bus had been on the road for thirty minutes, Paul sent a text message to his sister Rachel. It said, "Sorry, no flowers this time. Call me from a 'B' as quickly as you can. Need your help with the Briar Patch. Urgent!" He knew she would understand the text was from him. Paul worried that his sister would be concerned since he was breaking their established protocol. It could not be helped though. He would explain everything to her once they met. It had been several years since they last saw one another, and he knew she would be full of questions *and* she would want to *update* him on everything in her life. Paul understood his sister well. Though she was not like him, she was like him in many ways. Especially in her desire to serve. Rachel would call and she would know not to say much on the phone, burner phone or not. She realized and understood that since she was Paul Bannachek's sister she would always be under electronic surveillance. That meant computers, telephones, credit cards, debit cards and even tracking systems for her and her husband's vehicles. She would be smart enough to rent a car under her false identity Johnny Alston had provided Paul. And she only used it when she met up with her brother. Placing himself in a light rest, Paul waited for Rachel's call. Being semiconscious, he would be aware of all his surroundings while still resting his mind. His mind's eye would keep watch on the bus and everywhere within a mile. All he had to do was wait for Rachel's call.

The call came ninety-three minutes later. Paul heard his sister's frantic voice asking if he was alright. He told her he was, but he needed her help in meeting the Briar Patch. Rachel told him that it may not be possible as the Briar was not in a fully operational state. "I know all about it Rachel. We need to drive to the Briar now!" Rachel always understood that her brother knew things that most humans never knew. She understood and appreciated who he served. It was because of Paul that she was healed and who changed her life. Because of that change she met her husband and now had two children who were raised in the faith. She felt she owed everything to her brother; but she also recognized that it was not Paul, but God who had healed her and saved her. Unlike most people her brother interacted with, she understood that Paul was just an instrument of God and his Son Jesus. Rachel told Paul she would meet him one block north of the bus station in Boston. She asked what time he would arrive. Rachel also understood about cameras. She was extremely careful anytime she traveled to meet her brother. Rachel understood how bad the CIA and other governments wanted Paul as well as a certain corporation and a few specific wealthy men. She would never allow that to happen. That is, she would do everything in her power to not be the conduit to Paul.

The Greyhound bus arrived at 4:55 am - three minutes early! Paul told himself that was a good sign but then realized that even though he was watched and protected, the dark forces would always try and intercede for their Lord. He had learned to take nothing for chance and accept nothing as luck. He stepped off the bus with his backpack on, turned towards the bus parking entryway and started walking. Once at the entryway, he headed north to find his sister. It did not take him long to see her sitting in her rented Maserati Ghibli. She had aged a bit in the last four years. Her hair was showing some grey, which Paul thought gave her a look of distinction. She seemed to have put on about seven pounds though she still looked great as she had always been thin. Approaching the rental car Paul, saw Rachel start to get out. He could sense her excitement from even the twenty feet distance he still had to cover. He raised his hand waist high with his palm open, pushing it down as if he was saying relax and stay put. He knew the cameras would not see him, but if she jumped out of the car to welcome him, they would take notice and record it. Risking Rachel was something Paul could never do. He would die first!

Grabbing the door handle on the driver's side, Paul signaled for his sister to move over to the passenger seat. He figured she had been up for several hours and would need some rest, so he would drive first. Rachel moved over with a somewhat annoyed look on her face but quickly dissipated as soon as he sat in the seat and said, "Hey little sister, how are you?"

"I'm fine big brother! My question is, how are you? What is so important that I must get up at midnight, tell hubby I have to leave to help you, pack, rent a car and meet you here?"

"Rachel, all I can tell you is that there are two ten-year-old little girls whose life depend on me and Brian."

"Brian?! What does *he* have to do with it?"

Looking at his kid sister, Paul was in amazement that she looked so much older than him. He said, "Rach, I really don't know. All I do know is he will be instrumental in helping save those girls lives."

"Paul, Brian has been horribly wounded. He was wounded in Afghanistan by an IED. From what the doctors tell me, half his face has been burned off and he lost his spleen and part of his liver. His right leg has been almost completely destroyed and his right arm is paralyzed. How is he going to be able to help you in that condition?"

"I am more worried about his mental health and his emotional health Rach. If he is healed will he ever be able to accept and believe God not only exists but loves him? Will he be able to accept and believe Jesus, the only begotten SON of God came and died for him?"

"Paul, I told you that Brian refuses to believe. I actually think he does believe but because of all he has done in this war, he does not believe he can be saved."

"Well, he is wrong! *All* people can be saved. For now, I need you to introduce me to him. He still thinks I have long disappeared?"

"Yes. I have told him nothing of your existence or anything about us. It will come as quite a shock to him, you know. Also, I took the liberty of booking us two rooms at the Baymont in Orange Park. It's only three miles from the base."

"How do you plan for us to get on the base, Rach?"

"We don't have to Paul. Brian is being discharged the day after tomorrow. They gave him 100% disability retirement and the VA will be giving him 100% disability."

"How's he taking that"?

"Brian is angry, Paul. He didn't want to meet with me, but I told him I am coming, and he *better* meet me!"

"When did you call him?"

"I called him in his hospital room about twenty minutes ago. How else do you think I could tell you about him?"

Paul told his sister he had wished she did not call Brian. It may attract attention with agencies searching for him. He then told her, "Okay. I'll deal with anything that pops up." His sister knew Paul would do exactly that! As they drove down to Florida, Paul told Rachel he wanted to hear all about her first. She wanted to know what he had been doing but he insisted that she go first. She told him about Gary, her husband and how he left his company and started his own software company. Rachel then told him about his niece and nephew. Susan was now in sixth grade and a star in gymnastics. She also was a top student. Jamie was an excellent student as well, but his talents seemed to hover around art. Being in the fifth grade one could never know though. As for her, she had left her company so she could be a stay-at-home mom and be active in their church. Rachel told Paul she and Gary had decided that since they had saved her salary all those years, they could pay cash for a new house and buy two new cars. Having no debt made it easy to live off his salary and do so comfortably. She then asked Paul about his life over the past four years.

Not being sure how to tell his sister about anything, he just blurted it all out. He told her about Jerome Waller, the gangs, the prison. He told her about his encounter with the fallen at their parent's grave. He then told her about the time travel through the tunnel and about Germany and their parents. He started to cry when he told Rachel about Alisa and their short marriage and all she had done after they separated. He told her about the UFO's and the Bell-shaped time machine. He finally told her about Russia and the AI's, and all the battles and how he had placed history back on the right track so that their parents did not go to the death camps. Finally, he told her about his mission, at least what he knew of it. All through his story his sister held his hand trying to comfort him. She cried when she heard about Alisa telling Paul she was grateful he had experienced true love at least once in his life! Rachel explained that she knew nothing about their parents in the death camps which she was grateful for. She told her brother that he was doing wonderful things for the Lord and she believed he would be rewarded greatly in Heaven.

Normally the drive time to NAS Jacksonville would be almost seventeen hours. They made it in fourteen, arriving at 7 pm eastern time. Three hours of the drive had been consumed with their catching up. Then Rachel slept for eight hours. She had awakened from a nightmare about the Nazi's and the AI's. They had stopped at an HWY 55 Burger Restaurant in Hope Mills, North Carolina where Paul went in and ordered their food. He did not want to risk cameras spotting Rachel. Using his shield, he could prevent himself from being detected. They then filled the gas tank while Rachel ate her "Lil" double bacon burger, fries and strawberry shake. Once on they were back on Interstate 95 south, Paul ate his all-American burger with onion rings and chocolate shake. Rachel was again talking about her kids and Gary, but Paul fell asleep. Rachel woke him in the hotel parking lot in Orange Park. She told him she wanted to check them in but knew he would be upset. She was correct! Paul stepped out of the car, went into the hotel and checked them in for two different rooms from her reservation. Even though she had used an alias provided by Johnny Alston, Paul did not want to take any chances. Besides, he not only blocked the cameras from seeing him, but he also dismantled them as well. That way they could walk freely about the hotel, at least until the following evening.

After checking into their respective rooms, Paul walked to Rachel's room, next door, knocked and waited for her to let him in. They ordered Domino's pizza for a snack while they enjoyed one another's company playing gin rummy. They stayed up playing cards and talking, laughing and then Rachel took time to tell Paul about their parents' life after he was taken. She had provided him some information the last time they had gotten together but now she went into detail. Paul came to tears many times, though he was grateful to hear every word. He was happy to hear that his mother never lost faith. She always believed he was alive and had prayed for him every day. As Paul listened, he wondered about his life being so vastly different than his family's. Some would call his life exciting. He rather thought of it as necessary and uncanny. He refused to let himself feel sorry for himself, ever again. Paul Bannachek knew, understood and had finally accepted his purpose in life. Though he is every different from all other humans, his life was a necessity in the unseen battle between the forces of light and those of darkness. He wished, though, the war would end soon. He was tired!

Awakening at 6 am, Paul found himself sacked out on Rachel's hotel room couch. He looked over at her bed and saw it unmade with her gone. Using his mind's eye, he searched the hotel only to find she was nowhere around. Suddenly he saw the rental car pull up. Rachel stepped out with what appeared to be a large bag of takeout food. Paul pulled himself from the comfortable couch, went back to his room and showered. After a quick shower, Paul changed into a fresh pair of clothes from his backpack, brushed his hair and shaved. By then Rachel was knocking at his door. Letting his kid sister in, he listened to her tell him, "What kind of sleepy head he was." He did not have the heart to tell her that the past 60 years had taken a toll on him regardless of how "young and chipper" he may look. "Chipper? Paul you may have the strength and energy of a 26-year-old, but you act your age. You seem so tired."

"Been through a lot little sister. Been through a lot!"

Unpacking their breakfast, Rachel set a large croissant with two fried hard eggs and two large sausage patties and a large hash brown in front of her brother. "Eat Paul! You need your strength," she said. Then she sat down and pulled out a bagel with cream cheese for herself. She had purchased a large coffee for Paul with plenty of cream and sugar so he could mix it as he liked. She had purchased a Chai tea latte for herself. The siblings sat quietly eating their meals knowing the plan for the day. They had discussed it the night before. Rachel would go to the base where she would pick up Brian and bring him back to the hotel. Paul would keep watch to see when they arrived so he could leave the room he would share with Brian, so Brian was not aware of his presence. Once Rachel had Brian in the room, Paul would come over and knock so Rachel could let him in. From there they would have to take it one step at a time. Their whole plan would be fluid from there on out. Being wounded as badly as he was and fighting for twelve years as a Navy SEAL, Brian undoubtedly had a lot to deal with. Paul would try and help, but he could not force his brother to accept that help. Yet, Paul understood what was at stake. The twins were an all too important part of God's plan. For, Paul it meant everything to serve God. He would do whatever it took to get his brother's help.

5

Establishing the Plan

Knocking on the hotel room door, Paul had a strange sense of excitement and nervousness. He understood the feeling of excitement. It was, after all, the first time he was going to meet his younger brother. He had wanted this for years although he would not allow it. Paul understood that meeting Brian and bringing his brother into his life would be dangerous for Brian. Now, of course, that danger had been significantly reduced due to Brian's injuries and being medically retired; but now, more importantly, was the mission at hand. The twins had to have priority in everything. The nervous feeling seemed strange to Paul. *Why be nervous?* he wondered. Brian was his brother. They were of the same blood. Maybe it was because Brian was not a believer or at least that is what Rachel had told him. Or maybe it was because he was going to have to explain so much to his brother. How? That was the question nagging at Paul. "How do I enlighten my brother?" as the Spirit within him told him. Paul was to follow the Spirit's lead.

After a thirty second pause, Rachel answered the door. She

whispered, "Prepare yourself!"

"For what Rach?" Paul whispered back.

She again whispered that Brian looked horrendous from the burns. Stepping through the door Paul saw his brother sitting on the couch in the hotel suite. His brother was wearing a pair of shorts and a Navy SEAL t-shirt. He saw the man peer at him with his only undamaged eye. His right side was burned horribly. Brian had no hair due to the burns going over the entire circumference of his head. His right arm hung limp from his damaged shoulder which Paul could barely make out through his brother's t-shirt. Brian had a cane next to his left side for use walking as his right leg was badly burned and clearly six inches shorter than his left leg. "What are you looking at Mister!" Brian snapped angrily. "Who is this guy Rachel?" he asked his sister. Before Rachel could answer, Paul spoke up taking control of the conversation as Rachel closed the door behind Him.

"Brian, I am your brother Paul."

"What? Bull shit! My brother died years before I was ever born! Rachel, who is this con man?"

Rachel explained, "Brian, this really is our brother Paul. He and I have been in touch for ten years now. Listen to him, Brian! He needs your help, and he can help you."

"You mean to tell me you have known about him for ten years and never told me?!" Brian angrily snapped back.

"Brian, we thought it was best," Rachel replied.

"We? Who is we? You and him? If he is our brother, what right did the two of you have to not tell me about him? Huh!"

Rachel began to speak but Paul cut her off saying, "Brian it was for your own good! Believe me, it was for *your* safety."

"My safety? What the hell are you talking about Mister?!" Frustrated as well as time conscious, Paul said, "Brian, shut up and watch!" He walked over to his brother kneeling on one knee. He placed his hands over his brother's leg concentrating on the bones and the knee. Using his knowledge of anatomy, Paul began rebuilding Brian's leg using his telekinetic ability. He healed the burned leg forming new skin as well. Once the leg was healed, he moved his hands over his brother's abdomen concentrating first on what remained of Brian's liver. Paul understood that the liver could regenerate over time, but he needed his brother at 100 percent. He helped his brother's liver regenerate in a matter of seconds before moving his hands to Brian's spleen. The doctors had managed to save half of it, which was better than nothing. Paul regenerated the spleen. He then stood and ran his hands over Brian's shoulder repairing the bone and nerves. Running his hands down his younger brother's arm, Paul healed the nerves and muscle damage thereby giving Brian a whole new arm. Brian kept exclaiming, "Oh my God!" as Paul continued to heal him. Paul then stood and placed his hands over Brian's face repairing the damaged nerves first, then the burned skin, giving Brian his face back. He finished by placing his hands on Brian's skull, removing the burns and providing new skin and nerves.

As he finished Paul said, "In the name of Jesus Christ you have been healed!" "Now get up Brian! Go to the bathroom and look in the mirror" Paul commanded! Brian was up instantly, leaving his cane by the couch as he quickly walked into the bathroom. Paul and Rachel could hear their brother exclaiming over and over, "Oh my God! Oh my God!" as he sobbed.

After about two minutes Brian came out of the bathroom looking at both Paul and Rachel. He appeared white from shock. "How... how did you do that?"

"Brian, *you* need to sit down," Rachel told him. "There is much Paul must explain to you so that you will have a full understanding of what is coming."

Giving Rachel a smile, but a cautious glance at Paul, he walked back to the couch and sat down saying in a meek voice, "I'm listening.

Paul began to tell Brian his story. He told his brother about how he had been injected as an infant by Rebecca, the Mossad agent. He explained how he grew up with their parents until he was taken by Mary, the CIA woman. She had protected him and trained him, helping him learn about and refine his abilities. Paul told Brian about Beth and Stanley Frazier, and about being captured. He explained about the labs he had destroyed and how he had been hunted all these years. Paul then told Brian about all the people he had helped and provided the opportunity to choose. He spoke of his time travel to Germany, his marriage to Alisa, and what Alisa had done with her life. He told Brian about the billionaire Bowen and his experiments and the children that he had been rescuing all these years.

While Paul spoke, Brian saw Rachel simply smile a wonderful smile as she listened and looked at her brothers. He noticed his older sister have a look of sorrow while Paul spoke of Alisa. She seemed to feel sorry for their brother Paul. By the time Paul had finished speaking several hours had passed. Brian looked at his brother and said, "You don't really expect me to believe that do you? Granted, you just did something miraculous and amazing to me or rather for me, but what you just told me is so wild no one would believe it!"

Looking over at Rachel, Paul decided he would have place himself in great danger for Brian to believe and understand. He was going to have to share his memories with Brian. The problem with doing that is it would weaken him to a dangerous level of energy. He had already used thirty percent of his energy to heal his brother. Sharing his memories would drain another fifty percent, leaving him at a dangerous state of thirty percent. Still, Paul needed Brian to help him rescue the twins. His mission was his main priority and goal. Risk came along with service. He told Rachel, "I need you to look after me for the next twenty-four hours Rach. Will you do that?"

"Why Paul? What's going on?"

"Do you remember me talking about our parents and giving

them language abilities?"

"Yes. I remember."

"I am going to share my memories with Brian. But when I am finished, I will be at an exhausted state. I will need to sleep for at least twenty-four hours and then need a great deal of food when I awaken."

Brian interrupted by saying, "You're not doing anything to me!"

Paul fired a non-lethal stun plasma burst into his younger brother, placing Brian into an unconscious mode for at least six hours. "You know how I know he's our brother, Rach?" Paul asked his sister.

"Let me guess," Rachel said. "His pig-headedness?"

"Yup!" They both laughed together. Then Paul said, "I am serious Rachel, you need to keep watch over me. Okay?"

"I will Paul. I swear it! No one will hurt you. I won't let that happen!"

Paul smiled at his sister and then sat on the couch next to his brother. He placed his hands-on Brian's now healed head, concentrating as his mind moved into Brian's. Paul then began placing all his memories into Brian's short-term memory, like loading a disk or pin drive into a computer. After an hour he had shared everything the Spirit within him told him to share. Some things he would not share, just in case. When he had finished, Paul got up, staggered over to the bed where he collapsed, falling into a coma like sleep. His subconscious was aware of his surroundings, but his mental abilities were so weakened he could not even bring up his shield. Rachel would have to defend and protect him until he was awake and alert.

At 3 pm Brian awoke from his plasma stun to the sight of Rachel sitting in a chair watching both himself and Paul. She had moved the chair to a vantage point where she could keep an eye on both her brothers. He saw the exhaustion and worry on her face. She also had a look of fear. He saw Paul sleeping on the bed as if he were dead. Standing groggily, Brian walked over to Rachel and asked, "Are you okay Rachel? You look exhausted."

"I'm fine Brian. I just need to sleep. I have been sitting her for almost six hours watching you two. I was worried that neither one of you would wake up, and afraid that someone would come and try to take or hurt Paul." She wept as she told her younger brother how sorry she felt for Paul. She respected their brother but felt horrible for all he had been through and all the loss he had experienced in life. A life that was just beginning for Paul since he hadn't lived more than five percent of his life span. She wept harder when she told Brian how she and Paul had met and how Paul had healed her from the AIDS she had contracted from the man she was with then. Tears pouring out of her eyes, Rachel told Brian of her deep love for God and his SON Jesus because of what Paul had done for her because of THEM!

Brian knelt and wrapped his arms around his older sister telling her, "Rachel you don't know the half of it!"

"What do you mean Bri?"

"Paul shared his memories with me. I don't know if he meant to or not but those memories came with pain. He has had so much loss! He aches for his wife Alisa. He has such guilt for not being there for mom and dad! With all the battles I have fought and the things I have done in combat I thought *I* had a lot of baggage! But Rachel, Paul is in a lot of pain. He just buries it deep within himself and keeps going like that rabbit in the commercials we saw as kids."

"I know Brian. But his love for God and His Son Jesus keeps him going. He will never stop serving no matter what he loses. No matter what he has to sacrifice!"

"Rachel, why don't you go to your room and take a nap? I can look after Paul."

"Really Bri? All you need to do is keep guard. Make sure no one comes in to harm him. Okay?"

Walking over to his duffle bag, Brian reached in and pulled out a shoulder harness with twin 1911 colt .45 caliber pistols. He donned the harness, then pulled one weapon at a time loading a magazine into each weapon. He then chambered a round into each weapon, set the hammer and then attached the repressors his harness had for each weapon. Walking back to where Rachel sat, he looked deeply into her eyes saying, "No worries Sis, I promise you, if anyone tries to come for Paul, they will have to get through me first! I now know what he is and who he is. No one will harm our brother!"

Thanking Brian, Rachel stood from her chair hugged her kid brother. She then walked over to Paul, kissed him on his forehead and said, "I will be back in a couple of hours with some food for you. Paul will need a lot of food but not for several hours at the least until awakens."

"Rachel, I don't think it would be wise for you to leave the hotel. It would probably be better to order out, don't you think?"

"Agreed." See you in a few hours.

Paul opened his eyes at 11:30 pm to see Rachel and Brian both sitting in chairs at the end of his bed. They had pulled up a table which was loaded with food items. He could smell burgers, fries, onion rings, fried chicken and scalloped potatoes. Propping himself up, he saw three very large chef salads sitting on the table with several types of dressings. Next to the salads sat nine large bottles of Smart Water© and a small jar of Folgers© coffee. Unaware of the time that passed, he sat up asking, "What time is it?"

"You had me worried Paul," Rachel replied. "I checked on you multiple times. It almost seemed as if you were dead. I checked your pulse, but I could barely feel it. Your body was cold to the touch! Is that what happens when enter someone's mind?"

"Yes. Which is why I rarely do it. The first time I did it I almost died. Now *please* what time is it?"

"2330," Brian responded. Trying to be as nonchalant as he could, Brian said, "Not sure what you wanted for food so I ordered what I could from the memories you shared with me. I must tell you; you have had one interesting life! I thought I had a lot to deal with!"

"What you call life Brian, I call the world. For me, living in this corrupt world is just that. Accepting the world's terms as they come and fight when I have to and always try to help when I am called to. Food looks and smells good. Do you mind?"

"We ordered most of it for *you*," Rachel said joining in on the sibling conversation.

"Rach, I can't eat all that! I will take a chef salad, a couple burgers, onion rings and a couple bottles of water, if you don't mind?"

"Like she said Paul, we got this all for you," Brian chiming in.

Smiling, Paul pulled himself to the edge of the bed, swinging his legs over its bottom edge underneath the table. Grabbing a salad, he poured some Russian dressing on a salad large enough for two. Then lowered his head, whispering a silent prayer of gratitude for the food, for Rachel and their brother Brian. Before attacking his salad, he asked, "What have you two been doing since I have been out?"

"Just talking and playing rummy, whist, five card Omaha and some war. You know just playing and talking," replied Rachel.

"You know, just catching up," Brian added.

"Mmm," is all they heard from Paul as he demolished his salad. After swallowing the last bite, he said, "Never thought I would ever see the day where the three of us actually came together. It's good to finally meet you Brian. I have often wondered about you. And as for *you* little sister, I think of you often. Alisa told me I worried too much about you but hey, really can't help that, considering."

"Considering what, Paul?" Rachel asked.

'The agencies. I always worry one of the many agencies will go after you or your family to get to me."

"We have been smart about our relationship Paul. As far as any of them are concerned they must believe that I believe you're dead or in prison somewhere."

"Let's just make sure we keep it that way. And as for you Brian, if you agree to help me, when the mission is over you and I will have to act like Rachel and I."

"Meaning you must live your life as if you and I never met. Ever! It will be the only way to ensure your safety."

"Hate to say it bro, but I am quite capable of taking care of myself! Believe me."

"I do Brian, but not against these people and their *friends!* They have power and are like nothing you have ever come across. *Believe me!* Rachel, in the morning we go our separate ways. You go back to Boston and Brian and I will go where we must go, *if* he agrees to help me."

"I will help you Paul. There is no way I will let a child be hurt!"

"Why can't I help," Rachel asked?

Paul explained to his sister and brother that he and Brian were about to embark on an extremely dangerous escapade. There was a large probability that one or both of her brother's may not survive. And since what they were going to do was so danger-ous, Paul needed to ensure that at least one Bannachek survived to continue their lineage. And even though Rachel already had two children he would like her to live until the Lord returned. Both his siblings asked what he meant. Paul explained that they were in the last days, meaning the end times. He told them he believed the Lord would return within the next seven to ten years though he did not know that for a fact. Rachel asked him how he could make such a guess. Paul told his sister that the Bible was clear. The Clock started back in '48. "This current Pandemic is manmade, and part of the great apostasy foretold in scripture," he replied. He told them to start paying attention. He told them to watch and see how many Christians were leaving the church. "The numbers leaving will grow exponentially guys. Now no more about this. How about dealing me in?"

The two brothers were up at 4:30 in the morning. Having already said their tearful goodbyes to Rachel, they were on the road by 6:00 am. Stopping at the Waffle House in Orange, Paul had his normal steak and eggs while Brian chowed on large order of pancakes, sausage and eggs. They both knew they did not have time for leisurely travel, so they made sure they ate heavily. After breakfast, they were on the road. Taking I295 North to I95 North, then heading west on the Georgia State road 84 which turned into state route 38 to Hinesville, Georgia. Brian had asked why they were going to Hinesville. Paul explained that he was told that the Twin's grandparents lived there and that was where the girls had been taken from. He explained they needed to get the grandparents out of Georgia and get them to Townsend, Montana where they would be safe and protected. Paul was driving the rental car he had picked up in Orange Park and stopped at the TA travel plaza truck stop in Brunswick, Georgia to top off the fuel tank and purchase nine burner cellular phones. While there, he called Johnny Alston telling him to expect him plus one in twenty-four hours. He also asked Johnny to return his call from Johnny's current burner phone to the payphone next to him. "But make sure you call at least a block away from your offices," he reminded his friend and attorney.

"Like I am stupid or something? I call you back in five," was Johnny's response.

Knowing that names could never be used, even on burner phones, Johnny called Paul back as directed on the other payphone from his burner. Paul answered and explained that he needed one of the corporations, Johnny had set up for him, to purchase a home in Townsend, Montana as an investment. Once completed to have a rental agreement drawn up for the grandparents he was sending there; for whom Johnny would need to get new identifications for. He told Johnny he needed $4,800 dollars wired to him under his given name to the Western Union in Hinesville, Georgia and to purchase two bus tickets under the new aliases of the grandparents. He would call back for the departure time in two hours. Once Johnny agreed, Paul met back up with Brian at the fuel pump where Brian had just finished pumping the gas. "Let's go Brian. Time is running short," he exclaimed to his brother. Once they were in the car, Paul explained his plan to Brian.

The plan was simple, yet it had its complexities. Paul would meet the grandparents at their home and try to explain what was happening. Meantime, Brian would head over to Wright-Patterson Airforce base in Ohio. Brian's job there was to enter the base using his Navy retirement card and to tell anyone and everyone he was there to shop at the BX. Once on base, he was to find the legendary Hanger 18 and see how to make entry. If he could get access, he needed to find the mysterious "Blue Room" which was supposed to be impenetrable. If he made it that far he was to find all Intel on the Twins. They were now missing for ninety-six hours. Brian asked Paul how he knew what he knew. Paul explained that the Spirit within him was guiding him and therefore guiding them. "Paul, I have to tell you, I saw your memories and all, but I really don't believe in this sort of thing."

"You know what Brian? I really don't care what *you* believe and don't believe, but I promise you, when this is all over, you *will* believe! And, you will then have to make your choice."

"What do you mean by that?"

"Do you believe in aliens?" Paul asked his brother.

"Actually, I do believe there is other intelligent life out there. Why"?

"Like I said, when this is over you will believe. You will see what your "aliens" really are, and you will see what they are up to and doing. It and they will scare the hell out of you Bri. You will see what I know, which will make just as much of a threat as I am."

"A threat? To whom?"

"To the fallen. Sometimes they are called the Watchers by certain parts and people of the Government, and not just the American Government either. And since you will have this knowledge, you will become hunted like me that is if you survive!"

"Paul, why are these two kids so important to you? You have never even met them."

"First and foremost, they are extremely important to God and His SON Jesus, my Lord and Savior. Secondly, all children are important to me. Call them my weakness because I will always fight to protect them; or call them my reason for being, I really don't care. What I do know is they are extremely important for the upcoming battles and war."

"You're talking about that Armageddon, right?"

"No Brian. That will not come until the very end. What I am telling you is the soon to come changes in the world."

"What changes?"

"Okay Brian, listen carefully. Very soon the entire world will change. America has been changing for the past two generations. Soon there will be no more America. Then Christians and Jews will be hunted, slaughtered, arrested, and tortured or executed. The Twins have great powers or gifts which have been given to them by God himself. The children do not even realize this, but their powers will become evident shortly. We must rescue them before those powers show themselves. If we don't, the dark forces will try and manipulate the girls so that their powers are taken from them or misused."

"Paul, how do you know all this?"

"Again, you saw my memories. You know my guide Michael instructs me and the Holy Spirit within me gives me knowledge when I need it."

"I have to tell you Paul, those memories are fading. I guess I understand, but it is so hard when I don't get the messages from the Spirit or see this Michael guy."

"Brian, the memories I gave you will be completely gone very soon. I gave you those memories to help you accept that I, your brother, am alive and that I serve God and His SON Jesus, my Lord and Savior. If you want to have understanding, you must receive the Holy Spirt. And the only way to do that is to accept Jesus, as the only begotten SON of God, as your Lord and Savior. But Brian, and this is of the utmost importance, you must do so with true and pure desire! You can't just say you want this because the Lord knows every heart and every Soul. If you are not genuine in your desire, you receive nothing!"

Paul stopped talking as they approached Hinesville. He pulled over a mile from Ft. Stewart Army base and told Brian to get going. Once he had the grandparents safely on the road he would head to Wright-Patterson to meet up with his brother. He told Brian to use the burners only when necessary and to only call him. Paul hoped he would only be a few hours behind Brian but that would depend upon the grandparents. If they balked at him for his trying to rescue them, his job would become even more difficult. If they refused his help, he would have to come up with another plan of where to place the Twins and find people who would care for them. He told himself it would work out because Michael told him he needed to rescue the grandparents. The Spirit gave him knowledge on where to take the couple, so he figured it had to work out.

The Spirit led Paul to a house located at 202 Frazer Street. The house was a single story, brick home of about 1900 square feet. It had large, old growth pine trees in front with a five-foot-high chain linked fence attached to both sides of the house. The double car garage door was open. Within it sat a blue GMC pickup truck and a gold Toyota Celica. In the driveway sat a marked police car with two other unmarked cars parked in the street directly in front of the house. One of the unmarked cars had state plates and the other had Liberty County plates. Both the cars had pig tail antennas, telling Paul they were law enforcement. He wondered how long the cops had been there, and more importantly, how long they would be staying. He knew he did not have much time. He stood down the street scanning the rest of the residential area with his mind's eye. He found a rental house with several federal agents sitting inside, monitoring the grandparent's home. They monitored via listening devices and a couple of cameras they had installed at some point after the girls were taken. Deciding he needed to clear the agents out first, Paul made his move.

Circling to the back of the houses into the forested area, Paul sprinted to the back of the rental house. Keeping his mind's eye working at optimum, Paul saw he had not been noticed by any of the neighbors. Being 9:00 am, he figured many of the occupants would either be at work or on their way to their jobs. Watching the back of the makeshift monitoring station, Paul tried to get a mental grasp on just who these agents were. They were not FBI or Homeland Security. They were part of the CIA's Office of Scientific Intelligence, but not really. These men were different. They were part of a group that had no name. Then his mind found the information he needed. The agents were part of the "Specialty." A group that had been working with the Fallen known as the Watchers, although they believed they were working with aliens from another world. Paul could sense that all three of the men had been taken over or rather possessed by demons. The Spirit with him told Paul to attack. He was to destroy all recorded information and the men! Once that was accomplished, he could make contact with the grandparents.

Wanting to search the minds of the agents to learn more, Paul was about to extend his mind further and deeper. Suddenly the Spirit within him told him *no*! The Spirit told him that if he went deeper, the demons controlling the men would discover his presence. He had to go in and destroy the men as instructed. Paul charged through the back of the house, which lead directly into the kitchen. In one continuous movement, he fired a lethal plasma round into the agent standing there as he continued into the living room. There he fired to more plasma rounds into the agents who were sitting, listening in on the police and the grandparents. He felt the demons departing the now dead agents in search of other inhabitants. Paul then fired destructive plasma rounds into all the electronic equipment, ensuring no records remained. After searching the rest of the empty rental and finding nothing, he departed the house ensuring to sanitize it. Using his telekinesis, he repaired the back door he had crashed through and made his way back to his original position down the street across from the grandparents' house.

Only five minutes had elapsed since Paul had detected the agents. Standing there in the street his burner phone buzzed his pocket. Pulling out the phone he answered, "Yes?"

"It's me," he heard the voice say. The tickets are purchased for the 2:10 bus. Money has been wired."

Recognizing the voice as that of his friend Johnny Alston, Paul simply said, "Thank you. See you in about eighteen hours," before hanging up. Checking his watch, he saw that it was now 12:15 pm. That left him little time. He could not wait on the police to leave. Paul made his way quickly to the front door of the couple's home. Not being sure if he should knock, ring the doorbell, or just walk-in, Paul simply walked in through the front door. His entry startled the couple and the cops seated in the living room. Paul quickly fired non-lethal plasma rounds into the four police officers. As he walked past the now unconscious cops lying on the floor, he told the grandparents "Do not be afraid. I am here to help you and your girls!" The couple seated on their couch, glanced at one another momentarily before the granddad jumped up to charge Paul.

"Mister, you get the hell out of my house!" he yelled making his charge towards the intruder. Paul, using his newfound telekinetic ability while in Germany, fired a steady pulsating beam at the man, forcing him back to the couch where the beam kept him pinned.

"Oh my God!" his wife screamed as she sat frozen with terror.

"Please, listen to me! I am here to help you and your missing granddaughters! I promise, I will not harm you.

"What are you?" the woman exclaimed in a terrified voice. Are you an alien or something?"

"No ma'am. I am just as human as you, only a little different as I can do things other humans cannot do." Seeing that the grandad had become exhausted, struggling to fight the beam, Paul retracted it, allowing the man to relax. He then said, "Listen, are you Christians?"

"We are," the man said as he took hold of his wife's shaking hands. Why?"

"You may not believe this, but I serve the Lord. I have been sent here to rescue you and your granddaughters."

"We don't need rescuing!" the man angrily snapped back. "Our girls need to be found!"

"Sir. I have been instructed to get you two out of here and send you to a safe place so that I may go after the Twins and rescue them. I need you two in a safe place so that the girls have a place to hide."

"Why do they need to hide, mister?" the woman asked in a calmer voice.

"Your girls have been blessed with special abilities or powers by God himself. Very soon those talents will become known. If I do not get to them before those abilities show themselves, the forces of darkness will attempt to manipulate the children and use those powers for evil. I must get to them immediately. Time is running out!"

The granddad stared at Paul as if studying him, before asking, "What kind of powers? Neither Elizabeth nor Esther have ever shown any kind of unusual behavior. What kind of malarkey are you trying to shovel?"

"Sir, they have not shown it because they have not discovered their abilities. Now please let me help you!"

"What kind of abilities mister?" asked the woman.

Heeding the Spirit within him, Paul took the several minutes to explain what was coming and just how the Twins would be helping other Christians and Jews. He told them how he was instructed upon locating them that they would have a new home in Townsend, Montana with new names and enough money to live off and to provide for the twins. He explained how his brother Brian was already en-route to find the children. Paul told them that once the Twins were rescued, the agents used by the dark forces would be looking for them as well as the Twin's rescuers. He explained that no witnesses would be allowed to live. If only they would let him help them now, they would not be discovered and they could, if they practiced discretion, be secure for at least a few years before the final years began. The couple glanced at one another, understanding what he was speaking of. They were both well versed in their bible teachings. "Come on Joannie," Robert said to his wife. "I believe this man. I told you the end times were at hand. Let's pack a couple of bags and go with this man."

After explaining to the couple that he would not be going with them, Paul told them to call a cab, which he would take with them to the bus station. He explained about the tickets on standby and that they needed to stop by the Western Union to get the cash he had wired for them. The woman questioned what they should do about their home and the money in their bank account. Paul told her they were to leave everything, even their pictures. They were to take nothing but *some* of their clothes. They would be provided a nice home for which they would pay one dollar a month in rent. They could purchase new vehicles and all the furnishings once they arrived in Montana. He explained that they could have no connection with anyone they had ever known, not even their children. This was to ensure the safety and survival of Elizabeth and Esther no matter what. Knowing their thoughts as he spoke, Paul explained that they had to cut off all ties to their past and start anew. Many of those they thought of as Christian friends were not and would-be part of the apostolic crowd who would turn on them. They could trust no one except God and His SON Jesus. They would provide new people into the couple's life in Montana and the Holy Spirit would guide them.

While the couple each hurriedly packed a bag, Paul looked at the pictures on the piano. The picture of the couple with their granddaughters seemed new. The girls looked about ten years old. Both wore glasses and had long brown hair. They were truly beautiful kids. Their eyes had special look to them that Paul almost thought were eyes of pure knowledge. Knowing what they looked like would help him a great deal. There was another picture of the couple taken when they were younger. The grandad was a young Marine in his dress blues beside a woman wearing an attractive blue summer dress. The scene looked like they were at a dance somewhere during the '80s. Knowing the man was an ex-Marine told Paul a lot about the man's character. He was glad the man had some training though; he hoped the man would not be called upon to use it. Paul was used to working on limited information. He was told what he was told when he was meant to have the knowledge. For a brief moment he wondered if he would have made a good military man. "Maybe, in another life he told himself," as he waited for the couple to return to the living room.

The man came out of the back master bedroom first. He stopped short in front of Paul and introduced himself as Robert Veam, as he extended his hand in friendship. Paul took hold of the man's hand while he searched the man's mind introducing himself as Paul Bannachek. He saw the man's mind was genuine. There was honesty in the man, and he felt the man did in fact have the Holy Spirit within him. The man said his wife's name was Joannie, which Paul already knew though he played dumb. He did not want to say something that could give Robert pause. Joannie came out of the bedroom with her bag packed asking if they really had to leave *everything*. Paul explained that the police would be looking for them. But more importantly, there would be agents of darkness, who claimed to work for the Office of Scientific Intelligence, but in reality, worked for an unknown organization of men and woman who had been possessed by demons. They were the *most* dangerous! He told them it was better if they left no trace to themselves. Joannie shuddered at the explanation for a moment and then called for a cab, while Robert stood and studied Paul.

"Mind if I ask you a question Paul?"

"Not at all sir. Ask whatever you want."

"Well, I am just wondering Paul, how old are you? I mean you can't be more than 25 or 26 but you act and carry yourself like you were my age." As Joannie hung up the phone with the taxi service she listened to Paul's reply.

"I am older than you sir. Though not by a lot."

"No way!" the man replied. "I am 56-years-old. You can't be older than me."

How old are you really?"

"I am 60-years-old Robert. I was born in 1960."

"How can that be?" the granddad asked.

Paul decided to share limited information about himself. He told the couple about his birth and the Mossad agent Rebecca, how he grew up in Illinois until the accident, and Mary taking him and training him. While he did not go into all he had done or experienced, he did speak of what he could do. As he spoke, both Robert and Joannie displayed looks of sadness on their faces and in their eyes. Joannie asked, "So you will ever know the joys of marriage? You're always on the run?"

"Oh, I am married. My Alisa is waiting for me in Heaven," Paul replied.

Robert asked, "When did you lose your wife, if you don't mind my asking?"

Not wanting to lie Paul said, "Not too long ago." It was not a lie for Paul. He lost Alisa almost two months ago in his time even though she had really been gone for 58 years. He was glad he had given Alisa's ashes to Rachel. Paul knew she would place Alisa with their parents. He began to feel the gnawing emptiness in his chest as he thought of his bride. Paul told himself he could not think about Alisa right now because she would want him to concentrate on the girls. He told the couple he saw the cab coming down the road which caused Robert and Joannie to ask how he knew that since they could see nothing as they looked out the window. Just then the taxi came into their view. Keeping their astonishment to themselves, the couple followed Paul out to the cab and climbed in. The three of them did not speak until they arrived at the Western Union office where Paul told them he would wait for them. They exited and came back with a check telling the driver to take them to the bank.

After cashing the check at the bank, the taxi took the three of them to the Greyhound bus station where Paul told the driver to wait. Once they were in the station, he reached into his bomber jacket and pulled out a burner cellular. He programmed the number to one of his two burner phones that had not been used and told them to only call him in case of emergency, "Otherwise I will see you in Montana with the children."

Joannie said, "Please Paul don't let them hurt our girls! Bring them home to us safely."

As Paul shook Robert's hand, he said, "I will Ma'am. I will!" He then pulled Robert aside and briefly spoke to him in private. Once he was sure the couple was on the bus, Paul took the taxi back to their house. The stunned police officers were still out cold. He picked each one up and placed them in the unmarked county car, making sure no one was watching.

The neighborhood was still quiet. He then went back to the house and fired a destructive plasma round into the house. Once he was sure the house was fully destroyed, he took off through the forest behind the house, making his way into town where he bought a used car from one of the lots near the base.

6

Avoidance

The Greyhound bus pulled into the Columbus station at 4:10 am. During the trip from Hinesville, Robert Veam found it difficult to sleep. He thought about what Paul Bannachek had told him privately. Robert was not sure why he believed the young man or rather younger looking man; maybe it was because he saw what Bannachek could do. Or maybe it was because something inside him told him it was all true. He was not sure what that something was though. Was it his instinct or just his gut? Robert really wasn't sure. The one thing he was sure of was the fact that he and Joannie were in harm's way. He had to use extreme caution on their trip. "Avoid all cameras," was something Bannachek had forcefully told him. Bannachek had also told him about the agents. Robert had been warned that the agents were in fact men and women, but they did not work for any government agency regardless of what their identifications stated. The agents were possessed and controlled by demons. They all were cold, calculating, emotionless people who had been consumed by the darkness. They may have worked for the government at one time, but now they were controlled by the dark forces.

Stepping off the bus Robert tightly held Joanie's hand while scanning the entire area. He saw a camera on the building pointed downward towards the departing passengers. He ensured to keep his head down, but not away from the camera whispering to Joannie to do the same. Robert had shared most of what Paul had told him with his wife of 35 years. How could he not? They never kept secrets from one another, ensuring to keep pure honesty in their marriage. He felt blessed to have Joannie. She was indeed a good woman. Letting his military training from the Marines come back to his conscious mind, Robert began his quick reconnaissance of the bus station and the surrounding city block. He decided they should avoid the station until their next bus departed at 6:00 am. Spotting a café halfway up the block, Robert led his wife up the street reminding her to keep her head in a downward position. He quickly adjusted his Taurus .357 magnum snuggly situated in the small of his back and patted each of his coat pockets to ensure his seven round speed loaders were still there and ready. Robert hoped he would not have to use the weapon but knew he would if came down to it. He had **killed** before, but that was in combat and over 25 years ago. Robert knew that once a man takes a life, no matter what, he can always do so.

As the couple reached the café, Joannie asked Robert, "Do you really think we are in danger?"

"Darling, I think we are facing a danger like nothing I have ever seen. More dangerous than in the war. We just have to depend on the Lord to protect us or at least to help us protect ourselves."

"You know Bob, when Paul told us about the girls being special to God, I believed him. You want to know why?"

"Go ahead babe, tell me."

"Well by the time we received the girls, they had been through so much. The starvation, the neglect, and the abuse; they were just six years old. But they also had so much love in them. It almost seemed like they were love itself. They always seemed different from the other children, especially the kids they played with. Even the kids in our church."

"I know Joannie. I have always felt the same way. They always seemed different, like they were pure goodness. I miss them terribly and I am worried about them as much as you are, but I think between God and Paul Bannachek we will have Elizabeth and Esther back with us soon! Now let's get some breakfast. But remember to stay alert though.

Brian Bannachek made his way onto Wright-Patterson AFB using his retired ID. He drove to the BX, parking midway in the parking lot from the store. It occurred to him that he should meander around the store for a few minutes before making his way to the hangers on the other side of the base in the event the Air Police stopped to question him. He would simply show them his identification and say he was just checking out the Air Force's way of doing things. Being a retired Navy Senior Chief, he figured the APs would give him a break. At least until he came close to the off-limits secret and top-secret areas! There they would not care who he was. In those areas they would play no games. He knew this being a former SEAL and therefore expected it. Brian just needed to get close enough and then find a hiding place until dark. He would nap in hiding until it was time. His training would take over from then on.

After walking about two miles, Brian sotted another security gate which was part of the base but separate. A large sign on the twelve-foot-high fence said, "TOP SECRET. AUTHORIZED PERSONAL ONLY. LETHAL FORCE IS AUTHORIZED!" Brian thought to himself, "Yup, this is the place." He scanned the entire area looking to find a place to hide. Seeing nothing for at least a block, he had to back track to Facilities building and hoped he could find an entrance without being seen or caught. If he could not, he would have to keep retreating until he did find a place. Fortunately, he found a cracked window. Someone had violated security protocol by forgetting to close the screened window. It was not difficult for Brian to remove the screen and raise the window. He climbed in through opened window, replaced the screen behind him and then closed the window all the way. Brian did not want some AP discovering the security breach of a cracked window and drawing attention to his hide-out. He knew APs were fanatical about their jobs and security, as they should be.

Finding a storage room, Brian quickly made entry, slowly working his way around the boxes in order to find a good hiding spot. The last thing he wanted was some flyboy coming into the room and finding him. If he was discovered, he may have to hurt the person. He would do it if necessary, but he would not like it. Brian was like every other Veteran out there. He would talk smack about the other branches of service like they all did, but he would never go against fellow brother or sister Veteran. Civilians just did not understand Veterans or their code. There was no way they could.

After finding what he felt was the best vantage point and hiding place, he pulled out two of his three burner cellular phones. First, he texted Paul, writing, "Arrived at location for making entry. Will wait for you. Where are you?" He pressed send and waited for a response. Within a few minutes, the cellular vibrated with a message saying, "Three hours out. Will find you upon arrival." Brian texted back, "How?" Another minute passed before his cellular vibrated. The text was an emoji smiley face laughing with tears. It was followed by the text saying, "Trust me. I will find you."

Brian smiled to himself knowing his brother could do things other men could not. He then texted Rachel on his other burner. "Where you at?" Five minutes passed before that burner vibrated with a text saying, "Six hours out of Boston. Making good time. Where you guys at?" Brian was frustrated with his sister. She knew that he and Paul could never divulge where they were or what they were doing. He knew she was worried about them and what was at stake, so he simply texted back, "Never mind." Then texted, "Are you really going to take Paul's wife to our parent's grave?" Within a minute he received the text, "NO NAMES! Especially his! And yes, I am taking her to be with our parents." Brian cursed himself for using Paul's name. With all his years of experience in combat and on intelligence missions he knew better! He texted back, "Sorry! Be careful sis." A minute later he received a response saying, "Since meeting him I have always been extremely careful. You two take care of one another. Have to get back to driving."

Brian decided he would take his nap. He had been driving for twelve hours. Add the two and half hours walking around the base he felt tired. Since Paul had told him they may see and experience things he would not have ever believed, Brian decided that a good nap would help keep him mentally fresh. Closing his eyes, he tried to focus his mind on what Paul had placed into his memory. Most of the memories had disappeared but he did have a deep feeling of kinship with his brother. He wondered about what they were doing and if they were really going up against dark forces. He had seen how Paul had healed him, but a nagging thought kept crawling into his mind telling him that Paul simply had abilities that others did not understand. Brian began to wonder about God. Deep within himself he knew he did in fact believe in God, but he doubted he could ever accept Jesus as his savior. Their parents had raised Rachel and him in the church; but since Paul had been taken, they had kept him and his sister under such lock and key he just didn't have in him to be a believer. He rebelled and became a street punk. Brian believed in the Navy because it was the Navy that saved him from his street ways. His last thoughts before falling asleep were, "How can God forgive me? With all the crap I pulled on the streets and all the killing I have done as a SEAL, there is no way

God can forgive me. I can't even forgive myself."

Driving his newly purchased 2008 used Ford F150, Paul wondered how Brian was going to hold up when and if he saw what Paul believed he would see. He knew his brother was not saved, which put him at risk with the dark forces. If Brian did not get baptized and receive the Holy Spirit, he could become a liability. A liability Paul would have to deal with, brother or no brother. The Twins were his focus, yet he still feared what could happen with Brian. Telling himself not to think about it, he wondered about Rachel. They had only met up five times over the past twenty years and because of him she always had to take precautions. He felt sorry for his younger sister though at least, he told himself, she was saved. But even Rachel, like most Christians did not really believe or have an understanding about the battles and wars going on around them. They said they believed there was a devil but deep down they really didn't. Paul had met many such Christians or those who called themselves Christians. They were the ones who took the wide path. They simply could not accept what they could not see and therefore did not believe in the "Principalities" or the unseen things. They may recite the Nicene Creed on a few Sundays a month, but they clearly had no understanding of what was happening in man's world.

As he drove up Interstate 71, he saw a sign saying he was 45 miles away from the Wright-Patterson AFB. His energy was down to 93 percent since he had activated his shield the moment, he had pulled off the used car lot. Paul normally would be at 97 percent, but he was stopped by a State Trooper near Coal Fork, West Virginia. He had to do a memory wipe and place a false memory in the Trooper's mind so he could avoid detection. Paul liked or rather respected the police and would never do anything to harm a cop, at least not a good cop. He had dealt with enough dirty cops when he had helped those children in the past. It did not go well for those people. As he drove, his mind wandered back to Alisa. It had been only two months since they separated, though in reality or by this timeline, it had been 74 years! He missed his wife terribly, and he felt he needed her more now than ever. Alisa helped him understand things. She simplified things for him. Thinking of her, he could almost smell her hair. Tears started to form in his eyes, so he told himself to *stop*! He could think about her when the Twins were safe. "Who knows," he told himself, "maybe I will be able to go home and be with her. I am tired of the fighting. What am I saying… I am just tired!"

Twilight had just arrived by the time Paul had pulled his F150 into the rest area. He parked directly in front of the bathroom area, stepped out of the truck and sanitized it before he stripped away the vehicle identification numbers on the dashboard, the driver's side door and the engine block. Wiping the numbers using his telekinetic ability drained five percent of his energy though he was still at 92 percent. Paul walked to the vending area, purchased a roast beef sandwich, candy bar and a bottle of water before he walked over to one of the picnic tables nearest to the back of the rest area. Eating his tasteless, convenience store sandwich and washing down the disgusting, processed food with his water, Paul surveyed the lot. He had kept his shield on minimum to block the cameras from spotting him, but he was trying to go unnoticed. Paul wanted to make sure that any driver who saw him pull up had departed before he headed into the wooded area behind the rest stop. It took about twenty minutes before a lull had hit the rest area. As soon as the lot was empty, he picked up his backpack and dashed into the woods. Feeling his energy level back to 100 percent, gave Paul a sense of relief as he believed he might need it all where he was going.

Using his mind's eye, Paul traversed the woods to the back of Wright-Patterson. He stopped just short of the large two-mile clearing, scanning the area for sensors and cameras. Seeing none, he began to slowly move across the open field hoping a roving patrol would not stumble upon him. Halfway into the clearing, Paul stopped and scanned two miles from that point. His mind was now on the base. He scanned each and every building until he found Brian in building 754. Paul chuckled to himself at the numbering system on the base. It made no sense. He stopped his humorous thoughts when he saw the fence was electrified. Paul also uncovered 17 cameras which rotated at ninety degrees, each overlapping the other. He could see there was a 360-degree visual coverage from a quarter mile out from the base. His mind then found the motion sensors starting approximately 100 yards out from the fence. Paul knew he could pass through all the security measures without being detected but what about when he departed the base? He would have Brian with him. He could extend his shield around his brother but that would take up more energy. Depending on what they encountered, he may not have enough energy. No matter what happened, he could not be captured. The Fallen would love that even more than the Office of Scientific Intelligence. He understood that under no circumstance could he be taken. His total and complete destruction was the only viable option to him if capture was eminent.

Charging the installation's back fence, Paul made a mental note telling himself he needed to explain to his brother why his body would need complete and total destruction if they or he was captured. Covering the half mile in less than thirty seconds, Paul jumped the twelve-foot gate with one stride landing on the run to building 754. He found the building in about two minutes, making entry through the first floor, locked side door. He had to extend his mind even more to prevent the alarm from sounding in the security office. Using his mind, he forced the electronic lock to open in order for him to freely walk through the doorway. Slowing his pace, Paul found the storage room where Brian was sleeping in about forty seconds. Stepping through the doorway, he whispered out to his brother. Brian immediately awakened!

The years of training and experience had taught him well. Jumping to his feet in combat mode Brian saw his brother and said, "Took you long enough! What ya' do, stop for coffee?"

"As a matter of fact, I grabbed a horrible sandwich, candy bar and a water, smart–ass!"

"What? And you didn't bring me anything?" Brian said smiling with a cheesy grin.

"Where are we heading Brian?" Paul asked his brother ignoring the comedy.

"I have to tell you big brother, it's going to be tough getting into that part of the base we need to get to. They have excellent security!"

"You let me worry about that Brian. All you need to do is keep your hand on my shoulder. When we cross over the next security fence, you're going to have to get on my back. You will feel a strange energy sensation around you, so don't freak out. Okay?"

"On your back? Are you kidding? I weigh one-hundred and eighty pounds! You're a big guy, but there is no way you can carry me."

"I can and have carried heavier. Now listen, when we go over the fence and land, you need to jump off my back but continue holding my shoulder. And please try and keep up Bri!"

Thinking of the upcoming dangers, Brian felt his adrenaline rise. Years of training helped him control it but, he still felt antsy. "I hope you know what you're doing Paul," is all he said as they made their way out of the building. Creeping slowly from building to building, they made their way to the point Brian had scoped out earlier. Paul knew Brian could not even come close to his speed, so they could not run the block they would need to for cover. Instead, he turned right and headed west for a couple of blocks. It took them 35 minutes to stealthily transverse those two blocks. Fortunately, they found a better spot where they could cover the open one block area and not be spotted by sentries, unless a patrol happened upon them.

"Get on my back Bri. And hold on tight! We are going to jump that gate. Remember as soon as we land, keep your left hand on my right shoulder and try to keep up! From what I have seen, we have about a mile before we reach any cover, and the area is pretty open. Okay?"

Brian simply said, "Fine. Let's get it done!"

Once Brian was on Paul's back piggyback style, Paul charged the fence line at full speed, which was somewhat slower than he would have been able to without the Brian's extra weight. He was still able to cover the block, jump the fence and slowly trot to cover upon landing in less than 30 seconds. The brothers made it to the hanger area in less than six minutes, showing Paul that Brian was true to his SEAL training. His kid brother was in shape! They had been lucky. No patrols yet. The two patrols they had spied were easy to avoid. His shield had protected them from any of the electronic surveillance, but his energy was now down to 78 percent. The brothers found the legendary Hanger 18 at the rear of the hanger field. It stood out by itself at least 300 yards from the rest of the hangers. Since it was now only 9:30 at night the brothers agreed to wait until midnight before trying to make entry. There were still too many Airman around and going in after midnight would mean the second shift would have departed leaving only a skeleton crew, if any people were still working. Of course, that meant more security. Finding a dark, quiet spot Paul and Brian laid in the grease and dirt-filled ditch. They silently waited and watched.

Suddenly they simultaneously saw it! A shimmering object coming in from the south. It had no lights, but they could see it moving at an unbelievable speed! It came down from the sky at a speed Paul calculated around 4,000 knots, and abruptly coming to a stop. It hovered over, then behind the hanger for about ten seconds before dropping to ground level behind the hanger. "Did you see that fucking thing?" Brian exclaimed in an excited whisper.

"Yeah, I saw it Bri. Two things. Don't use that language around me ever! I mean ever, Brian. It is ugly and dark. Just ask your questions without the language. Understand?"

Feeling chastised, as he was, Brian whispered, "I am sorry, Paul. I didn't mean to offend you. It's just that's the way we talk in the SEALS."

"Understood. Just don't do it again. Number two. Yes, I saw it. What do you think it was?"

"I don't know. Aliens?"

"Brian you are about to get an unbelievable education," Paul whispered back. "What you and so many others think are aliens, are in reality the Fallen!"

"The what?"

"You know the Watchers. The Fallen Angels from Heaven. I really wish you would have read the Bible, Brian. It would make things so much easier."

"Paul, are you talking about the giants that are in the Bible?"

"No little brother. Those giants, as you call them were the Nephilim, the offspring of the Fallen. Now listen. What you saw are Fallen Angels. They have been around for many millennia and there are many of them. They travel the way you saw because they are not permitted to travel through time and space, at least not through the natural time and space created as part of the Earth by God. They have been interfering with humans, directing us into a world of darkness and thereby stealing our souls so those souls will never see Heaven. Through those many millennia, they have interacted with human leaders providing them knowledge and technology—information we not meant to have. And the more they give, the further away we are pulled from God. Understand?"

"No Paul. I do not understand, and I don't think I want to."

"Brian, I warned you that you would see things. This is just the beginning. Now if we make it out of here, I will explain everything to you. Or, at least, everything that *I* have been permitted to know. For now, we have to get moving. Prepare yourself mentally Brian, because you may see even more astounding things!"

The two brothers began to crawl across the grinder towards Hanger 18. Paul extended his mind to the four APs standing 50 yards apart from one another. Paul sensed they did not have the darkness in them, but they also were not saved. He could see their thoughts, discovering that none of them had ever entered the Hanger. Only the special unit of APs, nicknamed "The Squad," guard the inside of the Hanger, and they had their own special barracks. They did not socialize with anyone else on the base and the Base Commander had no authority over them nor the contents within Hanger 18. No personal were ever permitted around the hanger, especially the back of the hanger. Seeing this Paul, sent mental blocks to the APs standing guard. He and Brian would be able to walk right past them, though the blocks would only last a minute. The brothers had to hurry!

Stepping through the large metal hanger door, Paul scanned the entire hanger. Where there should have been offices on the second level, there was nothing but wall. It was made of some sort of translucent material. The floor of the hanger appeared as though it was made of concrete, but Paul's mind saw differently. His mind saw the floor had just closed as they entered. In the far-left corner, there was an opening hidden to the human eye. The opening was ten feet in diameter.

"Come on Brian, let's go," Paul told his brother. Then he said, "I hope you're ready to use those .45's." The brothers double-timed it across the hanger with Paul's mind's eye guiding them. They reached the opening within fifteen seconds. Paul looked down into the opening, seeing that it was some sort of lift system. He felt the Spirit within him telling him to move quickly, but to be careful *and* to be ready! Not knowing why, Paul grabbed Brian's arm and pulled his brother with him as he stepped onto the invisible platform. As soon as they stepped upon it the platform lowered itself with tremendous speed! The platform took about seven seconds to cover what Paul estimated as 1,000 feet. It slowed quickly before coming to a complete stop. Waiting for them was something Paul had hoped he would not encounter again!

Stepping off the platform into what appeared to be a never-ending tunnel the brothers were greeted by two AIs! The entities immediately raised their REMP weapons, but Paul was too fast. He fired two lethal and destructive plasma rounds into each entity blowing them into bits!

"Hurry Brian, grab one of those weapons and follow me!" Paul loudly whispered to his brother.

"What the fu..., I mean, what the heck were those things?" Brian said as he charged after Paul.

"Artificially Intelligent beings created by man with technology given by the fallen. Essentially, they are really advanced robots Brian. Now keep up!"

The brothers ran down the tunnel several hundred yards where they found an opening on the right. They peered inside and saw a train with three cars loaded with children and a few adults. Paul spotted the Twins immediately, but the train-like vehicle took off at an incredible speed! They had lost their chance. The brothers had to get out of there but were faced with a small army of 30 men running down the tunnel towards them. Some of the men were clearly agents, while the rest were the special APs Paul had learned about during his mind scan. Weakened to 58 percent, Paul began returning fire with his plasma shots while Brian unloaded his twin .45 caliber Colts. They killed many of the attackers though Brian had been hit twice. The kinetic energy from the numerous rounds hitting Paul's shield gave him a 15 percent boost in energy. Grabbing his wounded brother, Paul lifted him over his shoulder with his shield engaged to full and ran down the corridor-type tunnel back to where the lift had let them off. He hoped the lift was still there. Unfortunately, it was not!

Quickly calming himself, Paul listened to the Spirit within him tell him to place his hand on the left wall halfway up the wall to his shoulders. The Spirit then told him run the back of his hand against the wall in a semi-circle. While he and Brian waited the seven seconds for the lift to return, Paul kept taking fire and returning plasma rounds. He was being bombarded by M-16 rifle fire as well by two grenades! The explosions seemed to have no effect to the surrounding tunnel, but swiftly recharged Paul back to 90 percent. Glancing back, he saw the five AI entities coming at him at incredible speed! They opened fire, hitting his shield three times before the lift arrived for Brian and himself. Paul quickly stepped onto the lift riding the fast-moving system to the top. Those three shots from the REMP weapons sapped his energy level back to 75 percent! Reaching the hanger floor, Paul found himself confronted by 12 APs. These were dark ones! They opened fire on him as he unleased lethal plasma rounds in return killing all twelve! Worried that the demons from the twelve dead might try and possess Brian, Paul used his full speed and energy to get out the hanger door; receiving several rounds from the normal AP's as he ran at his top speed.

He managed to cover the two miles in less than three minutes nearly exhausting his energy to 30 percent. By the time Paul made the treeline and located his backpack, he figured he had little time to heal Brian. Knowing the base was now on alert for a security breach, Paul figured the local law enforcement would be notified thereby being prey for more hunters yet again. If he left this brother, he would have just enough energy to get away, but Paul could not do that. Not ever. He set Brian on the hard soil and began to heal the two bullet wounds in his brother's chest in the name of Jesus. Paul then fired a small energy plasma round into Brian giving his brother full capacity of his body and mind. The final charge into Brian dropped Paul to 15 percent energy. He had full cognizant ability and could even move at a normal pace, but his energy would quickly dissipate. Paul figured he could travel about five to ten miles at normal human speed but that would be it. He looked down at his recovering brother and smiled as Brian opened his eyes.

"Hey numb-nut, I thought you were a trained SEAL! Letting yourself take two bullets in the chest is pretty sloppy wouldn't you say?" he sarcastically said to his kid brother.

"Yeah well, we can't all be endowed with superhuman abilities, now can we?" Brian replied with his own sarcasm. "I guess we made it?"

"We made it off the base and I believe we are safe for now, at least from the Air Force Cops. I bet my left butt cheek that local and federal law enforcement are already looking for us though. And we missed the girls! A failed mission."

"Oh, I don't know Paul. We know they are alive! And at least I know what we are dealing with. You going to tell me now?"

"Tell you what Bri?"

"You know, about the fallen. The Watchers and the UFOS and all that stuff."

"Brian I am really weak now. I will tell you later when I have more energy."

"How bad are you Paul? Tell me what you need me to do."

"Brian, I need food and sleep! Just need food and sleep."

Not willing to let his long-lost brother kick it, Brian told Paul he would go into town and buy some food. He would be back as soon as possible. Paul told him he needed to be careful. He was sure they had their descriptions out or would have them out within the next ten to fifteen minutes. Brian simply smiled and said, "Not to worry Bro, we are in my world now!" He left Paul there as he started a high-speed jog through the forest to town where he could locate some food. Maybe he could even pick up some local Intel. One thing was sure, Brian Bannachek had seen some unbelievable things that night! He was trying to digest what he had seen as he trotted. The AIs frightened him, but the agents and the APs in the tunnel really scared him! They were human but he felt a coldness about them. Almost an evil. Brian was not sure what those people were, but he knew they were his new enemy.

Brian made it to town and back within an hour. He had purchased a loaf of bread, turkey and salami slices, mayo and mustard, apples, a couple of oranges and a pre-made large salad with ranch dressing. He also bought four 33-ounce bottles of Smart Water© knowing that was Paul's preferred drink. As he walked back to where Paul was resting, Brian told himself he needed to make a decision soon. He was out of his league with the war Paul was fighting but it was a war that felt right to Brian. Seeing what he had saw really made him question what he had come to know as truth. Real truth. He thought about being wounded. He thought about the AIs. If he was going to continue to help Paul, he would need a vest and more weapons! He just hoped that he did not run into anymore AIs. He saw what their blasters did to Paul even with his shield up. Being a normal human, Brian recognized that he, nor any other human, could survive such a blast. Reaching Paul, he sat down next to his brother and made Paul a quadruple decker sandwich with light mayo and mustard on the wheat bread he purchased and handed Paul some of the fruit with the water. He pulled out his twin .45 caliber colts, switching out the empty magazines with full ones, and sat back against the tree.

"You eat Paul. You eat and rest. I've got this," he said looking over at his exhausted brother.

7

Needing Friends Who Fight

Waking his brother for the fifth time so Paul could eat and re-plenish his spent energy, Brian made Paul another quadruple sized sandwich, along with some more fruit and another large water. He watched his brother eat as he scanned the area ensuring they were safe before Paul fell back to sleep. Brian wondered about Paul's life. He thought about what Paul had told him and what their sister had told him. He was angry that his brother was always alone, always on the run with no friends. He hated the fact that Paul was hunted by so many with such nefarious plans for his brother if he was captured. Brian thought about the conversation he and his older brother had as they drove from the hotel in Florida to Hinesville.

He was surprised at Paul's reaction when he asked, "What kind of God allows these things to happen to one of his serv-ants?" Paul did not react well to his tone. After he gave Brian a small tail chewing about respect and understanding, he told his younger brother that God was perfect and therefore his knowl-edge was perfect. He told Brian that God never allowed one of his chosen to suffer through more than they can handle. This caused Brian some deep reflection.

Waking up at 5:15 am, Paul sat up abruptly looking around. Seeing this, Brian's instincts and training told him to heighten his alert status. He knew Paul could see things far away. Things that no normal human could possibly see. "Everything okay?" he asked his brother.

All Paul said was, "Stay here. I will be back in a few minutes. Stay Alert Brian. Okay?"

Paul then walked deeper into the woods to a point where Brian could no longer see him. Brian wondered if his brother went to relieve himself or if something else was up. Either way, for Brian it did not matter. He had complete trust in Paul now. Not just because of Paul's abilities and not because of what Paul had spent his life doing, but because Paul had saved his life and healed him twice. And Brian respected his brother's outlook as well as what he did for others. Paul always put others first, yet he was relentless when it came to fighting evil.

"Where have you been Michael?" Paul asked his long-time guide.

Smiling, the Angel said, "Greetings my young friend. God, **Praise His Glorious Name,** sends His blessings. He is very proud of you Paul!"

"Yeah, well I didn't see you helping us back there. We missed the girls!"

"Paul, God, **Praise His Glorious Name,** is protecting the girls as we speak! No harm has come to them, yet."

"Michael, why doesn't God just come down and fix every-thing? I mean he could change all of this and make everything alright. Couldn't He?"

"Oh, my young friend, God **Praise His Glorious Name** knows your thoughts and feelings. You know that. This is why I have come now. To explain what you must do."

"Okay. Okay. What am I supposed to do Michael? I failed! I

failed God!"

"No Paul, you did not fail. You accomplished two things. First you now know what you're up against. And, your brother Brian has seen it for himself. He is trying to understand and digest all he has witnessed. Paul, God, **Praise His Glorious Name,** has special plans for your brother. In time your brother will have to make his decision. Either he will choose to give himself to the SON and become a warrior for God, **Praise His Glorious Name,** or he will not. Because God gave all humans free will, He does not know the answer of how Brian will choose but He does know what each path looks like based upon Brian's decision."

"I'm sorry Michael. But right now, I cannot worry about Brian's salvation! I am worried about those girls. And by the way you did not tell me about all the other children who had been taken, let alone the adults! We must have seen thirty kids on that train-like thing and at least fifty adults. What about all of them? You know I cannot just forget about them?"

"That is understood. It is also the reason why you will need your friends to help you."

"What friends? The only friend I have is Johnny Alston and he is a lawyer. I cannot place him in danger. He already takes great risks for me."

"Yes, he does Paul. He will take even more risk, but it will not be for you, it will be for God, **Praise His Glorious Name**. As we speak, an ally of yours within your native land's government is planning to meet Johnny. He will assist Johnny in helping you help those who have been captured. You will also need the help of your friend Diane."

"Diane? You mean Diane Dempsey? I have not had contact with her for over three years. How is she going to help? And what ally are you talking about? I have no allies except Brian and my sister Rachel!"

"Calm yourself Paul and listen carefully."

Paul's guide then informed him that John Danick had been alerted by an old program of human technology that was designed to track Paul Bannachek and it had sent him a message about the money transfer from Switzerland. Rather than share the information, Danick took it upon himself to track the money to Johnny Alston. He deleted the information from his system and told his staff that he was taking three days leave of absence, but they could contact him for emergencies.

Paul asked, "Why would this Danick guy do that?" Michael explained that John Danick had been baptized at the age of nineteen. He had been told by the Spirit within himself to keep his faith private. He has done so for the past fifteen years. Paul told his guide that he had spoken with Danick on a comm set in the Bahamas. He told Michael that Danick tried to capture him.

Michael said, "Paul, John must keep his true self hidden. He feels badly for you. He does not like what the Government is doing, nor does he believe "The Friends" are from other planets. He is very uneasy about them though he does not know why."

Paul asked why he needed to involve Diane in everything. Michael told him that Diane had become an expert in helping children hide and arrange their educations while placing them in good homes. He told Paul that Diane would be initially angry with Paul for not reaching out sooner, but she would help him help the children.

"And the Twins?" Paul asked.

Michael said "The Twins must be reunited with their grandparents at all cost. God, **Praise His Glorious Name,** has very special plans for the girls." He told Paul he must get Brian and himself away quickly because Agents were looking for them and they were using some of the unsaved to help them. He then told Paul, "You may not survive this Paul! You must develop your friends into a fighting force, each with their own talents! Now take my hand. You must have full strength my young friend!" Paul took his guide's hand, immediately feeling the energy surge. Michael then disappeared into the atmosphere as he usually did.

Hurrying back to his brother, Paul found Brian standing watch with his twin colt 1911 .45 caliber pistols drawn and at the ready. He told his brother they must leave immediately. They had to make their way towards Columbus where they would need to hop a Norfolk Southern Train west so they could then hop a Burlington Northern or BNSF train west. He told this to Brian because the Spirit within him instructed him that the brothers would have to get to Lake Pueblo State Park in Colorado. There they would be led to the entrance of the underground installation that the Fallen had built. A place of great horrors! The place where the Twins and the others were being held. As they journeyed toward Columbus, he would have to make contact with Johnny Alston and then Diane. While he revealed this information to Brian, the realization that Brian was fully onboard had struck Paul. He wondered to himself if he had a right to involve Brian in this battle and more importantly this war! Telling himself that Brian had been fighting for America for over twenty years as a Navy SEAL, Paul thought Brian had fought enough. But the Spirit within him told him that Brian was simply conditioned for what he must do, *if* he chose to serve. As far as Paul was concerned his brother's choice was just that. *His*!

The two brothers double-timed it for several miles through the forest. Daylight was upon them forcing them to move quicker. They could not take the chance of being spotted nor could they let themselves be captured. It was during this time together Paul explained to Brian why he could not be taken. Not alive or even dead. His body must be completely destroyed. No matter what! Brian, being inquisitive as he is asked why. Paul explained why he was hunted. They, the many governments and certain corporations, which were mainly pharmaceutical companies, wanted his DNA. If they ever had their hands on it, they would create super soldiers which would make the AI's seem like nothing. They would be mindless humans doing evil work totally controlled by their masters. They would have all human emotion programmed out of them. Brian asked how he was to destroy his own brother. Paul told Brian he had to first make sure there was no life left in him. Then he was to burn Paul at such an intense heat that even his bones would not survive. To which, Brian said, "That means I would have to heat your body to at least 1,800 degrees and even *then,* there would be fragments! I would need sulfuric acid to complete the job Paul. I would need a lot too." Paul told him he would need to do whatever he needed to do but Paul's body could not be taken. "You're asking a lot you know. I would think you should be buried with our parents like Rachel is doing for your wife."

Explaining why that could never happen because the dark forces would destroy their parents grave in order to get at his ashes, Paul told his brother that he depended upon him and him alone to make sure the necessary actions would be taken care of. "If I am alive, I will fulfill your wishes Paul. I promise!" Paul recognized that Brian had a hard time with what was being asked of him, but he also knew his brother was a hardened combat vet. He would do it *or* die trying. Paul thanked Brian for his promise and then pulled out the burner cell phone he had texted Johnny with. Paul sent a coded text so Johnny would be at a pay phone within a couple of hours. He figured at this time of the morning his friend was probably in the shower, but he would see the text by the time Johnny made his morning coffee. It struck Paul as interesting that those who were closest to him were all avid coffee drinkers. All accept Diane. She drank tea, or at least she *did.* Paul felt guilty for not being in contact with Diane though he told himself it would have been difficult for that year in the half he was in 1943 Germany. Too much had happened to him for Paul to have the ability to think about such matters. He cursed himself for not calling her before his trip to the Bahamas.

Knowing that the agents would be using satellites to try and track himself and Brian, Paul engaged his shield to a low power telling Brian to keep his hand on his shoulder. While waiting for Johnny Alston to call Paul began explaining more of what he knew. They discussed the Bible with Paul emphasizing that Brian must learn the word of God in the first Covenant and the Gospel of God's SON Jesus in the second Covenant. He then began to explain to his brother they were in the end times, when they actually started and what was transpiring. Forgiving Brian's human arrogance when he asked, "If this is true, can't mankind stop it from happening?" Paul continued his lessons to his brother. He told Brian of all he had seen and experienced over the past forty some odd years. Paul explained everything about the fallen who are sometimes called "The Watchers" and how they have been interacting with humans for millennia in order to drive mankind away from God. He explained what little he knew, from what Michael had told him, about time and space being part of the Earth's creation and therefore it was not permitted to have its use.

After an hour of teaching, Paul's burner buzzed in his coat pocket. Answering it, he heard Johnny's voice on the other end. His friend of over twenty years sounded tired. Before speaking and warning Johnny about Danick coming to meet him, he asked if Johnny was okay.

"Yeah. I am just tired, and I am bewildered with what is happening in the courts my friend."

"What is happening Johnny?'

"It is so strange. I used to win case after case because I stuck to the Constitution. Lately though I have been losing cases I should have won. It is almost like these judges have forgotten the Constitution and our laws. They seem to be ruling by the seat of their pants, usually against Christians. The only way I can win is to go to the Supreme Court but that takes a lot of money. And my clients don't have that kind of money."

"So, what are going to do Johnny? I mean is there anything

you can do?" Paul asked already knowing there was nothing his friend could do. All of the world was becoming corrupted, hating Christians even more than the Jews.

"I am thinking of retiring my friend. At least retiring from fighting for people in the courts. I will of course continue to help you."

"Can you afford to retire?"

"You have helped me become a wealthy man my friend. I do not need money. But I am only 51-years-old. I am too young to retire. I need a purpose!"

"Johnny, I am about to give you *that* purpose. Can you somehow get away in the next day or two?"

With excitement in his voice Johnny Alston said, "Sure! What do you need me to do?"

"First, I want you to go to a store. Make sure you avoid any and all cameras Johnny. Get to a store that sells burners. Buy a couple and buy a couple of sim cards as well. Once you have them charge them both completely and call me back at this number. Okay?"

"Consider it done my friend. I can call you back in about two hours."

"That's good Johnny, because in about four to six hours you're going to have a visit from the CIA?"

"What?"

"Don't worry Johnny! He is an ally. But be cagey Johnny. Be cagey. I will wait for your call."

If Johnny Alston had been anyone else Paul would have some concern for his friend dealing with the leader of the Office of Scientific Intelligence, but Johnny was smart! He knew how to think his way out of trouble. He knew how to handle people. Paul had a fleeting thought of, "Thank God Johnny's on my side. Hate to have him as an enemy," before pulling out his other burner to call Diane. He was not even sure if Diane had the same number. She might have moved away. Paul felt his stress and nervousness rise as he began to dial. "What if she moved away? Michael said she would be angry with me. What do I tell her? Michael also said she would help. Do I have a right to involve her in *this*?" The phone on the other end rang. He heard the voice of Diane say, "Hello?" in a questioning tone.

Twenty-four hours had passed since John Danick received the alert on his desk computer. He had never seen that particular type of alert. Investigating further, he found the alert came from an antiquated computer program which was designed to track any movements for Paul Bannachek. Danick's predecessor had ordered its design and implementation of the program. The system would monitor all banking information, telephone, email and wired communications. Anything that mentioned the name Paul or Bannachek would be filtered out and compiled with other information in order to track and locate Bannachek. Somehow, Danick's newly assigned computer had the old forgotten program. After receiving the alert Danick studied the information. He saw the wire transfer from Switzerland to the US and the within minutes the transaction had been converted to a buy order for stocks which within minutes was placed as a sell order with those funds then transferred to an attorney's escrow account. He spent fifteen minutes researching who was moving the funds finding the name of the individual was Steve McCormick. He then ran a computer check on McCormick finding the man had been in the Bahamas at the same exact time as Paul Bannachek. Too much coincidence for Danick! As far as he was concerned the man was helping Bannachek. "But why?" he wondered. "Was this McCormick person somehow one of the many people Bannachek had helped?"

Since Danick could find no further pertinent information about McCormick, he concentrated on the location of the final funds transfer. Before doing so he made a note about him in his private files, just in case the man's name came up in the future.

As his powerful computer worked, Danick destroyed the original alert file and then removed it from his destroyed files. Danick understood that nothing was ever destroyed but he could at least make it difficult for anyone else to find the information. The information led to the escrow account of the attorney. The name of the lawyer was Johnny Alston. Knowing he had seen the name before, Danick pulled up the Paul Bannachek file and ran a search. There it was. Alston from Spencer, Iowa. The same lawyer who had worked for the State Department who also had mysteriously resigned. Bannachek had been sighted in Spencer, Iowa twice back in the '80s and '90s. Clearly there was a connection and John Danick was going to find out just what that connection was.

Sending an IM alert from his desk computer to Marc Boyd, a man he did not like or trust, Danick requested him to come to his office. As he waited for Boyd to make his presence, he began to concoct his story. It would have to be verifiable so he would have to use his wife and kids. He would tell Boyd that while his wife Cindy was taking the boys to her sisters for an extended weekend, he was going to take a couple of days leave to see an old friend in Memphis. Knowing that the agency tracked the whereabouts of all senior leadership, he would not be lying. Cindy *was* taking the boys to her sister's; and he would travel to Memphis. He would make sure to lose any tail he might have so he could meet this Johnny Alston alone. Danick understood that withholding information about Paul Bannachek would be considered treason so he would have to be extremely careful. Deep down Danick did not really care though. From everything he had read in Bannacheks file, he had come to the conclusion that Paul Bannachek was not threat to America. Rather, it was the American Government that was a threat to Bannachek. Danick had always felt sorry for Bannachek. He had read the man's file many times. Yes, Bannachek had strange and unique abilities and if provoked, he could become very dangerous. Yet in over forty years, Paul Bannachek had never done anything to harm America or the American people. Yes, he had destroyed labs. But in hindsight, that act made sense to Danick. If he was in Bannacheks place, he would do the same thing. The simple reason of self-preservation would be enough for Danick to destroy the labs; although, he thought that idea did not fit the personality profile the agency had on Bannachek.

Giving the customary three quick knocks on Danick's door, Marc Boyd made entry into his bosses' office. "What's up John?" he asked in his disdainful voice. Danick could always feel that creepy darkness seeping from Boyd whenever he was near, so he wanted to limit their time together. He asked, "Where are we on Bannachek?"

"We think he is in Europe, but we are not sure. There is a meeting scheduled with our *friends* in two days. When the information is passed to us, we will know more."

"Good! We came so close to capturing Bannachek in the Bahamas I don't want to lose the scent, so to speak."

Boyd gave Danick a strange look of distrust as he said, "Don't worry. I think we will have him very soon. Is that all you wanted?"

"No. Cindy is taking the boys to her sisters for an extended weekend, so I am going to take two days leave to see an old friend in Memphis. I want you to run things while I am gone. Okay?"

Excitedly Boyd said, "Sure thing Boss! Keep you informed via cell?"

"Yes. Please do. I want this guy!" Danick lied.

"No problems on the home front I hope?" Boyd asked with a creepy sneer.

"If there were, which there are not, I certainly wouldn't broadcast them to my subordinates. Now get back to work! And Boyd, stay out of my office while I am away."

"Hi Diane. How are you?" Paul asked his oldest and dearest

friend.

"Oh my God! Is that you Paul?" she exclaimed in surprise.

Grimacing, Paul said, "Diane! The rules Diane. We have to keep with the rules. Okay?"

"I'm sorry P..., I mean I'm sorry. It *has* been several years you know!"

"Sorry about that. Believe me when I tell you I was unable to connect with you. How are you? How's the hubby and the kids?"

"I lost my husband a year ago to brain cancer. I really needed you then. Ya know?"

Feeling guilty, Paul could only say, "I am *truly* sorry Diane. Believe me when I tell you that a year and a half ago, I was totally unable to contact you. I wish I could tell you more, but I can't. At least not now. So how are your children?"

"All grown up! My son is in his residency in Boston and my daughter is an Associate Professor of Biology at the University of Chicago."

"You must be very proud of them! How about *our* kids? How are they doing?"

"So far every child you sent my way has done well. Many have graduated college and are on their own. Why haven't you called? Why haven't you sent more children? I know there are many more out there who are suffering just like I had when you found me."

"Again, I cannot explain that right now Diane. However, right now I will need your help again. That is if you're willing to help."

Angrily Diane said, "You know you beat everything! You know that?! I don't hear from you for a couple of years and out of the blue you call me asking for *my* help?! Where were you when I needed you? You could have saved my husband!"

Understanding why Michael had said Diane would be angry, Paul could only say, "Listen Diane. You of all people know I would not have dropped contact with you for any reason if I *could* contact you. And if I could, I would have helped you and your husband! But Diane, I was not anywhere around. So, I am deeply sorry. I wish I could tell you more. Now, if you do not want to help me with more kids, then just say so."

Sobbing, Diane said, "I am so sorry. I often forget about who and what you are. I will of course help you! What do you need?"

"I need you to write down the number I called you from. Then go out and purchase a couple of temporary cellular phones and sim cards and then call me back. Okay?"

"I will. Give me a couple of hours and I will call you right back. I promise!"

Pressing the off button to his burner, Paul placed the phone back into his coat pocket feeling very depressed. He wished he would have been there for Diane and her husband, but he also knew her husband was a saved man. He suspected God had made use of him to support and love Diane all those years she helped Paul with all the rescued children. He looked over at Brian who was shaking his head. "What's with you?" he asked his brother. "Who was that? I could hear her screaming at you from here!" Paul explained who Diane was. He told Brian how they had met, and all Diane had been through. Brian then said, "Yeah, well she sounds like a ripe bitch!"

"Brian! She is a human being like you or me. She has lost her husband and her kids have grown and moved away to live their own lives. She is alone and angry. I think she just needs to be needed again; and she *is* needed! She will help us with the children. *Believe* me, she is very good at this sort of thing."

Brian asked who *exactly* Diane was. Paul told him their entire story. How they met in Reno and how they rescued one another. Paul explained how Diane had spent years receiving kids he had rescued from Chicken Hawks, sex slave trader's and other evil, sick individuals. She arranged for them to go to private Christian schools, funding all their expenses. And how she consoled and counseled these kids, helping them, or at least many of them, come to the faith. Unfortunately, they could not all be saved. Some were just too damaged by what was done to them. He told Brian how much he loved Diane though it was not the love of a husband and wife. His love for her was more of the agape love. Brian asked what that was. Paul went on to explain the four types of Biblical love. It only took him thirty minutes before his brother seemed to understand. Then his other cellular burner buzzed in his other pocket.

"Hello?"

"Paul? It's Johnny. Now tell me what's going on?"

"Where are you at Johnny?" Paul cautiously asked.

"On Promenade Street near the Pyramid. Why?"

"Just being careful. As we talk, I want you to walk north to A.W. Willis Avenue and then head west to Mud Island Park. Okay?"

"That's a bit of a hump my friend, but I guess I can use the cardio. Okay I am moving. Now will you tell me what's going on?"

"The individual coming to see you is an ally, only he really does not know it yet. I have been told he is going to help you and us, especially now!"

"Been told? Who told you?"

"You wouldn't believe me even if I did tell you Johnny. All I can say is my source is the *most* reliable source one can have! Is that good enough for now?"

Thinking for a moment, remembering that his friend Paul Bannachek was not like a normal client and he was not even a normal human being, Johnny acquiesced his normal inquisitive nature. "I guess that will have to do for now. So, what are you into Paul?"

Johnny and Paul grimaced simultaneously when Johnny had mentioned his friend's name. He knew as well as Bannachek that a computer, monitoring all cellular communications in America, had a specific program within it to record all calls containing the name "Paul." That information would, in turn, be sent to another computer system which would refer the case to the NSA for further evaluation. Both men knew they had at most twenty-six hours before a human ear would hear the conversation. If they made no more mistakes when speaking on the call the computer may not even forward it. "Careful my friend!" Paul said.

"Johnny, I am into something very big. I will need at least thirty, maybe even more, special identifications. And no, they are not for me."

"Thirty?! Have you lost it?! I told you I am having difficulty just keeping you up to date! How am I supposed to get thirty?"

Thinking what Johnny must surely be thinking Paul tried to reassure his friend by saying, "It is going to work out Johnny. Don't forget, we have a new ally and I believe he will help you, at least to a point."

"What kind of specials are you going to need?"

"All I know now is the number. I also know they will be for different ages and races."

"Would you mind telling me how I can do this without the most basic information?"

"I need you to meet me and my brother at Pueblo State Park, Colorado in two days. And I need you to bring your computer. Can you do that?"

"You're talking about direct involvement! You told me a long time ago you did not want me involved. What's changed?"

"A lot has changed my friend. I have knowledge of things I never would have even dreamed of back when we met in Iowa. Things that will, if you decide to help these kids, truly enlighten you but also test everything you have come to believe. So, are you in, or not?"

"Kids and enlightenment? You know how to work me. You know I cannot not help children. And as an attorney, you know I am extremely inquisitive. Yes! I will be there. What about our ally?"

"Remember Johnny, he does not realize how much of an ally he is. Also remember that *all* allies have their own agenda. So, tell him as little as possible. You can tell him what you know about me and how we met, but I would not mention the State Department experience. Now I will see you in two days. Destroy that sim card and toss the phone at the river. Okay?"

"As soon as we hang up. See you in two."

Thinking about all Paul had just told him, Johnny Alston began to ponder. If Paul needed him directly involved, then whatever he was taking part of must be very important. Destroying the sim card and tossing his burner, Johnny headed back to his practice by hailing a cab. If his visitor was from the CIA, he did not want to take any chances. Ally or not, this Danick person could be dangerous to Johnny. That meant dangerous to his family. Reaching down to his belt he pulled out his I-phone from his hip case and pressed send for his preprogrammed number to his wife Karen. Johnny had never lied to his wife and he was not about to start now. Besides, she being an excellent attorney as well, would know if he lied. He would tell her that he had to meet a client and would be flying out the next day. Since he travelled all over the US to meet and defend clients in Federal court, Karen would not be suspicious. He did have to be careful though. She also knew Paul Bannachek and saw his capabilities back in Iowa too. Karen had told Johnny she did not want Paul in their lives after the Iowa incident.

Arriving at his office just as he hung up with Karen, Johnny moved quickly. He sent emails to all of his clients with scheduled meetings saying he had an emergency. He would contact them in a week to reschedule. He then filed an emergency continuance with the Memphis Federal court, copying the opposing attorney for the Veteran's Administration saying an emergency had occurred. He requested the judge set a continuance at the judge's discretion. Johnny knew the judge would grant his motion. The opposing attorney would be happy because then he could file for a motion later. Anything to not see the inside of the courtroom was the VA's motive. Johnny was passionate about all his clients and cases but this one at the VA gnawed at his craw. His client had suffered brutal harassment and discrimination because he was a Christian! That angered Johnny! However, as he had explained to Paul, the courts were making outlandish decisions towards those of faith. The activist judges were reinterpreting the law - more importantly, the Constitution! Sending his last email, he waited for his visitor from the CIA.

Sitting on a railroad tie beside the train tracks, Paul and Brian listened and waited for the 11:10 freight heading west. Paul knew it would be on time just as all American freight was on time. America was the one place where timeliness still had meaning, at least in business. Hearing the train coming from two miles east, Paul told Brian they needed to move into the woods and hide themselves from view until the train's engines were well around the bend. He looked at his brother and wondered if Brian was ready for this. His mind's eye had been able to clearly focus on the train now that it was within two miles of their location. He guesstimated the speed at 30 mph; but noticed it was slowly gaining speed. Paul figured the train would be at its' top allowable speed of 49 mph by the time the engine had cleared the bend. He could easily jump the train given his speed, strength and agility, but there was no way Brian could do so. "Look Brian, you are going to have to ride piggyback for a minute or so if we are going to jump this train. Understood?"

"Hey Paul. I have jumped some trains in my life! I think I can handle this without your help."

"One travelling at speeds between 30 to 49 miles per hour?" Paul asked.

Deciding not to argue with his older brother, Brian said, "Yeah, probably a good idea if I play horseman for a minute or two."

Once the train's engines were well around the bend, Paul

nodded to his brother, who jumped onto his back over his back-pack, and held on for dear life. He had been through this before and he did *not* like it!

Paul sprinted towards the train, running alongside it for twenty yards before grabbing the steel ladder on the train car. Pulling himself onto the ladder, his feet quickly found their respective places on the rungs and was able to climb. Brian slid off his back once they were situated on the train car's roof saying, "That sucked! Scared the bejesus out me Paul."

Laughing, Paul instructed Brian to go west along the top of the cars until he could locate an open one while he would go east and do the same. After several minutes, Paul saw Brian signaling that he had found an open car. He watched as Brian slid down into the train car, thinking his brother was foolish to try that without help. If Brian had fallen, he could have been killed instantly! Paul could not bring life back! He could only heal. Running and jumping from car to car, Paul swiftly caught up to the car Brian was in. He quickly followed suit by easily swinging down into the car.

"You know Brian, you can be really stupid! You know that?!" Brian just laughed at his older brother while he found a dry spot to make himself comfortable.

8

Convergence

The flight from Raleigh, North Carolina to Denver went without incident for Diane. It was uncomfortable having to wear that silly mask which she swore she would never do. It was necessary if she was going to meet Paul and the others in time. She needed to get there first so she could rent a 4-wheel drive SUV and a cabin that would sleep five. The cabin needed to be as far into the Pueblo State Park as possible per Paul instructions. Their conversation lasted less than an hour. Diane had to remind herself to always speak in coded phrases and to never use Paul's name. She learned a great deal from that brief conversation. Most importantly was a pair of twin girls. Fraternal twins who had been kidnapped. He did speak of the last couple of years though it made no sense to Diane. How could not be around, yet be there in a *different* place and time? How could he marry a year and half ago, yet his wife died back in '62? The idea that Paul Bannachek was somehow married bothered Diane. She knew that Paul aged at a much slower pace than most people. He had told her he could never marry because he could not risk passing on his genetic abilities.

Thoughts of jealousy clouded her thoughts! She had loved him dearly back when he rescued her, and she liked to believe that he loved her too. But she knew Paul did not love her in the manner in which she desired. His love was purer. Unlike every man she had met back then, he wanted nothing from her! He just wanted to give her a chance at life. Diane wondered about this woman Paul had married. She must have been very special for him to against marrying anyone. She wondered why she could not be *that* woman, but immediately she felt guilty.

She had had a *wonderful* marriage before Roger died. He had been a good husband and friend who always supported her, never mistreated her nor did he treat her like property! Most importantly to Diane was Roger had been a good Christian man who loved God's word and His SON Jesus. He was no Paul Bannachek, but he was wonderful. Exiting the United flight into the Denver air terminal, Diane wondered about the danger Paul spoke of. Of course, with Paul there was always danger, but he told her what she was getting herself in for was like nothing she nor most humans had ever encountered. She told herself she should be frightened, but Diane also knew that Paul would protect her just like he had before.

The CIA man arrived at Johnny Alston's office at 12:20 pm. Since he had sent his secretary home telling her he needed to work on a brief and wanted total quiet in the office, he had to let the agent in himself. The agent produced identification stating his name was Don Aspen as he introduced himself. Johnny suspected the man was lying because he had known agents back in his days at the State Department. Rarely did they ever use their given names and when they did it was only when they were away from their duties among close friends. Even then they may use aliases. Playing along, Johnny welcomed the agent with a feigned warmth, inviting the man to sit across from him at his conference table. As the agent sat down, Johnny studied him carefully. He was around 40 or 42, five foot ten inches tall weighing about 180 pounds. He had deep blue eyes with dark brown hair which was lightly greying at the temples. No visible scars. He wore jeans with Keen walking boots, a long-sleeved flannel, button down shirt and a jean jacket. Clearly all the clothes were brand new.

Offering the CIA man some coffee, which Mr. Aspen glee-fully accepted, Johnny stood and walked over to his beverage bar and plugged in the coffee pot. With his back to the man, he studied the agent closer, observing his reflection in the glass of the painting above the bar. Johnny then said, "I have to say Mr. Aspen, I am curious as to what the CIA wants from me? I am just a one-man law firm. I just practice employment law."

"Not true Mr. Alston, replied the agent. That is not true at all!"

Becoming nervous, Johnny kept his emotions in check while asking, "What do you mean by that?"

"Only that you also practice law by protecting folk's religious liberty at work and in general. Isn't that correct?"

Smiling a false warm smile, Johnny turned saying, "Is that why you're here Mr. Aspen? My practice in defending Chris-tians?"

"Mr. Alston. Do you record your meetings with clients or prospective clients?"

"I do not. I have an excellent memory Mr. Aspen." The two-cup coffee pot beeped three times signaling the coffee was ready. Johnny poured them both a cup, turned and set the cups on the conference table saying, "How about *you* just telling me what the CIA wants from me? That way we'll both know if your visit is a waste of time?"

"John, may I call you John?"

"Since you're taking the liberty, my name is Johnny."

"Fine, *Johnny*. I will come to the reason I am here. Tell me about Paul Bannachek."

"Who?" Johnny asked in response as he thought knight to rook three."

Reaching into his inner jean jacket pocket, John Danick pulled out a piece a paper and unfolded it. Looking at it he said, "Come now Johnny. Paul Bannachek. The man your escrow account received a wire transfer from."

Thinking he was caught Johnny kept doing what Paul had told him. He would be cagey as long as he could. He asked the agent, "May I see that paper please?" The agent handed the paper over to Johnny and sat quietly allowing time for Johnny to accept he was caught. But Johnny was not done playing. He still had some fight in him. He responded by saying, I have not checked my escrow account for some time." Johnny did not want to give an exact time frame on the oft chance the agent had his account's full record. If he had, he would know Johnny had transferred the funds right back out an hour after he received them.

"That is interesting that you say that because on this document I have here," the agent pulled out another piece of paper, "it says you transferred the money to a Paul Bannachek not even an hour after receiving the funds. Now tell me about this man Bannachek."

Realizing he was now caught Johnny decided to keep the game going. He asked, "What does the CIA want with my client Mr. Bannachek?"

The agent understood that Johnny was working his way to the attorney client privilege. He decided to play along by saying, "So he *is* your client?" in feigned surprise.

"I represent him on occasion, *yes*. However, I really cannot disclose anything to you about my work for Mr. Bannachek or any other client. CIA or no CIA."

The agent's facial expression gave away his frustration. He sat there looking at Johnny as if he was pondering his next move. He needed to get to Paul Bannachek, but he could not afford for the agency to find out he was withholding information. If they knew, he could possibly be made to disappear at the worst or fired at the least. "Do you know who this Paul Bannachek is, Mr. Alston?" the agent asked in frustration. He was now back to addressing Johnny as Mr. Alston. The agent understood just as well as Johnny he had lost the game.

"I know what I need to know about Paul. Why do you ask?"

Attempting to reestablish some sort of lead in their conversation, Danick said, "First Johnny, you need to know and understand that I am not a spy or anything. I work for the Office of Scientific Intelligence. Our office is interested in Mr. Bannachek for national security reasons."

"National security? What could Paul have done to make him an interest of national security?" Johnny asked.

Deciding to let Johnny in just a little bit, Danick told Johnny that the Office of Scientific Intelligence was only interested in Paul for scientific reasons. He had told Johnny they were responsible to study and track all past, present and possible future discoveries. They believed Paul Bannachek had information on a new discovery. All his office wanted was the information and nothing else. Johnny knew he was lying; that it was pure fabrication. He knew and understood why the CIA wanted Paul. They wanted to both own and control him, and if necessary, dissect him. He also understood why Paul could never let that happen. Johnny had sworn his allegiance to Paul and what Paul was doing in helping all those children. He also agreed that Paul must never let a lab be built or work to continue in making others like Paul. The human race would be doomed if *any* government had that kind of power. He decided he would go all in by saying, "Sorry Mr. Aspen. I cannot help you."

Reaching behind his back the CIA agent pulled out a .32 caliber pistol with a repressor already attached. He laid it on the conference table pointing directly at Johnny's chest saying, "Are you sure about that?"

Johnny thought back to what Paul had told him. "Be cagey Johnny, be cagey." He also thought back to conversations he had had with Paul Bannachek when Paul had told him if he was ever cornered, concerning anything about Paul, he was to give up all the information. Johnny also understood that if this CIA agent hurt or even killed him, Paul would come back with a vengeance. A vengeance with such force that the CIA would reel from the destruction Paul would cause. Paul Bannachek did not enjoy hurting or killing but he was also intensely loyal and would stop at nothing to avenge a friend!

"I'll make you a deal Mr. Aspen. You tell me your real name and why you really want Paul, and I will tell you everything I know about Paul Bannachek. I will explain to you how me met and what I do to help him.

Danick smiled saying, "You are not really in a position to make deals Johnny, but I have a strange feeling I can trust you. My name is John Danick and I want help Paul Bannachek."

Trying to explain to Danick just who exactly Paul Bannachek was and is had been more difficult for Johnny than he thought it would be. He explained how Paul had been injected by the Mossad agent Rebecca when Paul was only a day old at the Air Force Hospital. He then told the story as Paul had reiterated it to him. He explained Paul was always unusual as a child, but his abilities did not show themselves until Paul hit puberty. Johnny told Danick how Mary had taken Paul at the age of thirteen and taught him how to hone his abilities and control them. He told Danick about Beth, to which he said, "I am sure you know about her," as he continued his story. Danick just nodded thinking of the reports he had read from Agent Margaret Southerland who was a double agent and a traitor. As far as he was concerned Bannachek did the CIA a favor by eliminating her. *Besides,* he thought to himself, *Southerland was clearly an evil woman.*

As the Bannachek story continued to unfold, Johnny told Danick about all the children Paul had rescued and sent to a woman whose name or identification he did not know. That woman ensured the children were sent to private schools. Most of the kids accepted Jesus as their Lord and savior, though some were beyond saving. Danick asked how the woman could afford to provide such assistance. Johnny detailed how Paul made his money at casinos. He had made so much money over the past thirty years, he no longer needed the casinos because Johnny had invested the money for Paul, creating several corporations that did nothing but invest. Paul would contact him and tell him when to buy as well as when to sell. Bannachek paid him a ten percent commission, which more than funded his practice to defend Christians in lawsuits for their workplace harassment claims. Danick then asked how much money Bannachek had. Johnny explained that the last time he checked; Paul was worth over $40 million even after all he had spent helping the children. "You should know Mr. Danick, Paul does not use the money for himself. He uses the majority to help those who have been victimized!"

Seeing that Danick was becoming visibly uncomfortable as he continued on, Johnny wondered if the CIA man had guilt for hunting such a man as Bannachek. He then told Danick what Paul had shared with him about the fallen or the *Watchers*. He explained how they sent Paul into what could best be described as an energy tunnel full of darkness which for Paul was not to escape. But the forces of light released him, only to find himself in 1942 Poland. Johnny tried to explain the time travel as Paul had explained it to him. But since Paul didn't really grasp it and was still reeling from it, Johnny didn't understand it. Strangely, John Danick did. Johnny told Danick about the flying disks that Paul had destroyed although two got away. One of them he damaged. Danick immediately understood that that disk was the saucer that crashed in 1947 New Mexico. The idea of aliens came up by the intelligence of the Army Air Corp. He also understood that those intelligence people were working with what they thought were highly advanced beings. But that cooperation came at a cost. A cost that Danick did not agree with. A cost to human lives for experimentation by the so-called Aliens. After Johnny had finished it was Danick's turn to share.

Starting with what he knew from the reports and records, Danick began to explain how little they actually understood or knew little about Paul Bannachek. Danick had always suspected, since he came to be the leader of Office of Scientific Intelligence, Paul was in reality no threat to the United States. However, he had to do his job or at least appear to do it. He believed there was something sinister at hand within the Government and not just within the CIA. Danick never bought into the idea of aliens from other worlds, though technically that idea was not far from the truth. The fallen, or rather the *Watchers* were alien to the human being as they were not of the Earth and clearly not human. He had seen some strange things. Those things would give humans the idea these beings were human or at least humanoid. He told Johnny that he believed his assistant Marc Boyd was somehow controlled by these so called "friends" and that Marc Boyd did not trust him. "I have had to hide my faith for years Johnny. If I had not, I would not be in the position I am now. And lately, I get the feeling there is much darkness around me and even more so in the world."

Explaining that his duty was to hunt down and capture Paul Bannachek, he had a higher duty to God in Heaven and His SON Jesus who was John Danick's Lord and Savior. Since Danick openly stated those words, Johnny felt he could now place some trust in the man. Danick had said the words that are given in the Bible. No evil one can say those words. They may try and pervert the words in some sneaky fashion in an attempt to convince "Christians" they are one of them; but true Christians know and understand the idea of testing the spirits. True Christians are continually in God's word and would never fall for these diversions. They know an evil person cannot profess that, "Jesus is the only begotten SON of God our Father and Creator in Heaven and that Jesus is my Lord and Savior who died for me." But that same confession can also get a man or woman killed in certain places in the world. They spoke for another hour before Danick said he would help Johnny aid Paul.

Transporting Alisa's ashes to the Homewood cemetery was an honor for Rachel. She thought of all Paul had told her about his beloved wife thinking she was truly a heroine. Alisa had devoted her life to God by saving and protecting his people. She had given her love to Rachel's brother Paul. It seemed only fitting that Alisa be buried with their parents. Driving her rental car from O'Hare Airport down the I294 to Homewood brought back memories for Rachel. She stifled those memories to consider how she would place Alisa with their parents? If she went and inquired about having the dual grave opened to inter Alisa's ashes, there would be a record. Records meant questions. Questions meant possible surveillance which is something Paul had told her to avoid at all costs. She stopped at the Homewood Florist on Martin Avenue and picked up two dozen Calla lilies for the grave site. Many people placed fake flowers at graves for longevity but no one in the Bannachek family would ever do that! She wants live flowers, especially the Calla lilies, because they meant faith, purity, and holiness. This was something their parents knew a lot about, as did Paul and Rachel and she suspected Alisa knew and understood too.

Arriving at the cemetery, Rachel parked in the visitor's lot as close to the walking path as possible. She had not been to their parent's grave in several years. Feelings of guilt and even thought of neglect gnawed at her. It was one thing for Paul to not visit. He was after all hunted. A perfect place to lie in wait for him would be that place. He knew it just as she knew it. Rachel decided to use extra precautions. She did not want to pick up any possible tail. She knew there was of course satellites, but she told herself those hunting her brother would not simply watch the grave from space. With flowers in one hand and the small wooden box with Alisa's ashes in the other, Rachel walked the trail to her parent's grave.

Thinking she was foolish for wearing a dress, considering the work she was about to do, Rachel used the flower holder by her parent's grave to dig up a large piece of grass. Quickly glancing around to ensure no one was around to watch, she poured Alisa's ashes into the makeshift plot and swiftly replaced the grass. Rachel began to weep for her parents. She wept for Alisa because she had heard stories from her parents how Alisa and a strange man had saved them from the Nazi's. Her parents told both her and Brian that Alisa loved them as if she were their own mother. Protecting and caring for them across Germany, across the North Atlantic to New York City, and then to Ohio. They did not say much about the man except he could do strange and wonderful things. But they spoke of Alisa often, always grateful for her sacrifice and love.

Knowing that Paul and Alisa had a lifetime's worth of love in just a little over a year made Rachel cry even more. She was grateful to God for Paul finally being able to have some semblance of normalcy, even if it was for such a short time. Rachel quietly prayed to God and then she asked Jesus if it was all possible, could He bring Paul home so he could be with Alisa and their parents again. Rachel apologized for such a selfish prayer, though she reasoned to Jesus that Paul had always served Him and had sacrificed so much to serve Him and God. In Rachel's mind it was only fair though selfishly, she also didn't want Paul to really go home. She wanted to see him even more now.

Arriving at the Grey Hound Station in Clinton, Iowa, Robert and Joannie Veam took their newfound security precautions as they departed their bus. They had to transfer to another bus which was an express to Billings, Montana. Robert spotted them first! Two agents came toward them as they waited for their luggage being pulled from beneath the bus. The men identified themselves as Homeland security agents, though their mere presence made the small hairs on Robert's neck stand! Joannie had a strange cold sensation come over her as the one agent spoke. She looked into the man's sunglasses, swearing she saw only dark blackness for eyes. Shivering, she took hold of Robert's hand letting him know simply by her touch she was frightened.

The agent said, "Where are you going Mr. Veam?" Something strange inside him told Robert to say, "We are going to Cheyenne. We needed to get away after the girl's disappearance."

"Get away?" the agent said with a cold, emotionless pause.

"Yes, get away. Why?"

"It has been too much for us agent, what is your name again?" Joannie spoke up.

Ignoring Joannie, the agent said directly to Robert, "Why would you leave? We need to be able to contact you," pausing before saying, "In case we find the girls."

Joannie responded before Robert, saying, "We have the cards of our local law enforcement. We were told we could call anytime to keep abreast of the case."

Again, ignoring Joannie, the Agent asked Robert, "Have you contacted your local authorities since you departed?"

Thinking it was a valid question Robert lied and said, "Yes. And we were about to call them again, as soon as we received our luggage. What is this all about?" he questioned forcibly.

"Strange, we have no record of any calls from either of you. Why is that?" the agent responded in retort to Robert's forceful question. The agent's voice was still monotone and emotionless.

"I have *no* idea. I was not aware the authorities kept records of our communication."

"Mr. Veam, from this point forward you are to call this number, and this number only for information on the girls. We have assumed control of the investigation. The person at this number will answer your questions. Furthermore, you are not to speak of this incident with your granddaughters to *anyone*. Is that understood?"

Feeling threatened by this, Joannie spoke up in a forceful tone. She demanded to know why Homeland Security would give such orders. She told the agents they could speak to whomever they wanted.

The agent, still ignoring Joannie, said to Robert, "Communication about their disappearance could cause harm to both the girls and you." Robert demanded to know what the agent meant by that. The agent stated that they believed the girls were taken by a cult and if the culprits knew of Robert and Joannie speaking about this incident, they would have no incentive to keep the girls unharmed and alive. He then said, "They may even come after you two," in a cold, menacing tone. The agent then removed his sunglasses showing his black, cold, dead eyes saying, "We would hate to see that happen, Robert," in that same tone. The couple both felt the *implied* threat!

Before replacing his sunglasses, the agent looked into Joannie's eyes as he spoke to Robert saying, "Oh yes, may I see your tickets?" Terrified that he was caught in a lie, Robert had an overwhelming urge to show their tickets to Townsend, Montana. He produced the tickets letting the agent take them from him and study them. The agent put his sunglasses back on as he continued to look over both tickets. After a minute he looked back at the Veams saying, "So you are going to Cheyenne? We will be looking for you there." He handed the tickets back to Robert, nodded to the other agent and walked away around the bus terminal.

Joannie waited for about ten seconds and ran after the two men. She had reached the corner of the station, mere seconds later, only to discover the agents had vanished; she saw absolutely nothing— just an empty alley!

Walking quickly back to Robert, Joannie told him the men had disappeared. Robert was looking pale as a ghost, held up their tickets in front of him. "What is it Bobby? What's wrong?"

"It can't be Babe. It just can't be!"

"What can't be Bobby?" Robert showed Joannie their tickets. They both indicated a destination of Cheyenne, Wyoming! Then suddenly before their eyes, the tickets once again read Townsend, Montana.

After jumping three separate freight cars on three different freight trains, Paul and Brian made it to Pueblo, Colorado. They had done a great deal of walking and hitchhiking in order to make the rendezvous on time. Interestingly, the rides they received were all Christian drivers. They all had told the brothers they *never* pickup hitchhikers or strangers but something within them gave them the desire to stop and offer rides. Brian questioned this but Paul understood. He knew the Holy Spirit within the drivers was telling them to stop. Unfortunately for Brian, he simply could not or would not accept much of what he was told or what he had seen. Because of Rachel, he accepted Paul and his abilities because he believed it was science that gave those abilities to Paul.

During their walks Brian asked Paul many questions about his beliefs. He wanted to know why Paul actually believed there was a God. He told Paul that he believed in the Big Bang theory, but God seemed so juvenile to him.

Paul responded by telling Brian, "I will answer your question the best I can. First, the Big Bang states that suddenly there was an explosion and the universe formed. How can there be an explosion if there was nothing there Brian? Something cannot come from nothing! As for your idea that believing in God is juvenile, Jesus said quite clearly 'Let the little children come to me, and do not hinder them, for the kingdom of God belongs to such as these. Truly I tell you, anyone who will not receive the kingdom of God like a little child will never enter it.' And Brian

I do not just believe in Jesus or in His Father our God and Creator, I *know* Jesus is there watching, sitting next to God the Father! Beliefs can change Brian, but knowledge does not."

"Yeah, well I have to tell you that I sometimes think you people are really foolish!"

"Oh, and why is that little brother?"

"Look at your churches. Those people give their hard-earned money to those churches and what do they get in return? Nothing!"

"Brian, we do not tithe in order to *get something*. We tithe because God commands it. It all belongs to God anyway. Of course, there are many who do not tithe or do not tithe fully using the excuse they cannot afford it. Those people will have some answering to do in Heaven I assure you."

"Heaven? You really believe in Heaven? There is no rational explanation for a heaven."

"Really? Tell me Brian, how many dimensions are there?"

"Not sure. I know we live in a three-dimensional world though."

"Yes, we do. And yet we also know there is the dimension of time. And it is believed there may be up to ten or even eleven dimensions. I have already shared with you my time travel experience, have I not? So, if man can theorize ten or eleven dimensions how can you say Heaven is not in one of those dimensions or made up of all the dimensions?"

"Fine. You want to bring science into this? That would not be a fair conversation since I am not good at science."

"You brought up science by saying there was nothing rational about there being a Heaven. I simply made a statement of scientific fact which has clearly angered you. Why?"

"Honestly? I get tired of hearing about some God and Jesus and all that. Look! If there was truly a God that created all this," he said as he opened his arms into the air, "why does God let His world be so screwed up? Tell me that Paul! Tell me that!"

"Okay. I will tell you, but you will not accept my answer."

"Tell me big brother! Share your infinite wisdom on that!"

"Brian, God did not make this world. He made the Earth. He made the sun and the moon, the soil and plant life, the fishes and animals and then He made man and gave it all to man. Man became corrupted by the fallen, led by Lucifer who has many names. This world we are forced to live in is the way it is because of man. Not God! God our Father and Creator gave us free will Brian. It is *our* choice in how the world will be. *Our* choice."

"Are you going to say that you have never sinned Paul?"

"Not at all Brian. I have sinned many times. I have had sinful thoughts and I have done sinful deeds. I have probably sinned more than most."

"Then how is it you believe, oh excuse me, know you going to Heaven?"

"Brian, there is so much for you to learn with so little time. I am not a preacher or a teacher. However, I will tell you what I know as the truth. Jesus, God's only begotten Son came to the Earth to do several things. First, He shared His Gospel or teachings about His Father God, our God and Creator. He also came to teach us about Heaven and how there was only one way to get there. And finally, He came to die for *all* of our sins, Brian. But He does not take on your sin unless you are baptized into Him and receiving the Holy Spirit. And you must be called."

"What do you mean called?"

"Brian, Jesus said that no man could come to Him unless it was by His father."

"What does that mean?"

"It means that God must select or anoint those who will desire to come to Jesus. He does that at different times so one never knows when one will be called."

The brothers discussed God's word and the Gospel of Jesus for many hours as they walked and rode trains. Paul then shared with Brian what he had been told by both Michael and the Holy

Spirit. He told Brian about the forthcoming events in the world and what was going to transpire. He told Brian about what would happen to Christians and the Jews who have always been hated since the very beginning. Brian had become clearly agitated over what he was hearing. He did not like what Paul said in such a matter-of-fact manner.

Paul became quiet for several minutes. Wondering what was wrong with his brother, Brian asked if everything was okay. Paul told him that they would need more weapons than just Brian's two pistols.

"What do you mean? Why?" asked Brian.

"We will need weapons for the others who will join us. And I will need five grenades."

"*Grenades*? Why would *you* need any sort of weapon Paul?"

"Because. They are fantastic for recharging me."

"How do they do that?" Brian asked.

"It is hard to explain, so I will put it to you like this. If I have my shield enabled and an explosive device is set off near me, the kinetic energy of the explosion is absorbed by my shield. That energy recharges me. Just like when bullets hit me, they explode once they hit my energy shield thereby giving me a charge, albeit a small charge. Lightning will also charge me just like if I grab hold of electrical current. Different power sources replenish my energy but some of the newer power sources deplete my energy quickly."

"What kind of newer sources are you talking about Paul?"

"Brian, I do not know what they are. I just know they are from the dark forces given to the men who have been possessed and now serve the dark forces."

"Don't you have any defense against these new weapons, Paul?"

"I wish I did! They hurt like you would not believe. The only real defense I have is if I am in an open space. By moving quickly, I can try and avoid the shots and return fire to destroy those firing upon me. But Brian, where we are going there will be no open areas for me to run to."

"How do you know that?" Brian asked.

"The Spirit within me just told me. I was told about the layout and the weapons you and our friends would need. And Brian, you should know that I may not make it out alive! If that is the case you must, no matter what get the Twins out alive and anyone else you can help. You must forget about me!"

"*Paul*! How can I forget about you? You are my brother. And you have healed me and saved my life twice! I can't just leave you behind! I *won't* leave you behind."

"Brian, do you really believe it was me who healed you or saved you?"

"Of course, I do."

"Then you have learned nothing from everything I have told you! Understand this! I am led and sent to those who God chooses. I heal those who God chooses. I am nothing but a servant, Brian. I came to you because God wants *you* to assist in saving these children. Why do you think I have never attempted to meet you over these past forty years of your life? It is because I did not want to place you in jeopardy!"

"But you told me before I was to ensure no one was able to get your body. Has that changed?"

"No Brian. However, it is more important that the Twins are rescued than my dead carcass being taken and dissected. Of course, I will do everything I can to prevent that from happening. Mine, yours and our friend's main goal or mission is to rescue those Twins!

Not knowing much about weapons, Paul asked what Brian would need?

"What makes you think I would know where to get these weapons?" Brian asked. Paul explained that the Spirit within him told him that Brian knew someone who was nearby. That someone had served with Brian in Iraq. He told his brother that

Brian's friend dealt in illegal weapons for some militias and that he knew Brian was aware of this. Brian, shocked that his brother knew this, told Paul he did have a friend, but the weapons would cost a great deal of money. Much more money than the brothers had between them. After Paul had asked how much money they would need, he told Brian they needed to stop at a casino. They could stop at Bronco Billy's Casino in Cripple Creek, Colorado. He had been there several times a few years back when he needed cash replenishment.

Once the brothers arrived at the casino Paul did what he normally did. He placed a one-dollar bill into a slot and pulled the leaver. Concentrating on the machine, he ensured he hit the triple diamond on the first pull. He won $500. Paul cashed out his winnings, taking the payment ticket to the cashier cage and bought five hundred dollars of chips. Then he went to the roulette table and turned the $500 into $15 thousand within five minutes. Paul then moved on to the craps table and turned that money into $100 thousand in thirty minutes. Then he quickly ensured to lose back $50 thousand on one roll of the dice. Paul cashed out his winnings and the brothers left the casino. They walked a block north to a used car lot and bought a used Jeep Cherokee, then drove to Brian's friend's house twenty miles further west.

Waiting outside of the cabin, Paul wondered if they had enough time. He worried. So, Paul prayed for more guidance. The Spirit within him told him they must hurry. The Twins had not been harmed but they were scared. They had less than twenty hours before the girl's abilities would be discovered. Thankfully, Brian had not spent more than an hour at his friends. He came out smiling, loaded down with weaponry. Brian not only had six hand grenades, but he also had a 7.62 Tkiv 85 Finish Bolt Action Sniper rifle. He also purchased a Russian RPG-29 Vampire reloadable shoulder fire, Anti-Tank with Phosphorus shells and some C-4 with electronic timers, three handguns, a PTR91 .308

caliber semi-automatic rifle with ten large capacity magazines along with one thousand rounds of ammunition. He spent $20 thousand dollars, mainly for the M26 fragmentation grenades, C-4 and timers.

Paul drove while Brian loaded the magazines and other weapons. He explained to Brian that once they were within two miles of the cabin, they would have to dump the vehicle and walk because he would have to destroy their transportation. This upset Brian! He demanded to know why they had destroyed a perfectly good vehicle. Paul explained that he had not had enough time to destroy the digital camera information of him playing at the casino. Because of this he suspected the CIA already had the information via facial recognition and had reset a satellite to look for them.

"You mean we have one of those damn things watching us right now?" Brian asked.

"No. I have had my shield engaged as soon as we left the casino. They cannot see us or the vehicle, but we must destroy it regardless. If they find it once we park it, they will know our general location and send teams for the vehicle. If they find the vehicle, they may get my DNA which means they can make others like me. Others they can control!"

The brothers reached the cabin at 6:00 pm. They waited at the edge of the woods so Paul could scan the cabin and the surrounding area with his mind's eye. They had seen two SUV type vehicles parked outside the cabin. Paul had brought them to that particular cabin because the Spirit within him led them there. They noted some movement within the cabin though they needed to ensure it was safe. Paul scanned the cabin and the complete area doing a three sixty with his mind. The woods were deserted, as he expected for that time of year. Inside the cabin he saw Diane, Johnny Alston and another man. He was told from Spirit within that the man was John Danick.

Paul felt fear come over him. The CIA had hunted him for

over forty years and now one of their own was sitting in a cabin with his oldest and dearest friends!

9

Fast Movement

The cabin itself was remotely set deep within the Pueblo State Park. As cabins go, it appeared rather attractive on the outside. Being an actual log cabin, the appearance was quite rustic. Using his mind's eye, Paul noted there were three small bedrooms, a great room, one bathroom with a shower and a large steel tub. The kitchen was part of the great room. It had a wood burning stove and an iron sink with a hand pump for water. There was a small ten-gallon water heater for the shower. The furnishings were non-descript and well-worn, but for the purposes of Paul's team the location and setting were perfect. He knew from what he had been told by the Spirit within him the location for making entry of the underground facility was only a mile away. It was much deeper into the woods.

After deciding it was safe to make entry, Brian and Paul walked up to the cabin and entered. Upon entering through the front door Diane jumped up from the couch ecstatic with excitement at seeing Paul. John Danick was on his feet with his .32 caliber pistol drawn at the ready to fire, while Johnny Alston stood slowly as he recognized his old friend.

"Put it away John!" he told the CIA man. Your pistol will not harm nor have an effect on my friend Paul Bannachek!" As he said this Diane was in Paul's arms crying and hugging as she kissed his check.

"I cannot believe it! You look almost exactly the same as you did forty years ago! I am so sorry for how I treated you then and how I spoke to you on the phone Paul! Will you forgive me?"

"There is no need for you to ask Diane. I forgave you long ago and as soon as we hung up. You look well, especially for a 56-year-old woman," Paul teased.

"Thanks, I guess. But from now on will not discuss my age! Understood?"

Laughing Paul said, "Oh sure, sure. But can't I jibe you just a little?"

"No, you may not! Friend or no friend."

Standing there watching, Johnny asked who Brian was. Paul introduced him as his *younger* brother telling the small group he was there to help all of them. He then asked about the CIA man. Johnny introduced John Danick to both Paul and Brian saying he was there to help.

"I believe you can trust him Paul," Johnny told his old friend. Being cautious, Paul told Johnny the only people he trusted in the world were Brian, Diane, Johnny Alston and his wife Alisa who was no longer in this world. He did trust a man named Piotr, but he died over fifty years ago.

Looking at the CIA man Paul asked him, "Why are you here?"

"Paul, may I call you Paul?"

"Yes."

"I am here to help. That's all. I just want to help."

"Like the way you have been hunting me. You call that help," Paul barked angrily?!

Just then the atmosphere opened, and Michael stepped into

the room. Everyone in the room except Paul and Brian fell to their knees in fear. "Greetings my young friend! God, **Praise His Glorious Name**, sends his blessings to you and your friends Paul."

"Why are you here Michael? You told me you would not show yourself to others around me and yet here you are!"

"Paul, I am here to speak to your friends first. Then I will speak to you. Rise! All of you rise and seat yourselves. Do not take a knee to me. I am an Angel of God, **Praise His Glorious Name**, you bow to Him and to His Son your Lord Jesus, but not to me. After all, do you not know you will judge me in Heaven?"

Being shocked that his guide did not want him present for whatever he was going to say to his brother and friends, Paul left the cabin and took a stroll. He wondered what Michael was going to tell them, but he knew better to ask. After all these years Paul had learned to curb his curiosity when it came to God's commands. He knew Michael was God's Angel who came with word directly from God. It was not his place to know what he was not supposed to know.

"Friends of Paul Bannachek, and yes, you too, Brian Bannachek, have been chosen for a very important duty for God, **Praise His Glorious Name**. I can tell you that very few humans have ever been chosen as you have, so pay heed to my words."

Johnny asked, "Sir, what do you mean we will judge you? How can humans judge Angels?"

Laughing, Michael said, "You have not spent much time in scripture Johnny Alston! You should spend much time in the word of God, **Praise His Glorious Name**, for it is what you humans call a road map to Heaven. But only those baptized into the SON the Lord Jesus will understand because they have received the Holy Spirit."

Diane spoke up saying, "Do you mean what is written in 1 Corinthians?"

"Yes Diane. You have excellent knowledge of God's, **Praise**

His Glorious Name, word! It is awful the rest of you are not as knowledgeable as this woman! All of you should know this and much more. All of you, except you Brian Bannachek. Even now with all you have seen you still do not accept or know the truth!"

Brian, feeling embarrassed and self-conscious, said he just could not believe. Even then with Michael's appearance he had a hard time believing! He did not know why but he just couldn't. As the three others looked at him, Michael told him, "That is because God, **Praise His Glorious Name,** has not yet anointed you. Your time will come shortly and then you will have to choose. I hope you choose well!"

Michael then proceeded to give God's instruction to the four, explaining that it was vital to save the Twins and there would be other children they would want to save. He warned them against trying to save the captured adults, explaining that some were too far gone, and others had become consumed.

Danick asked what he had meant by consumed. Michael then explained that many who are taken are consumed or possessed by evil ones. "If you listen to the Spirit within yourselves you will know who they are," Michael told them. Danick asked if his assistant Marc Boyd was one of the consumed. Michael nodded affirming the truth about Boyd. He then went into detail about what they would encounter telling them to listen to and follow Paul's instructions at all times. Michael then told them that Paul would probably not make it so it would be up to Brian to get the Twins to Montana. Johnny, Diane and John Danick would be responsible to get any others they rescue to safety. For the children, Diane would do what she has always done only this time, she would need Johnny's help obtaining identities and John Danick would have to ensure Johnny was not impeded in his efforts.

"What do you mean Paul may not make it!" Diane excitedly asked.

Michael said he could say no more about Paul and told them

to have joy that God, **Praise His Glorious Name,** had chosen them.

"*Joy!*" exclaimed Brian. "How can you speak of joy when you tell us my brother may die? You are telling us we are about to face pure evil and we are to have joy?"

Michael then told the group, "Joy is not happiness my friends. Now *listen* to my words and pay heed."

Michael said, "What is joy? Well, it is not the same thing as happiness. Joy runs a lot deeper than happiness. Happiness depends on what happens, upon your circumstances, and those can be happy or sad. Joy, on the other hand–joy is not dependent on your circumstances. You can have joy even in the midst of challenging circumstances. There is Christian joy, even when things are going bad in your life. Happiness depends on what happens, and that can change. Joy depends on Jesus. Joy is found in the gospel of Christ, and that's a *sure* thing. See, so our life together in the church is a joyful gospel partnership. It is centered in, and flows out of, the saving gospel of Jesus Christ. There is nothing surer than that. There is absolutely nothing more joyous than that.

'For what is this gospel of Jesus Christ? It is the good news, The Good News, the greatest good news there can be! The gospel tells us what God has done for us in your Savior Jesus Christ. The person and the work of Christ for our eternal salvation—this is the heart of the gospel. The gospel that Paul preached back then is the same gospel that is or should be preached and you believe today.

'Paul says that it is the gospel "of your salvation, and that from God." For God has saved you in and through Christ. God sent his Son to save us from our sins and from eternal death. Jesus lived and died and rose again for your salvation, that you would be forgiven and live forever. Jesus Christ accomplished this by fulfilling God's righteousness on your behalf, living the perfect life we have not lived, the life of love, according to God's good law. Then Jesus suffered the punishment for all lawbreakers, which all sinners deserve, namely, death under God's judgment—again on our behalf, in our place.

'This is how your sins are forgiven: Christ died for them. You have his righteousness given to you as a gift. And through faith in Christ, you have life in His name, everlasting life. On the day when our Lord returns, you will be judged righteous, not guilty, because of Christ. And until that day, God will guard and keep you in this saving faith, as you continue in the gospel. This is why the apostle Paul said, in Philippians: *"I am sure of this, that he who began a good work in you will bring it to completion at the day of Jesus Christ."* It is through this gospel that you will be, as Paul says, *"pure and blameless for the day of Christ, filled with the fruit of righteousness that comes through Jesus Christ, to the glory and praise of God."* So, this is the gospel, and it is a joyous thing. Nothing better.

'The gospel is what you need more than anything else in the world. This is why the church exists: to be the home of the gospel. The church is where the gospel sounds forth for all the world to hear. The church is where the gospel of Christ forms you into a community, into a family of believers, where you build up and support one another in the faith. You have something special there. This is where Jesus is present, to forgive your sins and to give *you,* life. The gospel, in Word and Sacrament, is the church's very life. And it is the life you have been given, entrusted with, to share with the world. This is what all people need, whether they realize it or not: You need the gospel.

'Secondly, it is a partnership even in **prison.** Here I'm using "prison" as shorthand for "suffering," for all the adversities you face in life. These things do not break your fellowship, our partnership in the gospel, and they do not rob you of your joy. What are the prisons you are enduring? Do you feel trapped by our life circumstances? Are you struggling with chronic illness, yours or a loved one's? It can feel like you are in prison, with no way out.

But you have the sure hope of the gospel to sustain you. You have brothers and sisters here in God's family to help you or just to lend a listening ear. You have people who will pray for you, for it is God's help that you need most of all. You have a joyful gospel partnership, even when you are experiencing a prison."

After hearing Michael speak, he departed walking through the wooden door as if it did not exist. The four team members sat astonished trying to understand and digest what the Angel had just told them.

Finding Paul meandering through the woods, Michael approached his young friend. "Greetings my young friend! Why are you so glum?"

Paul explained to his guide that the Spirit within him had told him that he may not survive this ordeal. He was worried and frightened for the girls. He told Michael that even if the group makes it out, he was concerned that his brother may not make it to salvation. He wanted Brian to be in Heaven with Alisa and their parents.

"It will be *his* choice Paul," Michael told him, "just as it has been the choice of all those you were sent to."

Saying he understood, Paul told Michael that his brother Brian was different. "He is my brother Michael!"

Michael asked Paul if his brother was his *true* brother or merely his human brother. It was not a question Paul wanted to hear. He understood the difference and he understood it would be Brian's choice. But what if he chose wrong? Of course, Paul already knew the answer to that. Brian was a grown man. He had to take responsibility for his choices. He also understood that it matters little to God how much Brian helped in this mission. There was only one way to Heaven.

Good deeds did not afford people a free ride or ticket into Heaven for eternal life. Paul understood that God had sacrificed His only begotten Son for mankind. If a man or woman was so arrogant or foolish not to accept this gift, then *they* would be responsible for their choices. Paul had also witnessed many people who he had helped over the years choose wrong. He understood that when God made it their time to really choose, they must choose correctly. Many people think they had made a true choice but then turned their backs. They therefore were not true in their baptism and therefore would be destroyed. He asked Michael why the Angel was there. Michael told him boldly and forthrightly!

"My young friend, you were given great power back in your time travel experience. God, **Praise His Glorious Name,** wants to know why you have barely used it. You could have destroyed those evil beings you call AIs easily. Why did you not use what has been given you? Why do you stick to your older powers only?"

"What happened to me in Germany terrified me Michael! I am afraid of these new powers. What if I lose control? The destruction I could do would be horrible!"

"You will not lose control my young friend. Besides, if you use your new powers and abilities you will weaken near as quickly."

"I am not sure I know how to use these new powers Michael."

"Of course, you do. Just as you did back in time. Allow the Spirit within you to help you."

Still being fearful, Paul said he was not sure if he could do that. Allowing the Spirit total control. But Michael explained that the Spirit never had any control. The Spirit only advises and gives one desires. He told Paul that like all men and women Paul had free will. "You mean what I did in Germany was actually me?"

Michael said that was in fact the truth. He said, "My friend you often bewilder me."

"Yeah, how is that," Paul asked sarcastically.

"You were born and created to serve, heal, protect, and give people the opportunity to choose, yet you are still a man with man's arrogance. You were given more power and gifts than any man ever born to this world, yet you still have so much fear in you. How can you have such fear? Do you not love God, **Praise His Glorious Name?**"

Feeling guilty Paul said, "Of course I love God! How can you ask that of me Michael?"

"Because with love there is no fear my friend. No fear at all!" Michael then disappeared in his normal fashion by backing into the atmosphere.

Paul stood there feeling chastised. He knew Michael was right in all he said. He also understood that if he did not use *all* of his gifts the Twins may not survive let alone his friends and his brother. Paul now knew that he must place his full trust in God! He must place all of his want and fear in Jesus. If he did not, then the outcome could be catastrophic! Paul did not completely understand why the girls were so important, but he did know that they were born with powers of God. They were not like him who was simply injected with a serum meant for evil, which God intervened so that those powers would be used for the light.

10

The Attack

Having decided he must use all of his abilities Paul made his way back to the cabin. He had to establish a perimeter for the attack he was about to lead. And he needed to let each person know and ensure they understood their duties. Time was running out and Paul Bannachek knew it! He told himself that no matter what, those Twin girls *would* be rescued and brought back to their grandparents. He told himself that the Twins must be kept safe so they could accomplish whatever it was God had planned for them. Paul just hoped that his brother and his friends would all survive. That of course would depend on Paul. He had to relinquish his fear! He had to place his complete trust in his Lord Jesus Christ!

Arriving back at the cabin, Paul found Brian and his friends quietly talking. They were talking about Michael and their disbelief of what they had witnessed. None of them except Diane *wanted* to believe, especially Brian. It was Johnny who was saying he did not want to fall prey to mass hysteria. And it was Johnny who told the group they had either just been blessed with their newfound knowledge or they had been cursed! Diane spoke up telling the small group she believed they were blessed.

"For whatever reason God has selected all of us to help Paul. He sent the Angel Michael, and I for one will do whatever our Lord God requires! God does not curse man because God made man. Man curses man."

Listening to what had transpired, Paul told the group that both Johnny and Diane were correct. Changing the subject, he told his friends they were running out of time. They needed to get moving. He had a plan for each one of them and what they were going to have to do individually in order to save the Twins. "This plan will depend on each of you doing exactly as I tell you. I promise I will do everything I can to ensure we all get out alive, but we must all agree here and now that the Twins are more important than any of us or *all* of us." Looking at one another each member of the newfound team agreed. They all mad a pact saying they would do whatever it took to save the girls even if it meant death.

While describing the attack plan Paul expected some push back. He understood that they CIA man Jon Danick would want to have a frontal position since he was a trained operative. But Paul knew Danick was not a combat vet. Brian was the only person there with actual combat experience Therefore his brother would be up front with him so he could be part of the frontal assault. He told them about the AIs and that they appeared human. He also instructed them to fire at them just above the hip because that was where the entity's CPU was stored. Paul explained that the AIs could not be killed but they could be put out of commission. He also warned the group that the AIs were not run by their human creators as the government believed. They possessed their own darkness within them. John Danick began to question what Paul was saying.

"How do you know about these machines? They are classified."

"John, I know a great deal about the government's experiments and where they are getting the technology from!"

"How? These newer AIs were just given to us only six months ago?" the CIA man questioned.

"I cannot share that with you although I can tell you that I have come up against these beings before. What the American Government has are scaled back versions of what the Dark Forces use. They gave this technology to you to, shall I say, whet your appetite?"

Danick then said, "I have never been permitted to meet our friends and honestly I have had no desire. Something in me always told me to avoid them and the meetings they held with my superiors. But it is hard for me to believe these beings are from darkness. I mean you're saying they are of the devil!"

Considering what Danick had said, Paul replied by saying, "Listen to me all of you. You have met Michael. So, if you know Michael exists how can you not believe in Satan? I assure you; you will see things that will terrify you, but you must *not* be afraid! Darkness feeds off of fear! Hold tight to your faith and darkness cannot harm you, regardless of what movies and books tell you."

"So, what do we do when we see demons?" Brian asked.

"You cannot see demons, but you can see the fallen. Be careful though, the fallen or Watchers can take on any form. So again, trust in your faith. As for you Brian, I hope you are able to choose sooner rather than later. If you are consumed by a demon, brother or no brother, I will have to destroy you. None of us here can risk those girls. Do you understand me?"

"Enough of this rigmarole," Johnny interjected. "Tell me my position."

"You Johnny, will not be entering the compound."

"Why not? Paul, you know I can shoot. You have seen me shoot. I am a crack shot now."

"Yes Johnny, I know. That is why you will be placed in a

location to cover our retreat. You will take Brian's sniper rifle and lie in wait in a tree, covering the entrance way I will make. And Johnny, if anyone or anything comes out of that entrance way you are to kill it! If it is an AI, shoot it where I said to."

"But what if people come out of the entrance?"

"This may be hard for you to understand Johnny. If anyone comes out besides any of us or the Twins or any others that we rescue, I guarantee they are of darkness. Kill them!"

Looking down at the floor Johnny said, "I will do what I can Paul."

"I know you will Johnny. I *really* do know you will."

Danick wanted to know exactly what he would be doing. Paul explained that he would be providing cover for Diane. He told them all that Diane was key because being a woman the children would be naturally inclined to cling to her. They would trust her. He then told the CIA man that once they were out of the complex John Danick was to return to DC. Paul explained that he was aware that Danick would have to continue his hunt for Paul if for anything to maintain his cover as the Director of the CIA's Office of Scientific Intelligence. He did ask that Danick slow his hunt so Paul would have a chance, if that was possible.

"Give you a chance? We have not been able to capture you in forty years! Well, except that one time, but I believe you allowed us to do that so you could learn about the CIA."

The group left the cabin at 1:00 am. They walked due south through the heavy brush. It was late fall so the night air was becoming cold for the group. Paul recognized his friends were cold, so he fired small plasma rounds of energy into each one of them warming their bodies. He led them through the thick brush discovering only two sensors. Leading the group around the sensors Paul stopped abruptly. He told them, "This is the place." Brian asked how Paul knew that. Trying to explain to his brother just how the Holy Spirit led him was a waste of time. "I just know Brian. Okay?"

Using his telekinetic ability Paul raised Johnny Alston thirty feet into a large Limber Pine standing twenty feet from where Paul would blast an entrance. Checking to ensure Johnny was well hidden and secure in his sniper's nest Paul then told the others to stand back. He was not sure of how to use his new abilities fearing he could harm them. Concentrating, using a different part of his brain Paul conjured a beam of power firing it towards the ground. There was no sound with the exception of the ground moving and the rocks smoldering. He kept firing the beam using his mind's eye to control the powerful energy all the way down the seven hundred feet to just before the tunnel. Then using his normal brain usage Paul fired rapid shots down into the deep dark tunnel creating platforms in the rock so that he could jump from one platform to another.

Turning to look at his friends, Paul noted the shocked amazement and fear in their eyes. He wanted to calm them; however, he knew they were going to see pure evil very shortly. Paul had no idea what to say so he simply told his friends, "I will jump down. It will take me no more than a minute to reach our destination. I want all of you to stand around this opening. Once I reach the bottom level, I will lower each of you one at a time. First Brian, then Diane and then you Danick. From this point forward there can be no noise, no conversation. Only whispers. Does everyone understand?" They all quietly nodded. Paul then turned back towards the large hole in the earth and jumped the first hundred feet landing on the rock platform. Then he jumped to the next and the next until he reached the hard rock just above the underground tunnel.

Lowering Brian first, Paul used his telekinetic ability to lower his brother. The tunnel down was pitch black though through his mind's eye he could see Brian moving his arms and legs as if he were swimming, trying not to fall. Paul decided it would be best to lower the others quickly but to also use his mind to place them in a semi-conscious mode as they came down. He did not want them to feel the natural fear of falling nor did he want them to make any noise by accidently screaming. He brought down the CIA man next and then Diane. Once they were all standing on the rock above the tunnel, Paul brought them back to consciousness reminding them in a louder whisper they needed to remain quiet. He sensed their fear being down 700 feet in pitch blackness, so he fired a plasma round into the rock formation surrounding them energizing it so that it emitted a dull glow of light. He could sense his friend's relief, but also sensed that two of them had great fear of him—the CIA man and Brian. Diane, as expected, was becoming accustomed to Paul and his abilities just as she had years ago.

After the group had all nodded in agreement, Paul then engaged his mind's eye and scanned the subterranean complex just two feet below the rock they stood upon. He was shocked at what he *guessed* was the size of the installation. He scanned the tunnel to his left which he presumed was his east as he was disorientated either from the climb down or because of where they were. He could only see out two miles, which the tunnel far extended past his view. He estimated the tunnel was forty feet wide and thirty feet high. Paul had thought he would see cables along the sides of the tunnel for power, but there were none. He was amazed to see the tunnel was in the shape of a perfect square. There were no seams and the sides, top and bottom were perfectly smooth. He knew no human man had built this complex. There was no way.

Scanning to his right, his mind traveled about eight hundred and sixty yards or almost a half mile. There he saw movement! There were about 100 soldiers and airman and around 50 federal agents. They were assisting scientists who made up another 40 personnel. Then he saw the AIs, all standing guard or roaming as if they were inspecting what was being done. There were 20 of them! As he let his mind scan deeper, he saw the humans were all controlled by darkness. Their eyes were emotionless and black like that of death. He saw what the scientist were doing. *Terror* immediately struck him! Paul had never really felt terror although he had *experienced* fear.

What he saw sickened him to the point of vomiting! He saw men and women strapped to tables screaming for help as the scientist cut into them, sucked organs out of them and removed limbs! He also saw demons! He had not seen demons since his time travel experience and had hoped he would never see another one again. They were horrific appearing creatures who hovering about, waiting as if they were looking for hosts! Not wanting to see more, Paul forced himself to continue looking. He had to find the *Twins*!

Finally, after about two minutes he found the girls sitting in a cage without bars. They were with the other children he and Brian had seen on the train back at air base. The adults that had been with the children had already been separated and held approximately 200 yards further west. Then he saw them! The fallen. The Watchers were there! He guesstimated there must have been twenty of them, but they were not like the ones he had encountered before. Some looked humanoid, while others appeared as if they were some sort of reptile. Still others looked like a picture he had seen in the old texts. They were terrifying to look at. Many of them were sexually assaulting men and women before eating them alive. These beings seemed to thrive off the screams and begging of the men and women.

Rage surged through Paul as felt his energy ramp up past 100 percent. He told himself to calm down but the Spirit within him told him "No!" He would need all the energy he could muster to fight the scene he must enter, fear or no fear! He must engage and destroy, but he was to instruct the others that when firing on the possessed humans; they must fire to wound. Killing them would release their demons. Describing to the group what he had just seen and been told, he said, "If you were ever going to pray, now is the time!"

With Diane leading a quick prayer, Paul began to cut a hole into the last two feet of solid rock. As he cut the hard substance, he noted that only Diane and Danick had lowered their heads. Brian still refused. This worried Paul. Brian was the only one who was not baptized, so he was the only one the demons could enter. He could not worry about that right now. The priority was the Twins and any others they might be able to rescue. The Twins *had* to be rescued! Just as he had finished cutting a perfectly circular hole, Paul used his telekinesis to hold of the several thousand-pound hunks of rock and dirt. He raised it and let it sit in the long tunnel they were in. He jumped down the twenty feet to the interior of the tunnel and quickly lowered the other three.

The four-member team quickly headed in the direction of the girls. Paul kept scanning with his mind until they were just 50 yards from the area of death. It was the AIs who noticed them first! They charged at Paul and his group firing their REMP weapons in unison forcing Paul to use all his speed to shove everyone to the floor while he kept moving, weaving from side to side and back and forth firing his destructive beam from the back part of his brain. He was able to destroy all twenty AIs, but he had taken multiple hits, lowering his energy to 40 percent. The demon possessed soldiers and airmen began firing at the group hitting Danick in the leg and Diane in the left side of her chest cavity. Brian was rattling off round after round trying not to kill the rushing hordes while Paul knelt and swiftly healed Diane and the CIA man in the name of Jesus. He then rejoined Brian in the frontal assault, leading the group forward engaging his shield and extending it around the group.

Upon reaching the cage holding the Twins, Paul fired multiple beams into the nearby rock which had some sort of energy field keeping the children enclosed. The field immediately dropped! Diane ran towards the children, quickly grabbing hold of the hands of Elisabeth and Esther and telling the children to follow her. The children ranged in ages from about six to thirteen. She commanded the older kids to help with the younger ones while Brian, Danick, and Paul kept up their barrage on the charging evil. The Fallen had been alerted during the battle and came down the tunnel as such a speed that Paul could barely grasp sight of them. Knowing he could not destroy them, Paul fired multiple beams into the ceiling of the tunnel bringing it crashing down in front of the oncoming evil. He knew it would not stop them, but he hoped it would slow them enough to escape.

Suddenly Brian stopped firing! He turned his weapon on Danick and took aim, but Paul caught the action with his peripheral vision. He fired a stun round into his brother as he commanded everyone to run after Diane and the children. Picking up his brother, Paul slumped Brian over his shoulder and began charging east down the tunnel. He quickly caught up with Diane and the escaping children in mere seconds leaving Danick far behind. Screaming for Danick to hurry, Paul and the rest reached the entrance to the tunnel he had carved. Looking back, he could see that there were more agents and soldiers coming from the west chasing Danick. Being low on energy Paul had to consider if using energy was wise to save Danick. He had no choice. The man had joined them and fought with them to save the children. He *had* to help the man. Using his mind's eye for aiming, Paul fired a barrage of stun rounds down the tunnel hitting every single pursuer!

Seeing Danick was only a hundred yards back, Paul told Diane to form a chain by linking hands together with Elizabeth and Esther until all the children were connected. Realizing he was now down to forty percent energy, Paul recognized that using his telekinetic ability to raise the group would mean almost certain death for him, but he had no choice. "Besides, I still have my grenades!" he thought to himself. Concentrating as he had never done before; he raised the group to the very top of the hole.

The group was dizzy and nauseous from the speed of the travel. Collapsing with Brian on top of him, Paul realized that he was down to just eight percent of his energy. He could barely concentrate or even focus his eyes.

Danick arrived just in time to help pull Brian off of Paul. "You look bad Bannachek. You look really bad!"

"Listen Danick, pick up my brother and put him on your shoulders. I will lift you to the chamber!" Paul said as he began gasping for air. "Once you're in the chamber stand on the side away from the hole."

"Bannachek, if you do this you will more than likely die! You know that don't you?"

Smiling, Paul pulled out the six grenades from his inside coat pockets and said, "Not just yet Danick! Not just yet."

Lifting Danick and Brian into the entrance, Paul set off two of the grenades, dropping them on the other four he had lying next to him. Four seconds later there was a massive explosion! A millisecond later another then another! Paul was now back to forty percent energy. Still reeling from his mental and physical weakness he jumped the twenty feet into the entrance and then sent Danick and his brother up the tunnel. He was now back down to thirty percent energy. Paul started making minimal blasts into the rock creating for himself small ledges to grab a hold of while he climbed. Nauseated from weakness, Bannachek took over four minutes to climb the 700-foot tunnel. Once he reached the top, he fired massive energy beams into the long tunnel exploding rock and debris all the way down. The tunnel was completely sealed!

Lying on his back at just three percent energy, Paul Bannachek accepted he was going to die very shortly. Never had he been this weak or vulnerable and while he could barely think he did understand the battle was not over. He asked God in the name of Jesus to forgive him for failing and to help the others escape. Just as he felt himself start to slip away; he felt a small hand touch his. It was Esther! She was touching his hand while she held Elisabeth's. Smiling down at Paul she said, "It is not yet your time. There is still much you must do."

Paul felt a powerful energy form he had never felt. Within a minute he was back to one hundred percent. Though his mind was still groggy, he felt powerful.

Elisabeth smiled at Paul saying, "You should rest. We have some time. Esther and I will protect you and everyone else while you rest."

"No! I must get up and get you away from here. You are too important to risk!"

"We have the Spirit as well. You must rest your mind so you will be able to help the other children here."

"Help how? Don't you have what I have?" Paul asked Elisabeth.

Esther replied by saying, "No. We can heal bodies and we can provide you energy as well. We can remove demons from people too. We also can make a protective shield, but we were not given what you have. Yours is man-made. Ours comes from God in Heaven. Now please rest your mind! "

Amazed at the wisdom of these two ten-year-old girls, Paul asked, "What do you mean remove demons?"

"Your brother has two demons within him. If we do not re-move them before he awakens it will become dangerous for him. Please! Rest your mind for a few minutes while we look after your brother," Esther said.

Sitting back, Paul thought about what had just been said to him. He began to wonder how it could be. Then the Spirit within him explained that the girls were born with gifts directly from God the Father. Gifts that were hidden until now. These gifts were to be used to help protect the others who would have to go into hiding very soon. The gifts were not ever present until Paul actually turned them on when he engaged his shield. Once that happened the Spirit within them was awakened providing the children great knowledge and powers. This is why the girls speak the way they do at times. They are given these words from the SON, Jesus through the Holy Spirit.

Watching, the Twins place their hands on Brian's head, speaking in what Paul thought was Hebrew. He felt amazed at what the children were doing. He now understood what Michael had meant when he was told that he was injected by something that was created for evil purposes but God intervened so it could be used for good. The Twins however were actually born with God-given powers and abilities. That was the reason they had to be saved. If the Fallen had known who the girls were, they would have destroyed the girls because the Twins would not yet have known how to turn on their abilities. Lying back, he told himself he would rest his mind for several minutes. Paul understood that the danger was not over, and the Twins were not totally safe yet. Besides, the other children needed to have protection as well! The dark forces nor their government allies could ever afford to have those children running around with the knowledge of what they had seen. Even with Paul wiping their memories, the dark forces would not know that and still seek to destroy them.

As he rested his mind, Paul saw his friend Johnny Alston climb down out of the tree. He listened as Johnny, Danick and Diane spoke about what they had seen. They spoke of their terror and complained that none of them had signed up for *this* kind of unbelievable stuff. They all wanted to go back to the lives they had had. Even Diane wanted to quit as she was overwhelmed by the fear over taking her. She told herself she had helped Paul Bannachek enough. The CIA man told the group he could not be part of this any longer. He would give Bannachek a day's head start and then start hunting him again. Even Johnny Alston, after hearing what had transpired beneath the surface, wanted to get away from all of it!

Suddenly the girls spoke to the group. They formed a shield around all of them, including the other thirty children saying,

"There is a terrible disease afflicting our American people. It is not cancer, or heart disease, or obesity, or some dangerous viral epidemic. The disease we are referring to is 'I Trouble.' It afflicts people in the highest levels of government and in the largest financial institutions of our country. It afflicts our homes, turning children against their parents and husbands and wives against one another. It led Cain, Adam and Eve's first-born son, to kill his brother, Abel. It leads gang members to spray rival gang members with bullets. There used to be, before we were born, a popular magazine with the simple name of *Life*, then came *People*, then *Us*, and finally there was the magazine with the brazen two letters, *Me*.

'Remember the magazine *Others*? It never existed. In the '60s man was told: 'Know Yourself!' In the '70s it was 'Find Yourself!' In the '80s it was 'Express Yourself!' Then there were the '90s with the battle cry, 'Indulge Yourself!' Today our world is struggling to save ourselves from financial ruin. There is a book called *Generation Me* written about the epidemic of narcissism sweeping our country. Little children are given trophies for just showing up for soccer practice. They color in books with titles such as *I Am Special!* They attend princess parties that cost lots of money. Sports stars declare at press conferences that they enjoy being called selfish by the media.

'College students angrily confront a professor for not allowing them to retake a test on which they did poorly because of a hangover. Everyone can be a star through self-promotion on social media and by texting friends who seriously aren't all that concerned to hear what you had for breakfast this morning. It is so easy to see this problem of 'I Trouble' in others but so hard to see it personally in ourselves. We as people need to go to the emergency room of God's Holy Word. We have the much-needed prescription for curing 'I Trouble' and also the much-needed power for a cure. We shall give you the cure for 'I Trouble.' That cure comes from the Apostle Paul, who offers a prescription for curing 'I Trouble' with these words from the letter to Philippians:

If you have any encouragement from being united with Christ, if any comfort from his love, if any fellowship with the Spirit, if any tenderness and compassion, then make my joy complete by being like-minded, having the same love, being one in spirit and purpose. Do you have any encouragement from being united with Christ, any comfort in his love, any fellowship with the Holy Spirit, any tenderness and compassion built up inside of you because of what Jesus has done for all of us?

'Sure, you do. How often do we talk to our children about sin and how far we fall short of God's glory? And about Jesus and how He absorbed all our sins the way a sponge might soak up water. We talk about His suffering and death to forgive us and free us so we can have eternal life with Him. When you talk to someone about Jesus, or hear about what He has done for you, you have these feelings of deep love, compassion, tenderness, and joy that well up from inside of you, and sometimes simply overwhelm you. If you have ever been moved or touched by Jesus' love for you, then you can have that same compassion, tenderness, and love for other people.

'When you open the treasure of God's Word and see how much He loves you by giving His Son Jesus for you, it creates a love and tenderness and compassion for other people. Paul gave us all more in this prescription for curing 'I Trouble.' He wrote, 'Do nothing out of selfish ambition, or vain conceit, but in humility consider others better than yourselves.' Pride is our greatest enemy. Humility is our best friend. Pride loves to compare ourselves to other people. Humility compares us to Jesus. Pride covets the success of other people. Humility celebrates the success of other people. Pride is about what I feel, what I desire and what I want. Humility asks what others need and desire and what Jesus wants. Pride is about my glory. Humility is about Jesus' glory and helping others see that glory.

'Do any of you know a famous football coach, Gene Stallings from Alabama, who was fond of talking about his greatest moment in sports? He told about a time he attended a Special Olympics sports meet. The gun went off, the runners took off. Halfway down the track one of the boys fell down. One by one the other runners stopped running, turned around, and helped the boy who had fallen. They held him up and all together they crossed the finish line. The prescription continues for 'I Trouble, each of you should look not only to your own interests but also the interest of others.' How different these words sound from the language of today which speaks of self-absorption, self-fulfillment, self-actualization, and self-pity!

'When we are steeped in feeling sorrow for ourselves, then the problem of 'I Trouble' really grabs hold of us. We erect these horrible high walls around us and plaster them with pictures of how miserable we are, and we look at these pictures and then cry into our pillow. Man doesn't want to get up from bed and look out the window to see the mercies of God which are new each morning. Man doesn't want to see other people who are worse off than they are, because maybe God will touch our hearts and lead us to see that we each have tremendous value and worth not just as child of heaven, but a child of this earth who shines like stars in the universe. True greatness and worth come when we look on the interest of others.

'Jesus said, *'Whoever wants to be first must be a slave of all, even as the Son of Man did not come to be served, but to serve and give his life as a ransom for many.'* There was once a little boy named Chad who was shy and did not make friends easily. After his family moved to a new neighborhood, it was even harder to break the ice and make friends. Valentine's Day was approaching, and Chad decided to personally make Valentines for all the kids in his class. His mother bought him the glue and paper and even let him use her good scissors. She made fresh cookies that he could include with each Valentine. When he came home, she wondered if any of the children would remember Chad. As he walked in the door, he said to his Mom, 'Not one, Mom. Not one Valentine.' His mother's heart sank for him, until he finished the sentence by saying, 'I didn't forget to give one.' He found the cure for 'I Trouble.' To the selfish Christians, we remind you of our Lord Jesus's words, *'It is better to give than receive.'*

'The power for the cure of 'I Trouble?' We know what needs to be done; to be less selfish and more giving in our lives, but where will we find the power to change? That power is found in our Lord Jesus and his sacrificial love. Jesus was willing to submit Himself to death on the cross to make the ransom payment for our sin.

Martin Luther wrote in one of his hymns:

'The Son obeyed the Father's will,

Was born of virgin mother,

And God's good pleasure to fulfill,

He came to be my brother.

No garb of pomp or power He wore.

A servant's form like mine He bore, to lead the devil captive.'

'How far we fall short of God's glory because of our sin. Look at this picture of the Grand Canyon and imagine how impossible it would be to jump across that mighty canyon. So, it is impossible on our own to come back to God from our sin. His glory demands that we be perfect before He can accept us. But when we see Jesus and His perfect life as He always thought first of other people, and as He gave His life for us and for them on the cross.

'There we see our hope of being accepted by God and our hope of joining Jesus in glory. That is our strength, the power for putting others first in our lives. After giving His life for us, Jesus was raised again to glory. *'Therefore, God exalted him to the highest place and gave him the name that is above every name.'*"

When the Twins had finished speaking, the adults stood their mouths agape at what they had just heard. Such wisdom coming from two young children! And the fact that the girls had spoken in exact unison gave the adults chills. Not fearful chills but chills or rather warm shakes because they knew they had heard from Jesus through the Spirit through the girls. They felt ashamed of themselves for wanting to quit or to run! Even the other children listened in awe knowing they had heard great words. The younger kids did not completely understand but the older ones did! Most of them wanted to take part in the service of the upcoming war.

Brian had awakened from his sickness of the darkness and had also heard and listened. He began to realize that he had been wrong all his life. He began to realize that no matter what he had done, God loved him and would forgive him, if only he changed his ways. If only he could get over his human arrogance and teachings to realize just who in fact God and his SON, the Lord Jesus actually are! For Brian that was a difficult leap. He had been self-sufficient most of his life since the age of eighteen. To him, even if it was true, how could he believe that God would forgive him when he could not forgive himself.

11

Escape

On the surface the plan seemed simple enough. Split the team, get the children to safety and get the Twins back with their grandparents. Paul would lead the enemies after him believing they would think he was a better prize than the children. Paul knew better. He had been fighting almost his entire life. He understood that the secret government would never rest until they captured or eliminated the rescued children. He doubted anyone knew yet about Elisabeth's and Esther's abilities, but he could not be sure. Paul also understood the girls had immense power and yet they *were* still children. If they were ever taken before they reached a certain level of maturity, they could be used and manipulated to use those powers to harm rather than protect and heal. The plan needed tweaking!

It was decided John Danick would join with those pursuing Paul in order to slow the tracking or rather hunting of the government's prey. He would also use his laptop to open avenues for Johnny so he could arrange for totally new identifications for Elisabeth and Esther. That meant he would also have to create totally new personas for Robert and Joannie. Since Johnny was in control of the funding it was imperative, he leave first. He needed to get a flight to Helena, Montana so he could pre-pay for the hotel room at the Fairfield of Marriot for the Twins' grandparents. Johnny also needed to close on the home he had bid on. The home was a nice five-bedroom sitting on ten acres just outside of downtown Townsend. Paul had instructed him to ensure he bought a home with land so Robert could build a large underground bunker.

Once Johnny had the new identifications, he could have one of Paul's corporations wire two hundred thousand dollars to Robert and Joannie so they could purchase a car and furniture for their new home. Another corporation would actually own the home charging the grandparents one dollar a month rent. Part of the plan was for Johnny to use all the remaining funds in Paul's various corporations to keep the Twins safe and to assist Diane with the thirty other children. She would need several million dollars to provide the kids with private educations, medical and dental as well as find them homes. She had found many homes for children Paul had sent her over the years and believed she could continue to do so.

Diane looked at Paul and asked, "What about you Paul? You will have no money left. How will you survive?"

"Diane, my dear and oldest friend, you know I can always get money. Do not worry about me. Besides, you may never hear from me again, depending on how things go in the next few days."

"What on earth are you talking about Paul?" she asked.

"Diane. All I am saying is right now we must concentrate on getting these children out of here. The most important aspect of our mission is saving Elisabeth and Esther. You know how important they are, and you know there are very special plans for them. That is all I am saying. You should not worry about me."

"Paul, you seem like you're saying you're not important and

that is not true. Look at all the people you have helped over all these years."

"Diane, you know how I came about. You know my history. I am a simple man like anyone else! Only, I was given these abilities I have by an injection. That injection was meant for evil. Instead, it was used for good. The Twins are different Diane. *They* were born with very special gifts. *They* will protect and heal more people than I could ever help! Do you understand that? Do you understand we cannot allow any personal feelings, wants, desires or beliefs to interfere with saving the Twins?"

Because Diane did know she felt ashamed. She had such deep love and respect for Paul she had forgotten about what was really happening in the world. She had forgotten what was coming. She told herself she did not want to think about what was coming as it terrified her. But she also knew and understood that she was saved and no matter what would see Paul again. She would meet his wife and see her husband again. How soon she did not know but she trusted and therefore knew it would be soon.

Listening to everything being said Brian interjected. "What about me big brother? he asked with a smile.

"Brian, your job is to get the girls to Montana safely. You are an expert with weapons, and you know how to survive in the wilderness. You can afford them the best protection. Although, I have a feeling they will be protecting you," Paul said smiling.

Then Esther spoke saying, "No Paul, we will accompany you to New Mexico for your battle. When the battle is almost over, we will go to our grandparents. Mr. Brian will then escort us by plane. It is faster."

"What do you mean almost over," Brian asked in an alarmed tone.

"I am Paul's brother. If there is going to be a fight, my place is with him!"

At that moment several craft appeared over the group's hiding spot. They had been found! Paul immediately used his newer powers and fired steady streams at all the craft causing them to flicker. They all could see the craft were actually beings! The crafts took off to the west at speeds Paul guessed were the speed of light. He alone knew what the craft actually were. He had dealt with them back in Germany during his time travel experience. Paul decided it was time to get moving.

The group all agreed to the plan, though Brian had his misgivings. He had been trained to fight and believed his place was with his brother. Because he had not accepted the Holy Spirit he did not understand. Or rather, he refused to understand. The Twins, on the other hand, had an uncanny understanding for children of ten going on eleven years old. It was clear to Paul the girls had a much closer tie to the Spirit than he did. He could tell when the Spirit spoke through them, though it seemed to use Esther more than Elisabeth. Paul recognized the Spirit in them when they spoke.

Immediately the group broke ranks. Danick was already gone as he had to get back with the Government hunters. He had to keep his dual role hidden or he could help no one. He and Johnny had shared one of the vehicles to the airport leaving Diane the mini-van. She took off with nine of the children towards the airport as well. Brian, on Paul's instructions took five more of the kids with him so he could follow Diane. The remaining sixteen children stayed with Paul and the Twins, waiting for Diane to return. Paul had placed them all except the Twins into a heavy sleep with his mind. He could not take a chance at any of them becoming afraid and running or even wondering off. As the kids slept he listened to Elisabeth and Esther in amazement. Their knowledge was so keen and so pure he could do nothing but listen.

As Paul listened, he learned much he had not known. He learned just how important baptism really was and how it was so important to only be baptized once. He learned that there were many churches who would not accept baptism for other churches thereby controlling people's access to communion which was a gift from the Lord and not theirs to control. He learned how many in churches had been corrupted with false teachings just as scripture said would happen. He learned that many in churches condemned others because they did not truly understand the teaching of the Lord or of God himself.

The thought came across Paul's mind, "Why had not Michael told him these things?" The Spirit in Esther saw Paul's thoughts, so she told him told him that Michael only told him what he was permitted to inform him. She said," Mr. Paul, you are about see some wondrous things. You are about to know everything we know. "

"But Esther, why am I only being told now? Why not before?"

"Mr. Paul, Elisabeth interrupted, "you yourself know the bible says there is a time and a place for all things. You have spent your entire life serving the Lord and at the same time complaining. That must stop now! While you have served God, have you really served God? Or did you do so out of a sense of duty rather than love for God?"

Esther then spoke and told Paul, "We are about to receive some horrible news. You must accept this news with understanding! You must listen with your spirit, not just your mind or you will never completely understand."

What had been told to Paul by these ten-year-old girls was stressing! He had to admit to himself they were correct. He had to admit that he had done many wonderful things for people over the past forty years, but he did them out of duty. Not love! Thinking of Alisa, Paul saw what real love for God was. His wife sacrificed *everything* for God while Paul had never really sacrificed *anything*. "Sure," he told himself, "I have been hurt but since it is so hard for me to be killed, have I ever sacrificed anything?" A terrible sense of guilt and honesty came over him just as he heard a motorcycle come roaring up the path. He could see the driver was Brian with Diane hanging onto him riding the back of the bike. She looked pale. She looked almost lifeless as she clung to his brother.

Stopping the Honda 250 cc motocross bike with a slide, Brian could not catch hold of Diane as she fell to the ground. Her belly was bleeding profusely as if it had exploded. The Twins ran to her, dropping to their bare knees from their dresses. Elisabeth laid Diane's head onto her lap while Esther laid her hands upon Diane's open abdomen. Immediately the wound closed and healed. She has said loudly, "In the name of the SON, our Lord and Savior, you are healed." Diane slowly opened her eyes with a distant look. She looked up at the Twins who smiled at her while Elisabeth stroked her graying hair.

"What happened," she asked?

Walking over to Diane quickly Brian began to share the tail. Agents had found them at a rest stop where some of the children had needed to use the restrooms. The rest stop was nearly abandoned with the exception of one over the road truck driver who must have been sleeping in his cab. Six black SUV's pulled up to the rest area. Out jumped men dressed in black military uniforms along with six men in dark suits and sunglasses. Those men almost appeared to not be men. Their faces were expressionless, as if they were mannequins. The soldiers and these men immediately began chasing and grabbing the children dragging them to the forested area behind the rest area.

Grabbing his Remington .306 caliber rifle, Brian had opened fire. His bullets did not seem to have any effect on the suited men though he was able to take out about ten soldiers. They returned fire at him and Diane, both of whom had taken positions behind the pickup truck. Brian told them he kept firing trying to stop the agents from taking the children from the bathrooms but no matter how many times he hit the *things* nothing seemed to stop them. He said they must have had incredible strength because each of the six agents carried a child under each arm with one of the agents carrying three of the children. He told them the soldiers would fall to their deaths and then rise back up and continue their attack.

Brian said," Diane ran to the back forest after the children while I gave her cover fire. She had made it to the forest line. I saw her fall to her knees, so I ran to her unloading my Remington on fully auto at the soldiers. I just kept reloading and firing after each magazine was empty."

Then Diane spoke in a faint voice saying," I saw those *things* pull strange looking weapons from underneath their coats. They just fired into the children murdering every last one of them! They just slaughtered those sweet innocent children! Why?"

"It's true," I saw their little bodies all on the ground," Brian said in an angry tone!

"Then one of the, whatever they were, pulled another strange looking thing from under his coat and fired a beam of some sort which burned the children down to nothing," Diane said shaking.

Brian then said, "Those weapons cannot be of our world. I have seen and used flame throwers in combat. Bodies don't just disintegrate! They just don't."

After Brian had said that, he, Diane, Elisabeth, and Esther all looked at Paul. They seemed to wait for him to explain about the Agents and the weapons. He was surprised the Twins looked to him. Paul had thought they would simply know the answers because they were so in tuned to the Spirit. Esther seemed to understand his thoughts when she said, "Mr. Paul. What are those things and where do they come from?"

"You mean you don't know Esther?" Paul asked the younger of the two girls; younger being five minutes younger.

Elisabeth spoke saying, "Mr. Paul, like you we only know what we are told." Then in unison both girls ran over to Paul and grabbed hold of his waste and said, "We're scared Mr. Paul. Please don't let them get us!"

Suddenly, the atmosphere opened and Michael stepped through the opening saying, "Greetings my friends. I have come from God, **Praise His Glorious Name**, to help and explain. Do not be afraid as all is happening is it is meant to happen."

"Michael, where have you been?! Do you know fourteen children were murdered?! Why didn't you help them?" Paul demanded.

"Paul, those children are not dead. You yourself know that once a person here on earth dies, they are, in a blink of the eye, with the SON; if they are his."

"And what about those who do not belong to the Lord, as you say?" Brian asked.

"Ah. Those go to another place to await judgment."

"You mean hell, right?"

"No. Hell is not until after their judgment. They go to a place and wait for that day. They do not even no they are separated as there is no time in that place just as there is no time in Heaven. Some have been there for millennia and think it is still the same day they arrived."

Brian then asked, "What do they do there?"

"Different things for different souls. Now I did not come here to speak of that I come to speak about what must happen next."

"Wait a minute," Brian said. "Are you saying all those children are with Jesus?"

"No. Most of them are, but two are not. They went to the other place."

"But I thought all children were saved?" Brian asked.

Looking at Brian intently, Michael said, "Until the age of atonement they are. But after that age if they have not made their choice they are like all others."

"Well, what is the age of atonement?" Brian asked again.

"Read your scriptures and learn the truth. I will only say this last thing about it. Many of men believe they have time. They believe they have all the time in the world to decide. But they do not know when their time is up. It can happen slowly so they have a final chance to make their decision, or it can happen quickly where they have lost that chance to decide. For them, they go and await their judgment."

Paul interrupted asking, "I am sorry Michael, but why are you?"

"Ah yes. I have to come to explain what you must do next."

"Well, we have a plan or at least a partial plan, "Paul replied.

"Yes, you did Paul. How has that been working out for you?"

Sheepishly Paul replied, "Not so good I guess."

"That is correct! You planned to use your own knowledge and thoughts. You should have prayed, and the Spirit would have told you what I am about to tell you. Because you did not, all this has happened."

"I know you're right Michael, but I have been left to my own devices almost my entire life, at least until you have showed up."

"Not true Paul. All you ever had to do was pray and God, **Praise His Glorious Name**, would have answered you through the Spirit within you. Why do you think I have had to come to you so many times?"

"Because God wanted me to succeed in what I was doing for him!"

"Wrong! God, **Praise His Glorious Name**, has sent me because you do not pray, or you rarely pray. If you had I would had never had to ever come. Your plan is NOT going to happen, or rather most of it will not happen! Now come with me now Paul so that we may speak. The rest of you keep guard. Look after the children Diane. Brian, you are to keep guard!"

Even though an entire day had almost past, as it was now evening and the sun was lowering, Paul went with Michael. They walked for what seemed to be hours but, in the reality, they had only been gone minutes. Paul had been told a great deal during their walk. He had learned that Brian still had an opportunity to make his choice, but his time was running out. He been given a plan that must be carried out and that he could only share some of the plan with the others. Michael had told Paul he was soon to be given a choice. No matter what he chose God would look favorably upon him if he chose with his heart and not his mind or his instinct. When Paul asked what the choice would be, Michael said, "That is not for me to say or even know. But I do know I will never see you here on *this* earth again."

The plan was not something Paul would expect. At least not for how he would be used. He figures something more elaborate would be needed. Then again, he thought to himself, *that is how I would think.* He understood that with all his experiences and all the knowledge he had gained, he was still just a man. A man who, while extraordinary, he was just a man. He also understood the Twins and Michael had been correct. Paul had rarely prayed. He always did things his way unless Michel had shown up to direct him in other ways. It had dawn on him that he himself had not really done anything in the world. What good he had done, the people he had helped and rescued, that all came from God. He was just a servant. But just a servant was not truth either. Nor was he just a tool. Paul Bannachek was needed these last forty-five years to help people prepare for what was coming. And what was coming would terrify the world!

The world had plenty of changes over the past eighty years, since 1948. The day Israel became a nation state. Almost all of the biblical prophesies had been fulfilled. Paul understood the current Pandemic was not a pandemic and he understood that it was man made unlike other pandemics which had come from God. He also understood the world had adopted a rational which it called "woke." Under that manner of thinking anything was good. Thoughts were now controlled by the media; churches were being burned, and Christians were being killed in other churches. He knew that this was the time Christ had spoken of. Paul also understood that whoever won the American Presidential race in 2020, the outcome would be the same. America would fall. It had to in order to rush in the new Government which the United Nations had started planning on back in the fifties.

Seeing the "great falling away" by Christians had initially bothered Paul. Then he grew to accept the only the truly faithful would stick to their faith. Michael had told him long ago how and what was going to happen. He knew that people could lose their jobs if they expressed their thoughts or beliefs which contradicted the "wokeness" of the world. Paul also recognized the majority of people he had provided the opportunity to choose, chose poorly. But a few choose wisely, and they, themselves, helped others choose. The ripple effect was growing but it was also affecting the churches. He expected that within a year, maybe eighteen months the world would fall under one system of government and the United Planet of earth would elect one leader who control everything. Knowing this, many Christians had begun to form small groups of no more than twenty. They were pooling their resources to stockpile food, medical supplies and weapons for their common defense. They were also stabling lines of communication via shortwave and good old-fashioned letters. They could not trust technology in any form knowing that it was already monitored.

12

Led to Confrontation

Being late at night now, Michael was informing Paul what must occur. Paul's plan simply would not work. His plan could not ensure the survival of the remaining sixteen children. Nor did his plan even begin with any sort of massive destruction of the small, amassed group of dark forces. He simply figured he would the forces away so the others could take care of the children and get the Twins to safety. As usual, he did not even consider there were other plans, better plans, which came from Heaven. Plus, never had Paul ever been instructed to go look for a fight, especially a major battle which would be so threatening to himself. But now he was. Now Paul had to lead the dark forces to a place where they could amass and attack him *and the Twins*. It made no sense to Paul at the moment. He thought he was supposed to rescue the Twins before their abilities were discovered. He thought he was supposed to get them back to Joannie and Robert so they could hide until needed.

He asked Michael, "Do the girls know this?" as he looked over at the Twins.

"Yes, my young friend. They know *and* they understand."

"But they do not seem frightened at all! How they are not afraid?"

"Because Paul, they have so much love within themselves. Godly love. For each other and for those they are meant to protect. You do know what the scriptures say about love don't you?"

"Of course, I do Michael. The Holy words say with love there is no fear."

"You are correct my young friend! Are you afraid of what you must do? Even if it means you will die here in this world?"

"No Michael. I am not afraid! I just thought I was supposed to be here until the Lord Himself returns."

"As I said Paul, I do not know anything about that. I do know the Twins will be here in this world until the SON returns! They will be taken up with the last remaining living Christians. All Heaven will cheer these children because they are exactly what the SON told man over two millennia ago."

"You mean when Jesus said, 'Verily I say to you; unless you are converted and become as little children, you shall not enter into the kingdom of Heaven. Whosoever therefore shall humble himself as this little child, the same is greatest in the kingdom of heaven. And who so shall receive one such little child in my name, receiveth me'?"

"So, you do understand the word and the spirit!" Michael responded. "I must leave you now and take these sixteen with me. I will bring them to the place where these children will reside. Your friend Johnny is being instructed, as I speak to you now, to arrange for these sixteen to have homes and attend school through a particular church at the place you call Helena. That church has families which take in these children and the church will give them education and love from God, **Praise His Glorious Name**! I will come for the Twins at the appropriate time. Now you must go and prepare for battle. You may have more than one."

"But what about Brian and Diane?" Paul asked.

"My young friend, I cannot speak to your brother Brian as he has not accepted the free gift. I do not know if he will. But Diane's name is already in the book of life for the SON is proud of her and loves her very much. She has done so much for the children over her life period here on earth. Now I must go!"

At that moment Michael walked from Paul towards the now awake sixteen children and vanished with all of them. Brian, having stayed on watch, had kept his eye on Paul and Michael. When he saw the angel of God disappear, he ran towards Paul to find out what was happening. At the same time Diane walked over towards Paul quickly. She also wanted to know what was happening.

Suddenly, all hell broke loose! A barrage of bullets came at Paul, Brian, Diane, and the Twins. Looking quickly at the girls Paul saw they had taken positions on the grounds holding each other's hands. They had engaged their shield! He knew as long as they were together and holding hands nothing could harm them.

Immediately, Paul's shield had enabled as he began firing lethal plasma rounds at the charging forces of men in black fatigues! Brian had turned and fired in such a swift motion as only a true combat hardened SEAL could. As Paul fired, he watched his younger brother move with speed and accuracy as Brian unleashed an onslaught of fire at the enemy. He saw his brother take two rounds, one to the upper left shoulder and one to the lower right leg. He was amazed that Brian kept moving and charging towards the enemy as if he had not even been hit! Continuing to fire his Plasma rounds Paul took hit after hit from the many bullets being sprayed him. The rounds simply hit his shield recharging him slowly from the kinetic energy created as the bullets exploded into his shield. Out of the corner of his left eye he saw it.

A soldier of the dark forces carrying an Italian Beretta ARX160 fired; the attached 40×46mm NATO low-velocity grenade launcher sending the round directly into Brian chest exploding his brother to virtually nothing. Screaming, "No!" Paul unleashed the most devastating force he had ever let lose. He fired more plasma rounds and destruction explosive rounds as that one moment than he had in his entire life. By the time he was done, there was nothing left standing! Not even the trees. The ground was scorched black with the air smelling of nothing but death.

Looking over at the Twins he saw them kneeling over Diane. They were crying. Paul, being exhausted and down to fifteen percent of his available power, staggered to the Twins. Falling to his knees he saw his oldest and dearest friend lying on the ground with half her head missing. Knowing he did not have the energy left to heal his friend he asked the girls, "Please. Please heal her!"

Esther took his hand in hers and said, "Mr. Paul. We cannot. Her body is dead."

"But can't *you* fix that," he asked with tears streaming down his cheeks?!

"No, Mr. Paul," replied Elisabeth. "Like you, we cannot bring life back to the body. But you should know she is already with the Lord our Savior."

Knowing that Elisabeth had spoken truth from the Spirit within her, Paul's tears changed to tears of joy. He knew his friend Diane was now with Alisa, his parents, Diane's husband and all the others who had left over the past two millennia. Still, he also had a sadness within him. He had rescued Diane over forty years ago from the bikers. She had overcome so much! She had changed her life and had helped hundreds of children he had sent to her over all those years. She had done so much good in a world that did not deserve her! Just as it did not deserve his Alisa. But then Paul understood that they were meant to be so they could do what they did. Who was he to judge the world? The Lord would be doing that very soon.

Not wanted to look back at what remained of his brother, Paul told the Twins in an exhausted whisper, "We must leave now."

Esther took his weakened hand in hers and then took hold of Elisabeth's hand saying, "You need a recharge, Mr. Paul." Immediately, Paul was at one hundred percent, though emotionally he was beaten down to nothing.

Nodding his head and then thanking the girls he said, "Let's get moving. But first I must collect some items we will need." Paul then quickly gathered two heavy coats from two of the dead soldiers, some canteens full of water, and some meal rations. He put the coats on the shivering Twins and picked each one up in his left and right arms and started to run south by south west. He needed to get as much distance between them and the small battlefield. He knew where they were heading. The Spirit within him had told him. They were going to Aztec, New Mexico, population 6448. Or at least the above ground human population.

Joannie Veam had just finished checking herself and Robert into the Fairfield Inn in Helena, Montana while Robert parked the used care they had purchased in Billings. They had departed the bus in Billings because that which is in Joannie told them to do so. After their experience with the agents, they did not want to take any more risks. The couple had now learned to really listen to the Spirit within themselves. Working as a team, as they always had, they knew they could survive and get to their granddaughters.

Turning from the check-in desk, Joannie saw a man looking at her. He was wearing a denim jacket, jeans, and hiking boots. Over his shoulder was a laptop bag and an overnight bag on his other shoulder. He walked up to her and introduced himself as Johnny Alston. She recognized the name offering her hand as an introduction. He had a firm trustworthy handshake. She immediately felt as though she could trust this man. He told her that plans had changed and asked if they could speak outside. She nodded and followed Johnny out to where Robert had parked their used, 2008 Ford Eco-Sport. She introduced Johnny to Robert as the men shook hands. Then Johnny spoke.

"I want you both to know that the Twins have been rescued. They are safe and unhurt."

"Oh, thank God, Joannie said, and then asked in a hurried, concerned voice, 'Where are they then?'"

"Joannie, the last I saw of them they were with Paul. Believe me, as long and they are with him, nothing can hurt them. No one will hurt them! They will be here soon. For now, I need to go over some changes to the plan."

"What changes?" asked Robert.

"You two need new identifications."

"Again?" asked Joannie.

"It cannot be helped Joannie. Also, you will need to stay here for about twenty-eight days. I will pre-pay your rooms and leave extra on your room's account so you can rent movies and other necessities. Also, I will be opening you a joint checking and savings account in your new names as soon as I have your identifications ready. You will have access to two hundred thousand dollars. I am in the process of closing on your new home in Townsend. It is a five-bedroom ranch on ten or twelve acres. Sorry, I cannot remember the land size exactly. You will be required to pay Paul's corporation one dollar a month in rent. He told me to tell you Robert, that you should start building an underground bunker on the land. Funds will be made available to you for this specific purpose."

"Startled Joannie asked, "Why is this happening, sir?"

"Your granddaughters are of utmost importance Joannie. Paul wants you to send them to a particular church school here in Helena. And don't worry, their education will be paid for by the church. You will need to go buy yourselves some furniture for your new home and I will purchase you a new car in your new names. One or both of you will need to get jobs and live as though nothing has happened. And remember, you may not have *any* contact with anyone from your prior lives. Ever!"

"We encountered some strange men on our trip up here Mr. Alston. Do you know anything about that?" Robert asked."

"What kind of men?"

After Robert described their experience at the bus station, Johnny told them the truth. "Those were not men folks." Thinking they needed to really understand, he explained to the couple what was happening and what was about to transpire."

The three of them walked around the hotel towards the back which had an empty lot. The false pandemic had reduced traveling America by almost sixty percent. Just as Joannie was about to ask Johnny, "How this could be?" Michael appeared in his normal fashion with the sixteen children!

"Fear not," he said to Joannie who had grabbed hold of Robert! "I am here to bring these children to you. They were with Elisabeth and Esther when Johnny and Paul rescued the Twins. You must look after them until you are contacted."

"How are we to do that?" Joannie asked.

"My friend Johnny here will help you with the money. By the end of the next day, in your time, a Pastor will come to see you. He will help you find these children homes. Your granddaughters have sworn to protect them for, and through, what is coming. Johnny, you must get these children rooms for three days."

"Of course, Michael. But where are the other kids?"

"Most are with the SON, two are not."

"What about the rest Michael? What about Paul and Brian and Diane. How about the Twins?"

"My friend, I can tell you that Diane is with the SON. Paul and the Twins are en-route for battle. As for Brian, I am not permitted to say."

"Battle!" Joannie exclaimed in horror.

"How can anyone expect two children to go to battle?!"

"Woman," Michael said, "You know not who your grand-daughters are! They have the protection of God, **Praise His Glorious Name**, Himself! I myself will bring them to you very soon." Michael then disappeared into the atmosphere leaving the three of them standing there with all sixteen kids.

The journey to Aztec, New Mexico only took Paul and the girls two full days. Paul would run carrying them for twenty miles and then walk for five miles. He would repeat that travel timing until his energy had depleted to twenty percent. By that time, it was the first morning since escaping. When the girls awoke, he set them down so they could stretch and gather their thoughts. Luckily, they were near a deep stream so the girls could bath. He asked them to recharge him so he could heat an area of water for them to bathe, while he prepared the rations he had taken off the soldiers. He did not want to see the girls naked as they bathed so he moved up stream to an area covered with heavy brush telling them to bathe there.

Once they had recharged him, he fired plasma rounds into the water making it very hot. As the current mixed with the steaming water, it cooled enough for the girls to bathe. Though they had no soap with them, they could at least feel clean. Listening to the children frolic in the water Paul then went about heating their breakfasts ensuring to keep his mind's eye on the perimeter. After about ten minutes, the Twins called out to him saying they were freezing so Paul heated their jackets with plasma rounds tossing them into the heavy brush saying, "Use your jackets to dry. Then get dressed and bring the damp coats to me and I will heat them so you can wear them again." The girls did as they were instructed quickly emerging from the brush area shivering from the cold morning air. Paul immediately took their coats laying the items on the ground and heated them dry with plasma rounds. He then helped the girls put their coats on and took them both into his arms and warmed them.

"I have your breakfasts ready girls. Sorry about having to eat out of the packages but the food is hot so eat quickly."

Sitting down on the once cold ground Paul had heated with two plasma rounds the Twins began attacking their meal. "Mr. Paul," Esther asked, "How long until we get there?"

Laughing to himself as he thought all children were alike, even if these two were special, he said, "I believe we will be there by tomorrow afternoon. Are you in a hurry?" he asked.

"No Mr. Paul," Elisabeth replied, "We like being with you. You are nice. Besides tomorrow is scary!"

"Oh, how so Elisabeth?" Paul asked.

Esther then chastised Elisabeth telling her, "You know we cannot talk about these things, Beth. Mr. Paul, she should not have said anything. I am sorry, but sometimes we know things and don't always understand them so we accidently blab." She then started to cry and Elisabeth started to cry also.

Taking the children into his arms Paul said, "It is okay. I do understand. There is no need for you to cry. Okay? Whatever happens will happen."

Holding the girls in his arms he kissed each on the forehead telling them they must get going. He told them they could walk for a while but then he would have to carry them on the run and then need recharging. So, they each took one of his hands starting to skip and sing songs, as if nothing had been said. Paul skipped with them and tried to sing their songs. He felt so wonderful then. He himself felt like a child somehow forgetting what was coming and all he had ever known. He felt innocent and clean for the first time since his escape with Mary before she was killed.

After a half hour of this the girls became bored so Paul picked them up and started to run. He covered about twenty miles in fifteen minutes before stopping to walk and rest himself. The girls asked him how he was able to run so fast. He then began telling the children his story. He was able to cover all the main points of the past forty-five years in two hours. The girls cried when he spoke of Alisa, both wrapping their arms around his waist to hug him. They said they were sorry. They said his life sounded hard but they also understood how important he was to God. Not knowing how to react Paul simply picked up a girl in each arm and began to run again. This time he pushed himself hard. He covered forty miles in twenty-two minutes, trying not to think of his Alisa.

Since he had pushed himself to complete exhaustion the girls had to join hands and re-charge him. They then said, "Mr. Paul we are here."

"Here where?" he asked.

"Just over that hill is Aztec," Esther told him.

Listening to his spirit Paul knew they were correct. He decided to make camp in the wooded area just that side of the hill at the bottom. It was still late morning so Paul wanted to set a camp and camouflage it. Then he wanted to reconnoiter the area in order to see where the battle would take place. Instructing the girls to stay hidden in the makeshift fort, Paul left them ensuring them he could keep an eye on them while he was away. They girls seemed to understand what he could do with his abilities accepting his word. They just decided to play with sticks by drawing in the sandy dirt.

Slowly creeping up the large hill Paul used his mind's eye to both keep an eye on the girls and to scan the entire area. Once on top of the hill he could see the town of Aztec. It was a small town, though it seemed somehow strange. Even though it had a population of just over six thousand, there seemed very little traffic on the town's main road. For some reason he felt a chill come over himself. It was not the type of chill one feels when cold either. He could feel the evil in the area. He had felt that same feeling back in Germany during his time travel. Paul had an overwhelming desire to pray at that very moment.

After praying he walked back down the hill to the hideout he had made. The Spirit within him told him that he needed go no further. The battle would take place where he stood the next morning. It would not happen in late afternoon after all. He began to feel nervous as he approached the hidden entrance to their fort. Esther had prepared their dinner from the remaining rations Paul had taken from the soldiers, while Elisabeth used large sticks to dig a small hole which both girls could lay down in.

Wondering why Elisabeth had dug the hole, Paul asked, "What are you doing Elisabeth?"

Looking at her sister Elisabeth asked, "Can I tell him now?"

"Yes Elisabeth. It is okay to tell him but no more."

"Tell me what?" Paul asked.

"This is where you must make your stand, Mr. Paul. I dug this hole so Esther and I can lay inside of it and not be seen. You must stand close to us for your battle, Mr. Paul. We will be able to recharge you by touching your ankle, but you must stay close to us! Do you understand, Mr. Paul?"

"I do Elisabeth. And I promise I will stay right next to you."

Esther said their dinner was ready so the three of them sat on the ground Paul had warmed eating their final rations. Paul was amazed at the Twins. So much of the time they were children while at other times they were leaders. One would listen to them and just know they had an understanding that even Paul did not have. They seemed, at times so strong with the word of God, having keen understanding while at other times they were just two beautiful little girls who played and sang. Paul found it funny that the two would even snap at each other yet they seemed to have a deeper fit together than regular Twins. They seemed so interconnected, as if they knew they would always be together.

A small sense of envy came over Paul. Minus the time he had with Alisa, he had been alone since he was sixteen. Even though he knew in his heart he had truly not been alone he still felt that way. Looking at the girls he felt nothing but love and admiration.

Paul did not know if the Twins knew or understood who they were though he suspected they did deep down. He watched them quietly bicker like any sisters at that age as he ate his last ration. Paul began to wonder if it would be his last meal ever. Shaking off the defeatist thought he chose to simply warm the ground with a few plasma rounds and call the girls to come lay down to sleep.

That night he had wonderful dreams of Alisa. His dreams were of their past and what he thought could have been their future. He dreamed of his parent's both as adults and as children when he had rescued them in Poland. He had dreams of everyone he had ever met. Then his dreams became strange. They seemed to show him what the people he had helped would be like if he had never met them. He saw them have lives that were not meant for them. Lives full of distrust, loss, pain and hardened souls. The dreams became like nightmares waking him up in a sweat! It was early morning as he opened his eyes. He saw both Elisabeth and Esther with their hands on his chest. They were just sitting there with their eyes closed. Then their eyes opened suddenly.

"What are you doing girls?" Paul asked.

In unison the girls said, "Help you understand, Mr. Paul.

"Understand what?"

"You have been allowed to see what would have happened if you were not made to be who you are," again they replied in unison. "It is time now, Mr. Paul. They are coming from behind us. And they are coming from our left and our right!"

Jumping to his feet Paul saw agents and soldiers dressed in their black uniforms coming at him from the north and the east and the west. The south was too his back. Quickly the girls laid down in their hole and began whispering prayers. They took hold of each other's hands forming their impenetrable shield. The oncoming deluge of forces opened fire with repressed weapons hitting Paul's own shield. He returned fire with a barrage of plasma rounds. Lethal plasma rounds, destroying all that came at him! Then he was hit with an REMP weapon of huge force. It was a cannon being fired from the north though it was more like a beam of energy. The blast knocked him to the ground just next to the Twins. He stood up and used his other weapon firing the beam which destroyed the cannon.

More soldiers and agents came at him firing the smaller versions of the REMP weapons. Each hitting him with blast after blast! He returned fire destroying all that came with a ferociousness that he had never felt before. In the back of his mind Paul wondered why he had not weakened and then he felt Esther's hand touching his ankle. The Twins were recharging him enabling him to keep the fight going. He already destroyed no less than fifty soldiers and twenty agents. Then the AIs came at him from the east and the west. Their speed as they charged was incalculable. They fired their mini- REMP weapons hitting him with over fifty shots. Paul returned fire with his newly acquired gift obliterating the AIs. Suddenly coming from the south, he saw what appeared to look like three tanks. They all had large REMP weapons mounted on their turrets. He also saw John Danick and his assistant Marc Boyd riding in a Humvee just to the east of the tanks.

Danick had jumped out of the Humvee first speaking into a head device waving at the tanks to stop. He appeared to be ordering the tanks not to fire. Two more Humvee's pulled with two agents stepping out of each vehicle. The slowly walked over to Marc Boyd and spoke something to him. Paul watched as Boyd pulled a pistol from his hidden shoulder harness and shot Danick in the head. Enraged Paul used everything he had destroying the tanks! He felt completely weakened. Looking down to the girl's hole he saw they were not there. Looking around as the four agents fired their mini- REMP weapons hitting him multiple times, Paul saw the girls walking to the top of the hill under the cover of the thick foliage. At the top of the hill in a cluster of some large trees he saw Michael standing there.

Falling into the girl's hole, out of site of the agents, Paul gasped and quietly shrieked in excruciating pain like he had suffered in Germany. He knew he could not survive. Trying to think, but unable to he saw the atmosphere open. He looked up and saw Alisa smiling at him. He then saw his parents and his grandparents. He saw Diane and her husband. He saw John Danick. Behind all of them he saw thousands of people all smiling and waving at him to come to them. He did not see Brian though. A huge sense of loss was upon his heart when he heard Alisa say, "Do not be afraid my husband. It is your time now." Shaking his head, no, Paul said in a weak whispered voice, "It can't be my love. I must serve."

A hand appeared to reach through the opening as a voice, gentle but strong said, "Take my left hand and you may come home now." Then the other hand came through the opening and the voice said, "Or, you may take my right hand and stay. I will heal you and strengthen you. I will move away from here, but you will have to be on your own from now on." Paul saw that both hands had holes in them.

He knew who was speaking to him feeling the joy and the love like he had never experienced before. Not even with Alisa. He said, "But I am supposed to serve you. That is why I was made."

The voice said, "You have served me well. My father and I are proud of you, Paul. Now make your choice. We will not judge badly no matter which choice you make."

With his last bit of energy, Paul expelled his last breath reaching and taking the...

About the Author

Bruce Blanton (the pen name of Philip W. Tullis) grew up in the Midwest. He joined the Navy at the age of seventeen serving for seven years.

After being medically discharged for wounds and injuries, Philip went on to attend Fort Hays State University in Western Kansas, and then completed his education at the University of Illinois where he majored in History, Business, and Literature.

Philip has worked in various careers before retiring early to write. He and his family lived in Europe for several years for his wife's active duty before returning to America. Philip writes Christian Action-Adventure books under the pen name of Bruce Blanton to honor his brother Bruce Blanton Tullis who lived a short, hard life.

Philip and his wife, both disabled veterans, work to support veteran's groups, Christian organizations, and unplanned pregnancy outlets, which help young woman have their babies. They are very active in their church and have three grown sons. They live on their small ranch, north of Helena, Montana.

Philip has written **PROGRAMMED** and **SHIFTED** and now **The TWINS** as a trilogy under his pen name, which are Christian Action-Adventure novels. He has also written **CONFLICTED**.

His non-fiction book **Got Attitude So Do I** is written on corruption in the work world and that of American society. He also has written a non-fiction book titled, **Christian or In Name Only?** which is an argument for trust over belief—an argument of what Christians are *supposed* to be.

Made in the USA
Las Vegas, NV
13 March 2021